Praise for earlier Tim Maleeny novels

Stealing the Dragon

An Independent Mystery Bookseller Association
Killer Book of the Month

"Tough, original, compelling—a perfect thriller debut."
—*Lee Child, NY Times* bestselling author

"Tim Maleeny makes a strong entrance into crime fiction with *Stealing the Dragon*. There is hardly a drought of Asian-themed mysteries, but Maleeny gives readers a fresh and fast take that enthralls."
—*Crimespree Magazine*

"Tim Maleeny captures not only the bright atmosphere of San Francisco but also the darker aspects of its soul, in a manner perhaps previously matched only by Dashiell Hammett." —*Bookreporter*

"Combines a gumshoe mystery in the tradition of Dashiell Hammett with the exotic action of Trevanian." —*Mystery Ink*

"Characters and plot twists bring back memories of Ian Fleming's 007 series." —*Cherokee Sentinel*

"Readers will want to see more of Cape and Sally." —*Library Journal*

Beating the Babushka

"Maleeny's second Cape Weathers mystery engages the reader without insisting that it be taken too seriously....The snappy writing and a parallel plot of drug-dealing Italian and Chinese mobsters keep the pace lively and will resonate with Elmore Leonard fans."
—*Publishers Weekly*

"With an obvious understanding of the traditions of crime fiction, [Maleeny] has created a series that tips the hat as it modernizes the plot line. A plot that sizzles from page one and keeps cooking until the twists at the end. I can't wait to hear more from the very talented Maleeny."
—*Crimespree Magazine*

"The vivid characters…enrich the suspenseful plot, providing a perfect reading experience."
                                                        —*Fresh Fiction*

"A new San Francisco treat. This series manages to suggest both the quirky characterizations of Elmore Leonard and the take-it-to-the-mat derring-do of Robert Parker."
                                                        —*Thrilling Detective*

"The second coming of Travis McGee."
                                                        —*Bookgasm*

"…A highly entertaining thriller…Cape and Sally make an engaging pair, and Maleeny does a nice job showing us the cutthroat side of the movie industry. Keep 'em coming."
                                                        —*Booklist*

Greasing the Piñata

"Tim Maleeny's *Greasing the Piñata*…is madcap entertainment—funny, fast, and fab. A tequila-soaked adventure that makes for a terrific read."
                                  —John Lescroart, *New York Times* bestselling author

"Maleeny is the kind of writer that makes you want to jump in the passenger seat and go for the ride—okay, maybe with eyes jammed shut and your hands gripping the arm rest—but then you want to go again."
                                  —Don Winslow, bestselling author of *The Dawn Patrol*

"Maleeny smoothly mixes wry humor and a serious plot without sacrificing either…An appealing hero, well-crafted villains, snappy dialogue and an energetic plot show that Maleeny…is a definite contender in the private detective subgenre."
                                                        —*Publishers Weekly*

"Tim Maleeny holds a razor to your throat from page one through the final breathless chapter. Snarling, fast, and relentless.…"
                                  —Brent Ghelfi, award-winning author of *Volk's Game*

Jump

Books by Tim Maleeny

The Cape Weathers Series
Stealing the Dragon
Beating the Babushka
Greasing the Piñata

Jump

Jump

Tim Maleeny

Poisoned Pen Press

Copyright © 2009 by Tim Maleeny

First Edition 2009

10 9 8 7 6 5 4 3 2 1

Library of Congress Catalog Card Number: 2008937739

ISBN: 978-1-59058-574-0 Hardcover

Poisoned Pen Press
6962 E. First Ave., Ste. 103
Scottsdale, AZ 85251
www.poisonedpenpress.com
info@poisonedpenpress.com

Printed in the United States of America

For Robert C. Maleeny
Who at my side was ever near

Jump (verb)
1. to spring clear of the ground or other support by a sudden muscular effort; to leap: *to jump out a window.*
2. to ignore intervening steps or deliberation: *to jump to a conclusion.*
3. to enter into an activity with great energy and enthusiasm: *he jumped at the opportunity; she jumped at the chance.*
4. (Colloquial) to attack suddenly; to pounce: *he was jumped in a dark alley.*
5. (Film) to change the point of view suddenly, moving from one scene to another abruptly and without warning.

Chapter One

The scream tore through the building like a pregnant nun on her way to confession. It bounced off the walls, rattled the windows, and woke up everyone in the neighborhood.

Ed Lowry plummeted a hundred feet before he made any noise. The fire escape on the twentieth floor was two hundred feet off the ground, so accelerating at thirty-two feet per second squared, he was falling at nearly forty miles an hour and covered half the distance to the ground before he grasped the real gravity of his situation.

It was probably the sight of the penguin that jolted him back to reality and knocked some air back into his lungs.

The penguin was a sculpture, rising up from a fountain that sat dead center inside the main courtyard of Golden Towers Apartments. Baby penguins nestled on either side of the mommy penguin, who had her head back, beak pointed triumphantly toward the heavens. A soaring symbol of the strength and nobility of motherhood, carved lovingly in marble and bronze. It was conical, shiny, and sharp as a mother's tongue.

Ed realized he wasn't merely going to hit the driveway, but was headed straight for the penguins. He let loose a scream that could wake the dead, though it didn't stop Ed from joining their ranks.

He twisted in midair and struck the penguin back-first with a sickening, wet noise that one witness described as the sound of a whale being dropped from a skyscraper. Ed didn't look much like a whale when it was all said and done, but he was skewered like a fish by the upraised beak of the penguin. Blood flowed down the marble body of the mother penguin, pooling at the feet of her young, turning the water of the fountain a deep wine red.

Sam McGowan was on the twentieth floor when it happened, so he wasn't too surprised the cops wanted to talk to him. After all, he'd been a cop himself. He'd worried that he would miss the job when he retired, but so far life as a civilian was full of surprises. Like your landlord taking a header off the top floor of your building.

Sam's first day of retirement, and already they wanted him back on the job.

Chapter Two

Sam could feel his balls getting squeezed and didn't like the sensation one bit. They weren't caught in a vise, but the gentle pressure of guilt was gripping each testicle like a hand and making him squirm. After more than two decades as a cop, he was finding it hard to say no to a fellow officer.

"I told you, Rodriguez, I'm retired," he said for what must have been the fifth time.

The man sitting across from him said nothing, just looked at him with those cop eyes. Unreadable, totally devoid of emotion. For Sam it was like looking in the mirror.

Sam shook his head and pushed himself out of his chair. It was a worn leather recliner, set at an angle so you could face the TV in the corner or the person sitting on the couch to your right. Marie had always spread out on the couch, one pillow under her head, another for her feet, while Sam changed channels and told her about his day.

Sam blinked away the memory and looked down at his uninvited guest. "You want something to drink?"

Danny Rodriguez started to shake his head, then checked his watch before saying, "What've you got?"

Sam walked past the short counter into the kitchen, which was really part of the same room, separated by a change in the overhead lighting and the sudden disappearance of the carpet. Sam's head disappeared behind the counter as he bent down to examine the contents of the refrigerator.

"Orange Juice, iced tea, and Rolling Rock," he called. "And tap water and ice cubes."

Rodriguez didn't take long to decide. "Rolling Rock."

Sam grabbed two bottles, twisted the caps, and handed one over before reclaiming his chair. The room was large, almost twenty by twenty. The wall behind Rodriguez was made entirely of glass, two sliding doors leading to a short balcony. Tonight you couldn't see anything besides a layer of fog against the night sky, but during the day Sam had one of the best views in San Francisco, an unbroken vista from the Bay Bridge all the way to Alcatraz.

"This is a nice place, Sam." Rodriguez raised the beer in acknowledgement before taking a long swig. "Marie do the decorating?"

Sam nodded but didn't say anything.

"She was a good lady," said Rodriguez, raising his beer.

"The best," replied Sam, tilting his own green bottle in acknowledgment but not really inclined to get into it. Almost two years, and still he forgot sometimes that Marie was gone. He'd known other people who had lost someone to cancer, but it always seemed like they had time to prepare. What did they say in the movies? *Get your affairs in order.* Marie came home from her doctor with the news, and three months later she was gone. So sudden it was as if she'd gone on a trip. Sam still woke in the middle of the night, convinced he'd heard her keys in the front door.

He blinked, realizing Rodriguez was saying something.

"Great location, just a couple blocks from the Ferry Building, in the heart of downtown, connected to the shopping center next door by pedestrian bridges. Must set you back a bit each month, no?"

Sam shrugged. He couldn't really afford it on his pension but their savings and Marie's insurance made it possible. Besides, he wasn't ready to move yet. "Rent's not as bad as you'd think. The place has amazing views, but it's old. Almost thirty years now. Newer buildings have gone up in the neighborhood, the views just as good. And the landlord, Ed, hasn't done much to keep it renovated. Always said he would, but never seemed to get around to it."

"Guess he won't be getting around to anything," said Rodriguez. "'cept maybe an interview with Saint Peter."

"Going to be a short interview."

"Yeah?" Rodriguez sat up a little straighter on the couch. "This guy was an asshole?"

"Your cards are showing, Danny."

Rodriguez held up his hands, the half-empty beer still clutched in his right. "I'm off-duty, remember? Just asking."

Sam took a drink, watching his old friend over the upraised bottle. He nodded as he swallowed.

"The first month we knew Marie had cancer, she got really weak, really fast." Sam's eyes turned dark with the memory, his wife unable to lift a carton of milk. "And the front doors to this building are as heavy as anchors, the springs really old. I practically threw my shoulder out just opening the door, and Marie couldn't budge them but an inch or two."

"So you talked to Ed?"

"Right, we said something to the landlord. Turns out, a lot of other people had, too, over the years. There's plenty of older people living here, some over eighty, and they'd all complained about the doors."

"What did the guy do?"

"Said he'd think about it."

"*Think* about it?"

"How about that?" Sam nodded. "We ask again a week later, and he says it would be *cost-prohibitive*, and there's no obligation on his part unless the city makes it a requirement."

"He know Marie was a lawyer?"

"Don't think he cared." Sam frowned. "He knew tenant law, and he wasn't going to spend a dime unless someone forced him to, and who's got enough money, let alone time to take a guy to court over a door?" That was the one thing he and Marie didn't have enough of, time.

Rodriguez leaned forward. "But did Mister Ed know you were a cop?"

Sam smiled, but his eyes were hard. "He found out."

"You get rough?"

"Nah." Sam shook his head. "He wasn't worth it. But I did call the local precinct and have his car towed, every day for a week. I heard they scratched it some."

Rodriguez laughed.

"By accident, of course."

"Guess he fixed the doors?"

"Yeah, he got around to it," replied Sam, his smile fading. That was a good week, in the midst of everything happening with Marie. At least he felt like he was *doing* something. That had been the hardest part, being useless, unable to change or control a damn thing. "Made me real popular with the old ladies around here."

"I'll bet." Rodriguez smiled. "But you were always popular with the ladies, Sam. You could always get them talking, anyway."

Sam grinned. "I'm a sensitive guy, Danny, you know that." He looked at a wall clock before he added, "Anything else you want to know?"

Rodriguez drained his beer but didn't get up to leave. Sam sighed inwardly. The cop dance. *But who's leading?*

Rodriguez spread his arms across the back of the couch. "So I guess he won't be missed, huh?"

Sam fetched two more beers, handed one across the coffee table. "You're relentless, you know that?"

"He piss off anyone else?" asked Rodriguez. "More recently?"

Sam shrugged. "Couldn't tell you, but I doubt he was on anyone's Christmas card list, not if they lived here. I heard there were at least three lawsuits against him."

"What for?"

"Don't know, really—Marie had asked around. Small Claims Court, I think. Refusing to return deposits to people moving out, that sort of thing. Chickenshit stuff."

"But you're not sure?"

Sam shook his head. "Nope."

"You talk to your neighbors much?"

Sam hesitated. "What, you mean about Ed's little swan dive?"

Rodriguez shook his head. "No, I mean *ever*. How well do you know your neighbors, the other folks living on this floor?"

"What do you think, Danny?"

"Not at all, huh?"

It was what you'd expect from a cop. Sam kept odd hours, leaving for work in the middle of the night, coming home and sleeping while everyone else went to work. Homicide wasn't a nine-to-five job, and it wasn't conducive to casual banter in the elevator. Sam didn't take it personally. Nobody feels comfortable around cops, even the innocent. Especially when the cop in question reeks of death. Most people just nodded at the man in the rumpled suit smelling of formaldehyde.

"Maybe they'll talk to you now," said Rodriguez. "You being retired and all."

"Your guys didn't make the rounds?" Sam already knew the answer but wanted to see how Danny handled it.

"'course we did," replied Rodriguez a little defensively. "Everybody was home. Everyone heard the scream, but nobody *saw* anything."

"Typical."

"That was your story, too, right?"

Sam nodded. "Heard the scream, then yelling from the courtyard. Few minutes later, I saw the flashing lights through the window, bouncing off my ceiling. Took the elevator downstairs just as the meat truck arrived."

"Pretty gruesome, huh?"

Sam shrugged. "We've seen worse."

"But not that dramatic," said Rodriguez. "*Espectacular!* You think the penguin happened on purpose?"

Sam looked at his friend, feeling the pressure build, wondering when he was going to get to the point. "Danny, would *you* aim for the penguin, if you decided to jump?"

"Fuck, no."

"But?" prompted Sam.

"But I might try for it, you know, if I was throwing the *pendejo* off the fire escape."

"So that's your theory?"

Rodriguez shrugged. "Just an idea. Not a theory yet."

"So check it out." Sam thought, *here we go.*

"How long you been retired, Sam?"

Sam looked at his watch. "Not counting the weekend? Maybe twenty-four hours."

Rodriguez nodded. "Right. So last time you were on the job, what was the Mayor doing?"

"Busting our balls." Sam replied without hesitation. It was all over the papers. The new mayor of San Francisco was a press-magnet—young, good looking, and opinionated. His latest crusade for the papers was fixing the "dismal" rate of homicide closures. Never mind budget cuts that had slashed the size of the force. Forget that most of the deaths were gang-related, occurring in parts of town that the Mayor's administration had turned its back on, in terms of manpower. There were too many suspects, no help from the courts, and no witnesses. The local residents didn't trust the cops, because the force was spread too thin to have any real presence in the neighborhood. But those were cop problems, not the Mayor's.

The press took the bait like sharks to chum, and now the police were second-guessed on every investigation, no matter what they did. They were under a microscope until a case was closed. It was a catch-22. No more funding until the closure rate improves, but without more funding, they couldn't get the manpower to work the cases they already had.

"*Si, cabron.*" Rodriguez nodded sagely. "Nothing has changed since you retired. Our balls are getting busted by that pretty-boy asshole, so a new case just means more pressure. And I must tell you, my friend, my balls can't take much more pressure."

Sam shifted in his chair as the pressure got passed across the room, invisible but insistent. His friend was asking him for help, and his conscience was telling him to say yes. He drained the last of his beer.

"You think the guy got some help," he said noncommittally. "Maybe a little push."

Rodriguez spread his hands. "I'm just saying it's a possibility." He smiled sheepishly. "I say more than that, then I gotta write it up as a potential homicide. Start an investigation."

"But if you leave it alone…" Sam let his voice trail off.

"No paperwork," said Rodriguez. "Not for me, at least. Just another jumper with second thoughts."

"And bad aim."

"Maybe, but I got my doubts."

"The body tell you anything?" It was too soon for the autopsy results, but the crew at a crime scene usually had some theories before they bagged the body.

"No, and it probably won't," replied Rodriguez. "You saw it, remember?"

Sam nodded. The penguin hadn't left much evidence. As thorough as the guys in the meat truck had been, he suspected there were still bits and pieces of Ed hanging off the trees and bushes in the courtyard. He eyed his empty bottle before looking Rodriguez in the eye.

"So what exactly do you want me to do, Danny?"

Rodriguez drank off the last of his beer and set it down on the table, leaning both elbows on his knees. "Say it was murder."

Sam shrugged. "OK, it was murder."

"Easy to say, right? But you and me, we know there's no case without establishing *motive*, right?"

"Right."

"But to do that, I gotta start asking questions. You know, all that cop stuff."

Sam nodded. "And if the case is open, but you can't close it…"

"I'm fucked," said Rodriguez. "Even if I can't close it as a homicide because we discover the asshole jumped, I'm still fucked."

Sam smiled at the perversity of the situation. "The mayor and the press will say you're just trying to cover up your incompetence by changing your story, claiming it was a suicide."

"*Exactamente.*"

"So what do you want me to do?" Sam repeated half-heartedly. "I'm retired."

"The guy fell from this floor," said Rodriguez. "And there're six apartments on this floor, right?"

"Yeah, so?"

"So that's where I'd start."

Sam asked the question, just to hear the words. "Start what, Danny?"

"Getting to know your neighbors."

Sam sighed. "There's a problem with your theory."

Rodriguez frowned. "What?"

Sam held Danny's eyes for a long moment before answering. "What if I killed him?"

For an instant Rodriguez didn't react, just stared at Sam with those cop eyes, but then his broad face broke into his trademark grin. "Then I guess it'll be a short investigation."

Chapter Three

Larry was wondering if he could stab his brother under the table without anyone noticing. It was only a passing thought, a spur-of-the-moment plan, abandoned as soon as the waitress brought their food, but it kept him calm just thinking about it.

Larry's brother, Jerome, was beaming across the table, his features obscured by the steam coming off his plate.

"*Fajitas*," sighed Jerome, looking like he'd just won the lottery. The plate set before him was iron, heated close to its melting point before a cornucopia of shrimp, chicken, and vegetables was dumped onto its surface. The iron plate was set in the middle of a black plastic tray divided into three sections. On the left was the guacamole and sour cream, on the right black beans and rice. There was no room for the flour tortillas, which were stuffed in a wax paper bag and dropped unceremoniously onto their basket of chips.

"What did you say?" asked Larry testily.

Jerome spread his hands like Moses, inviting his brother to gaze in wonder upon the awesome power of the mix-and-match combo.

"Fajitas!" he cried. "*Fah—HEEE—Tas!*"

A couple sitting at the table to their left glanced over. Larry scowled at the woman before turning the look on his brother. He leaned across the table, getting close enough to feel the steam on his face. He wanted to get a good look at Jerome's pupils.

"I know they're fucking fajitas," he growled. "Now the whole restaurant knows it, too. What's the big deal? You order them every time we come here."

"Lighten up, man." Jerome grabbed the bag and yanked a tortilla free of its waxy embrace. "You want some?"

Larry didn't say anything, just scanned the restaurant.

Jerome kept talking, oblivious. "I just like the sound of the word, is all." He lowered his voice to a conspiratorial whisper. "Makes you happy just saying it."

Larry did not look happy. "Are you stoned?"

"Just say it," insisted Jerome. "Fah—*HEEE*—Tas."

"No."

"C'mon, it'll cheer you up."

"I asked you a question."

"What?"

"I said, I asked you a question."

"Right, what's the question?"

"Are…you…stoned?"

Jerome ignored the question, instead concentrating on getting some black beans onto the surface of his tortilla without spilling them. Another plate would help. Maybe he should flag the waitress. She was cute. A little wide in the hips, and a little too gringo for a Mexican restaurant, but nice. Maybe he'd ask her out, right after dessert. He jerked his head toward his brother but didn't look him in the eye. "You want a marguerita?"

Larry shook his head and grabbed his beer, a Dos Equis. He looked at the marguerita glass sitting in front of his brother, big as a fish bowl, the ice melted, the green liquid swirling around in the colored glass. It had to be ten inches in diameter.

"I'm not drinking margueritas," he said evenly. "And you're stoned."

Jerome looked up defensively and then shrugged, his pupils like two solar eclipses. "A little."

Larry nodded, his jaw set. "You realize every ounce you smoke is one less ounce we sell?"

"Math's not my thing, Larry." Jerome ladled some guacamole on top of the beans, then jammed the wrapped tortilla into his mouth. "That's why *you* handle the books."

Larry shook his head in disgust. *Then why do we split the profits fifty-fifty?* He kept the thought to himself as he sipped his beer. Jerome leaned forward and slurped loudly from his marguerita bowl. Larry just kept shaking his head, the throbbing in his temples a metronome of budding rage.

Larry and Jerome Siegel were known around town as The Sandwich Brothers, an entrepreneurial venture started in their kitchen almost four years ago. The concept was simple enough, an inspiration born of having been fired from perfectly respectable jobs in several small to midsized companies.

Part of the reason they got fired was because they were both fuck-ups. Larry realized that now. He'd matured.

But he also realized a big part of their ineptitude, came from being constantly malnourished. He and Jerome didn't eat lunch, so they were lightheaded, so they fucked up. When you work in an office in San Francisco, you basically have two options for lunch. You can go to a nearby restaurant, which costs you half your weekly paycheck—unless you order a salad, in which case you won't go broke until the middle of the month. Only top executives, overpaid financial types, and tourists ate at swanky cafés lining the downtown sidewalks.

The other option was bring your lunch, but who wants to walk to the fucking grocery store, make a sandwich, wake up early to pack your bag for work, and then eat at your desk? OK, so women in the office did it all the time, no big deal. *But that's what chicks do, isn't it?* Go on stupid diets, make their own food, and starve themselves during the day so they can eat like pigs when their sap boyfriends take them out to dinner. Larry didn't have a girlfriend and hadn't in quite some time, but he was pretty sure that's what chicks did.

So you've got all these half-starving, half-broke guys moping around cubicles all over San Francisco, looking for something to eat. *Why not make them lunch?*

It was a brilliantly simple way to make a living. Sleep until ten, then go to the grocery store, make a bunch of sandwiches that cost maybe a buck each, stuff them into a cooler, and sell them to the rubes in the cubes for five bucks each, unless they want to spring for chips, in which case you charge them another dollar.

Word spread, and within a few months Larry and Jerome were delivering sandwiches to offices all over the city. They even had t-shirts with The Sandwich Brothers logo emblazoned on them. It wasn't glamorous work, but it paid the rent.

Then one night Larry was struck by a bolt of inspiration.

He was trying to do the books while Jerome sat on the couch watching reruns of Scooby Doo, smoking a blunt the size of Montana, ash falling on the carpet while smoke curled in the air and stained the ceiling yellow. It drove Larry crazy when his brother smoked in the living room, so he started to say something when he was struck by an idea that seemed so obvious, he wondered why it hadn't occurred to him earlier.

Larry had stopped smoking pot years ago because it made him nauseous. Jerome always said that was because Larry was too tightly wound. (Larry always told Jerome to go fuck himself, to which Jerome said, *see what I mean?*) But looking at his brother sprawled on the couch—a slack, doe-eyed expression on his face—Larry realized that most people their age were more like Jerome. Though he hated to admit his brother was right, most of their friends would say Larry *was* too uptight. Most of their friends smoked pot. As a general rule of thumb, young people would rather get stoned than balance their checkbooks.

Therein lay the opportunity.

They were visiting offices all over the city, staffed by young men and women in their twenties, most of whom liked to party. Many of whom smoked pot, based not only on Larry's personal experience with his brother but also national statistics. The Sandwich Brothers already had a distribution network which made them invisible, so why not sell weed along with cold cuts and chips? Slip a joint next to the ham-on-rye and take a twenty off the guy instead of a five. For bigger sales paper bags worked just fine, and soon Larry was setting up regular accounts with lines of credit.

Within two months The Sandwich Brothers had quintupled their income, and their reputation spread through underground channels across the city. Interoffice e-mail was fueling their fame and paving the way for new sales.

And Larry would be the first to say that he needed Jerome—at first. The key to the whole operation was spotting the person in the office cool enough to approach for the first sale. Jerome could spot a fellow pot-smoker a mile away. They could be across the room and Jerome would say, "yeah, that's our guy," and ten times out of ten he'd be right. Jerome would ask the guy where he could buy some weed, just to see if he was using, then turn it around and offer him a regular supply.

Yes, Jerome had a gift, but of late he'd become a liability. Buying clothes. Leaving big tips at restaurants. Bragging to girls in bars, hitting on waitresses, telling them he was a player. Fortunately, he didn't look the part, so most advances were rebuffed with a snort of laughter, but the key to long-term success in this game was anonymity. The Sandwich Brothers had to keep up impressions, two hard-working boys feeding the future managers of corporate America. The cover was good, but it would crumble if you looked too closely.

If they started *acting* like drug dealers, they'd get busted so fast they wouldn't have time to shit before they were suddenly behind bars getting ass-fucked by some Aryan monster named Bruno.

Larry didn't want that to happen.

"So what happens now?" asked Jerome, talking around a mouthful of chips.

Larry shifted in his chair. "What do you mean?"

"Our landlord's dead."

Larry looked at the couple next to them to make sure they weren't listening. The woman was laughing at something the guy had said. Larry thought it looked like a forced laugh, but

she was hot, and Larry was sitting over here with his dumbass
brother, so what did he know? Maybe the guy was funny.

Larry leaned over the table. "I know he's dead. What's your
point?"

"So who do we pay?"

"What do you mean?"

"Well, the dude was blackmailing us, right?"

Larry frowned. "We had an *arrangement*," he said impatiently.

The arrangement started like this: one day about six months
ago, Ed the landlord let himself into their apartment to check
on a water leak that was called in by a tenant downstairs. The
brothers were out, but their month's supply of pot was laid in
neat packages on top of their kitchen table. Ed threatened to
turn them in, but Larry figured Ed would have already called
the cops if he didn't have something else in mind. Ten minutes
later they had a deal, Ed had supplemental income, and The
Sandwich Brothers had a silent partner they were paying every
month to stay silent.

"Right," said Jerome. "An arrangement. So who's our partner
now?"

Larry's mouth opened and closed a few times before he
could get the words out. "*Nobody*. How much did you smoke,
anyway?"

"You changing the subject?"

"We only paid that asshole because he threatened to call the
cops. Now he's dead, so we keep all the money ourselves, just
like before."

Jerome blinked for a minute, thinking about that one.

"*Swweeeeet!*" he said, a little too loudly. The couple next to
them glanced over before turning back to their conversation.
Then Jerome added in a not-so-low voice, "Did *you* kill him?"

Larry clenched the dinner knife in his right hand and almost
went for it right then and there, a quick jab across the table, a
mad dash out of the restaurant, a plane ride to the Bahamas, and
home free. Jerome face-down in his fajitas. Larry would have to

tell their Mom eventually, and she usually took Jerome's side, but Larry knew in his heart that she'd forgive him if she only knew what he'd put up with.

A voice from above changed Larry's mind. It changed a lot of things.

"Hi, guys."

Larry turned in his seat, the knife still clenched awkwardly in his hand. Jerome looked up from his marguerita. It took them both a second to place the guy.

Midfifties, bald with black sidewalls, tan face, and a paunch that looked like it had been there a while. Deep lines around his eyes and nose, a wry smile beneath a shiny black mustache. He lived two doors down from them, one of the one-bedroom apartments on the twentieth floor. Larry squinted as he tried to remember the guy's name. Willy. Wally. Wilson. Something like that.

"Walter," the guy said.

"What?" both brothers said at once.

"That's my name," the guy said. "You were trying to remember my name."

Larry tried a recovery, took the surprise out of his voice.

"We were?"

"Sure. My name's Walter. I live down the hall."

Jerome played it wrong, the vestiges of his high mixed with tequila giving him false confidence.

"Good for you, Walter," he said. "What's that got to do with us?"

Walter shrugged, the smile still there. "I was sitting at the bar over there." He gestured over his shoulder. "And I thought I should come by and say hello. You know, get started on the right foot."

Larry got a sick feeling in his gut, but Jerome jumped in before he could say anything.

"Right foot, left foot," sang Jerome. "No offense, Walter, but what the fuck are you talking about?"

Larry closed his eyes, waiting for the answer.

Walter's smile got bigger. "I'm talking about our business arrangement, Jerome. You are Jerome, right?" He switched his gaze. "And you're Larry."

Jerome shook his head and turned to his brother, irritated. This guy was ruining a perfectly good buzz.

"Larry, who is this fuckin' guy?"

Larry studied Walter, now leaning in close, crowding the back of his chair but still smiling. *Now we're fucked.* Larry sighed, answering his brother's question but still looking at Walter, his gut hanging over the edge of the chair.

"Jerome, meet our new silent partner.

Chapter Four

Sam was floating three feet above his mattress and spinning slowly clockwise. Or maybe the room was spinning counter-clockwise around him. He couldn't be sure. But that's what it felt like when he closed his eyes and tried to sleep.

It was four in the morning. Danny Rodriguez left just past midnight, but Sam didn't go to bed for another two hours. Instead he sat at his kitchen counter and drank the rest of the beer in his refrigerator. It wasn't much by standards of his youth, but it was too much. Hence the spinning. Middle-age had struck with a vengeance, his metabolism had changed, and he'd become a lightweight.

Maybe he was just out of practice. Since Marie passed, he drank erratically, going for weeks without touching a beer, then forcing himself to go out and sit in a bar, and, on those occasions, probably drinking too much. What he needed was discipline. A consistent, moderate consumption of alcohol to keep his liver in shape and his wits about him.

He reached across the bed with his right hand and felt the sheets, confirming the suspicion he wasn't really levitating. Though he had the whole bed to himself, he still slept on his side. He put a pillow lengthwise down the middle when he slept, so he could rest his hand there, the way he had across Marie's hip. He was a back-sleeper, but she always slept on her side. He once read that said a lot about a person, how they slept, but couldn't remember the specifics. Maybe sleeping on your back meant you were always looking up. An optimist. Marie said he was an optimist, the only cop she knew who wasn't a cynic at heart.

But he wasn't a cop anymore. He took time off when Marie got sick, a leave of absence. When he came back to the job it wasn't the same. Not having someone at home had taken away the motivation, as if Marie's chemotherapy was killing his ambition instead of the cancer inside her body. No longer was her voice in the room, telling Sam to hang in there, convincing him that what he did really mattered.

Now he looked at his job differently. He put bad guys behind bars, but the courts just let them go again. And two out of three scumbags committed another crime within a year of getting released, usually worse than the first time around. Some guy beat up his girlfriend, next time he killed her. Nothing Sam could do about that.

Not while wearing a badge, anyway.

They asked him to reconsider, and he did. Hung in there almost two years. Tried to get lost in his work, new cases piling up all the time. But with each new arrest, it seemed to matter less and less. He wasn't making a difference, and there was no one in his life that could tell him any different. He wasn't a cop anymore. Since Marie's passing, Sam wasn't sure what he was.

Maybe you're lonely.

The thought struck him like a blow to the chest. A heavy, dull thud of awareness that knocked him back into the mattress and caved his head in. Not because it depressed him—he realized he was already depressed, and had been for some time. But the realization demanded action, and Sam had grown quite comfortable in his private cocoon of self-pity. He might not be happy, but he wasn't vulnerable, either. You care about someone, then part of you dies with them. Between the job and Marie, Sam had seen enough death for one lifetime.

But having acknowledged that he'd become a loner, a social misfit, he couldn't just ignore it. Sam was a fixer. Something was wrong, he took action. Even if he knew it was hopeless.

He closed his eyes, but the bed stopped rotating. The amusement park of despair had closed down for the night. No more spinning. He felt as heavy as a bag of cement, pressing down against his twisted sheets.

Get to know your neighbors, Sam. Danny Rodriguez had said it again before he left.

A simple request. A call to arms. A problem Sam could solve.

If only he could get himself out of bed.

Chapter Five

The Sandwich Brothers considered adding murder to their menu. One minute they were back in business, able to profit from the addictive properties of cannabis in the spirit of a free-market economy, and the next minute they had some fat fuck breathing down their necks for his share of the spoils.

"His share?" yelled Jerome from the couch. They were back in their apartment, Larry pacing furiously in the kitchen, Jerome slouched on the couch, his face and half the room obscured by great halos of smoke. "His fucking share of what? He didn't do any of the work."

Larry stopped pacing and caught a glimpse of himself in the chrome on the refrigerator. His face was distorted by the curve of the handle, his features twisted and angry. Then he saw himself across the room, in the mirror over the couch, and realized he really looked like that. He was stressed beyond belief, struggling with a sudden, overwhelming urge to get stoned with his brother. He knew it would make him sick, but it might be worth it. Sit down next to Jerome and smoke all his troubles away.

But they weren't going away. Walter was real, and he had them by the short hairs. Larry had felt the guy's belly brush up against his back as he leaned over their table. He shivered at the memory. The guy was a pig.

"What did he say he did for a living?" called Jerome from the cloud of forgetfulness. "Besides ripping us off?"

"He's a producer," said Larry. "He makes movies."

"Like what?"

"B-movies," said Larry dismissively. "Like *Revenge of the Scorpions.*"

Jerome sat up straighter on the couch. "*Scorpions* was a cool movie. This giant scorpion, well, it starts out small, but then a nuclear bomb goes off in the desert. Well, this fuckin' scorpion gets big, and I mean really big—and then it gets loose and, well, it pretty much *eats* Scottsdale, Arizona."

Larry shook his head impatiently. "That was *Scorpions.* Walter didn't make that one. He made the sequel, *Revenge of the Scorpions.*"

Jerome shrugged. "I don't think I saw that one."

"Neither did anyone else," snapped Larry. "He made some other movies, too, all direct-to-video shit. That's why Walter needs to supplement his income by blackmailing us."

"Oh." Jerome nodded. "Still, *Scorpions* was a fuckin' good movie, bro. Maybe this guy isn't so bad."

Larry squeezed his eyes shut and counted to ten. Jerome kept talking.

"I'm just saying, maybe we could work out a deal."

Larry's eyes snapped open. "Walter's already worked out the deal for us, you moron."

"He did?" said Jerome. "That was nice of him."

Now counting down from ten.

"No, it wasn't nice," replied Larry. "Apparently he went drinking one night with Ed, our recently deceased landlord and former business partner, and dumbass Ed spilled his guts to his new drinking buddy." Larry visualized Ed's big toothy smile. It reminded him of Walter's smug grin, back at the Mexican restaurant. Smiles of victory. *We'll see, you fat son of a bitch.*

"And he wants two percent?" asked Jerome.

"*Twenty* percent," corrected Larry. He watched Jerome from across the room, waiting for it to sink in. He counted. Jerome's eyes bugged out after eight seconds.

"Twenty?" said Jerome, on his feet now. "Twenty fucking percent?"

"Twenty." Larry nodded. "Or he goes to the cops."

Jerome blew out his cheeks. "Maybe we could run over him with our truck."

Larry enjoyed the visual for a moment, Walter's big gut dragged under the grill, his eyes wide as they disappeared under the hood. The SUV lurching as four-wheel drive kicked in and they ran over him, a minor speed bump on the road to success.

Larry blinked away the image and shook his head. "Too messy. Might be witnesses."

"Baseball bat to the head?" asked Jerome, trying to be helpful.

Larry was suddenly back in little league, squinting under the brim of his cap, his arms cocked, his hands tight around the bat. Stepping forward on his left leg, he realized that the pitcher had not thrown a baseball after all, instead substituting Walter's head, shrunken down to ball-size, tiny seams stitched across his forehead.

A home run!

Larry reluctantly let go of the image. "No, even worse than the car. We'd be behind bars by the end of the day."

Jerome frowned and returned to the couch, this time lying down. His cheeks sucked inward as he took a deep hit on the joint. "So we're just going to pay him?" he asked in a strangled voice.

Larry shook his head, his jaw set. "Who do we buy our pot from, Jerome?"

Jerome responded immediately, proud to know the answer to something. He slapped his hand repeatedly in the air against an imaginary buzzer, like a Jeopardy contestant having a seizure.

"Buster!" cried Jerome.

"Buster is the middle man," said Larry softly, not wanting to dampen his brother's constructive energy. "The go-between. Where does Buster get the pot?"

Jerome nodded, ready for the challenge. A two-part question. No problem. It took him a few seconds, but his hand shot up again, slapping wildly in the air.

"Zorro!" he shouted. "Fuckin' Zorro, man."

"That's right," said Larry, as much to himself as his half-baked brother. "Zorro."

Zorro. The Spanish word for fox, an apt name for a predator. Larry smiled, feeling in control of the situation again. He walked over to the couch and sat down next to his brother, moving Jerome's feet with surprising gentleness.

"Jerome, one more question," said Larry. "This time for double points."

Jerome sat up, his bloodshot eyes bright with excitement. "Shoot."

"Who's scarier, that fat bastard down the hall...or Zorro?"

Jerome's hand shot into the air like a rocket and slapped the imaginary buzzer again and again. But he didn't need to say anything. He just looked at his brother with a big, lopsided grin.

The Sandwich Brothers both knew the answer to that one.

Chapter Six

The old lady accosted Sam before he was ten feet down the hall.

Mud. Mudding. *Muddridge.* That was her name. A nice old woman, according to Marie. Always smiled at Sam on the few occasions he'd seen her in the hall. But today she had her door open, apparently waiting for him to emerge from his apartment.

"Hello, young man," she said warmly. "I've been waiting for you."

"Ma'am?" Sam reflexively moved into polite cop-speak but let his confusion show.

"Come in, come in." She opened the door wide and waved him inside. Sam looked over his shoulder once, then shrugged and followed her into the apartment.

The layout was identical to his own, except in reverse. The view looked over the park next to the building and the nearby skyline instead of the water. From the foyer Sam could see the Transamerica building piercing the morning fog like a rocket waiting to be cleared for launch.

Sam stopped short of the living room where a couch and loveseat were separated by a table already set with coffee and a large silver tray full of cookies. His hostess sat down on the loveseat and smoothed her skirt, looking expectantly from Sam to the empty couch. He started to say something, but she cut him off with an upraised hand.

"Call me Gail," she said abruptly, then lowered her hand. "You had that look about you."

Sam tried not to sound defensive. "What look?"

"Like you were about to call me Mrs. Muddridge, or even worse, *Ms.* Muddridge...God, I hate that. Thirty years of feminism and that's the result? My husband was the greatest man to ever live, let me assure you, but he's been dead and gone now ten years, and I had a name before I met him, and it was Gail. Still is, unless I decide to change it."

Sam smiled. "I wouldn't change it, Gail. It suits you."

Gail nodded once. "You bet your ass it does. Want a cookie?"

Sam gave into the situation and stepped over to the couch. "No thanks, Gail," he said, shaking his head. "Not ready for breakfast yet."

"Don't know what you're missing." Gail pointed emphatically at the silver tray. "These are almond cookies—to die for, believe me. Those have cherry filling—take forever to make but really pack a punch. These are chocolate mint, great with coffee. And those—those are macaroons—coconut's not my favorite, but I do love saying *macaroon*."

"I don't blame you," replied Sam. "But thanks just the same."

"Suit yourself." She gestured past the tray. "Coffee?"

"Not ready for that, either."

Gail narrowed her eyes. "Hung over, are we?"

Sam leaned back on the couch. "You don't miss a thing, do you, Gail?"

"Not much," she agreed, sitting back with her coffee balanced delicately on her lap. "I'm going to send you home with one of each in a Ziploc, for later. Unless you don't like cookies."

"Who doesn't like cookies?" Sam noticed the age spots on the back of her hands and the folds in her neck. He put her in her late sixties, though everything else about her radiated youthful energy. Her pale blue eyes were practically backlit, and the wrinkles on her face made her more expressive than any girl of twenty. Sam felt energized just being near her. He was a mere mortal, tired and hung-over, and she was a Sun Goddess, bearing gifts of warmth, hope, and macaroons.

"You going to ask why I dragged you in here?" she prompted, a bit abruptly for a Sun Goddess.

Sam shrugged. "Figured you'd get around to it—you don't seem particularly shy. Is your name spelled with an 'i' or is it G-A-L-E, like a hurricane-force wind?"

Gail laughed, a high-pitched sound like parrot squawking. "Well said, young man."

"Call me Sam."

"Fair enough," she replied. "I knew your wife; she was a lovely woman. I was sorry to see her go."

Sam sat up straighter on the couch. "That makes two of us."

Gail's voice got quieter. "I used to talk with her sometimes, if I saw her in the elevator or in the hall. You could tell she was a good person."

Sam didn't say anything.

"I'm telling you this because she told me about you," said Gail, the energy in her voice picking up. "How wonderful you were, how hard you were working all the time. She told me you were a policeman."

"I'm retired."

"I heard."

Sam looked at her quizzically before putting it together. "Lieutenant Rodriguez told you."

"Was that his name?" asked Gail. "The handsome man who knocked on my door? Had those Latin-lover eyes."

"Yes," said Sam. "Danny Rodriguez. He was the officer in charge, making the rounds to see if anyone saw or heard anything unusual."

"Like our landlord jumping off the top of the building?"

"You think he jumped?"

Gail's eyes lit up. "You think he didn't?"

Sam shrugged.

Gail nodded, once. "That's why I wanted to talk with you."

"Why, exactly?"

"Well, that policeman wouldn't tell me anything, but when I asked why you weren't working the case—being our neighbor and everything, at first he wouldn't answer. So I asked him if you were a suspect."

Sam smiled despite himself. It explained Danny's big smile when Sam suggested the same thing. "You said that?"

Gail blushed a little before continuing. "You said it yourself. I'm not shy."

"So he told you I was retired."

"I think he didn't want me or anyone else getting the wrong idea about you," said Gail. "He must like you."

"We were partners for a while," Sam said simply, as if that explained everything. For a cop, it did.

"But since he didn't seem to object to my question about there being a suspect, it made me wonder…" Gail let her voice trail off.

"Of course," said Sam. "If the cops won't tell you what's going on, who better to ask than an ex-cop?"

Gail demurely sipped her coffee.

Sam laughed. "Are you typically this nosey, Gail?"

She wrinkled her nose at the suggestion. "Aren't you curious?"

Sam thought about it. "Not really."

"How can you say such a thing?"

Sam hesitated before answering. "You go to the grocery, Gail? The one downstairs?"

Gail frowned. "Yes, I do. But what's that—"

Sam held up a hand. "You ever go to the bank?"

"Of course."

Sam shrugged. "I work—*worked*—with death every day. My lists of things to do never had groceries or checks on them. Murder and suicide were the files on my desk, the paperwork I had to fill out before I could come home to Marie."

Gail watched him over the rim of her cup.

Sam continued. "I'm not numb, if that's what you're thinking, but after a while, only certain ones get under your skin. Sometimes it's a dead person, and it's just awful. And sometimes…it's just a corpse."

Gail slurped her coffee before setting the cup down. "And Ed really was a cocksucker, wasn't he?"

Sam coughed reflexively. Gail was obviously a live wire, but the voltage was getting higher by the minute. A woman like that certainly deserved a straight answer.

"Yeah," said Sam deliberately. "He was."

Gail pursed her lips in satisfaction. "I never did thank you for getting those doors fixed. I should have mentioned that when you first came in."

Sam blushed despite himself. "It was nothing."

"He tried to run me out of this apartment every year for the past ten years, you know that?"

Sam shook his head. "How?"

"This place is rent-controlled," replied Gail.

"Yeah, I know," replied Sam. "Our rent—my rent—hasn't changed more than twenty bucks a month in the past five years, if that."

"Well, I've been here *twenty-five* years," said Gail. "Fifteen with my husband and ten since he passed. Wanna know what I pay in rent?"

Sam shrugged. "A helluva lot less than they're charging me."

"Damn right," said Gail decisively. "And a lot less—and I mean *a lot* less—than that dead bastard Ed would have charged to rent this place to a new tenant."

Sam nodded slowly. "So he wanted you out."

"One year my asthma started acting up, and the next thing you know, the air conditioner in my apartment breaks. Guess how long it took Ed to fix it?"

"I have a feeling you're going to tell me."

"Five months, and only after I threatened to sue. The next year, I had an ant problem."

"The six-legged kind?"

"Hundreds of the little fuckers," said Gail. "When I complained, same story. No response until I threw a fit."

"Didn't anyone else complain?" asked Sam.

Gail shook her head. "No one else had the problem, at least not for the first few weeks. I think Ed planted them in my apartment."

Sam whistled. "No offense, Gail, but that sounds a bit—"

"—paranoid?" Gail cut him off. "That's what I thought, but then it was the fuses. Every time I turned on a light in the kitchen, the whole apartment went dark."

"And no one else had this problem?"

"Not even the pretty young things down the hall, and you just know they're running their blow dryers and stereo overtime."

Sam's brow furrowed. "I don't know the sexy young things."

"I said pretty, not sexy," Gail corrected.

Sam blushed again. "My mistake."

Gail waved it off, mischief in her eyes. "Tomato, *tom-ah-to*," she said. "You should meet them. They've had their own run-ins with Ed."

"Such as?"

Gail shook her head. "Better to let them tell you. My point is, well, you get the point, don't you?"

Sam nodded. "You didn't like Ed much, either, is that your point?"

"No, young man," replied Gail, sounding like a disappointed school teacher. "If you had problems with Ed, and so did I, don't you think other tenants did, as well?"

Sam chuckled. "Believe it or not Gail, that had occurred to me. But it's nice to know you're trying to make my job easier."

"What job?" said Gail. "You said you were retired."

Sam ignored the question and looked up at the ceiling, talking to himself as much as his host. "How well do you know your neighbors?"

As Sam turned his eyes back toward Gail, she was smiling. "This might take a little while," she said in a forced whisper. "Sure you don't want any coffee?"

Sam looked at the service on the table and gauged the motion in his gut.

"Sure," he said. "Guess it's about time I opened my eyes."

Chapter Seven

Walter grabbed his cock in both hands and tried to get a steady stream going.

Ever since his fiftieth birthday, taking a piss was like reading a mystery novel. You never knew what would happen next. One day straight as an arrow, loud enough to wake the neighbors, the next day a halting stream, one pitiful drop at a time. When he was eighteen, he could hit a silver dollar from six feet away and hold a case of beer in his bladder for hours. Now he had to piss every ten minutes, and half the time it was a false alarm.

A doctor told him it was normal for a man's prostate to enlarge as he got older, making the simple act of urination challenging at times. He said it just like that, *challenging at times*, while twisting his finger around inside Walter's ass. As if there was some double meaning there, like getting Walter to change sides and turn homo was going to be a challenge. That was the last time Walter visited that particular doctor, pretty sure the guy was a fag. Not that Walter had anything against gays, mind you. Lots of them worked in the movie business, and on the whole they seemed to work as hard, if not harder, than the straight guys. And Walter definitely didn't have anything against lesbians, based on a couple of videos he rented last year which clearly demonstrated that lesbians not only enjoy having sex with other women but also enjoy having sex with men at the same time, especially if the guy happens to be a repairman of some sort, like a plumber.

But Walter's plumbing was shot. He realized that every time he took a piss, but he would wait until his prostate exploded before going back to that doctor. It was one thing to work with gays on a job, but it was another thing entirely to pay someone to stick his finger up your ass. That was crossing a line Walter was *not* prepared to cross.

He gave himself a shake and turned sideways to check himself out in the mirror. His gut had kept him from seeing his cock for some time, so every once in a while he made it a point to look in the mirror and make sure everything was where it was supposed to be. And there they were, two plums and a banana. Or maybe two raisins and a carrot that sat in the sun for too long on the dashboard of a car in the middle of August.

Fuck, he was getting old fast.

Walter zipped up and wandered back to his living room. The drapes were open, revealing a remarkable view of the Oakland Bay Bridge and the water. A huge container ship was moving slowly under the bridge, a wide strip of shadow throwing the forward cabin into darkness and revealing the true size of the vessel. Must be longer than a football field, end to end. Walter sat down heavily on his couch and watched until the ship emerged into the light on the other side, wondering briefly what was in the containers, and how something that big could float.

It made Walter think about his bowel movements.

That was another bit of medical advice Walter had received recently. *Your stool should float.* Walter was struck dumb when he heard it, since he'd gone to see a specialist about a ruptured disk in his back, not his shit. He'd pinched a nerve in his back, which sent electric jabs of pain down his left arm and side every time he carried something heavier than a milk carton. He figured a back surgeon would want to do back surgery, so he decided to try some alternative medicine instead. Normally not his style, but friends who had undergone back surgery always seemed to end up in more agony than before they went under the knife. So Walter asked around and got a referral for some Asian dude named Master Ling.

Ling's office was really the back of his house, a small clapboard up in the Sunset district. He treated four or five people there at once, laid out on massage tables, all of them looking about as out-of-shape and miserable as Walter.

Master Ling started off with a back massage, which was OK. It was better than OK—it seemed to be helping, but then he rolled Walter over on his back and started poking him in the stomach, hard. Told him he's constipated—that's where all his trouble started. The belly and the back are two sides of the same coin, said Ling, and Walter needed to respect his stomach. Walter almost busted out laughing but caught himself, seeing the serious look in Master Ling's eyes. But when Ling asked, when was the last time Walter ate steamed vegetables, fasted for a day, or eliminated meat from his diet, Walter told him the truth.

Never.

That did it for Master Ling. No more back massages for Walter. Instead the guy sat down and wrote out a shopping list, told Walter to change his diet and then return after four months, once his stool started to float. *Show me you want to change, Walter.*

No meat. No booze. Nothing fried. He pretty much put X's through everything Walter normally consumed in a twenty-four hour period. *You will know you are reaching inner balance when your stool softens.* Only then could Master Ling work on his back.

Walter crumpled the list on his way back to the car, threw it in the back seat and drove away, realizing Master Ling was a whacko and the only solution was to avoid any heavy lifting. Put it in perspective. He'd rather have back surgery than eat nothing but steamed vegetables the rest of his life.

Now he had groceries delivered to his apartment once a week. Problem solved. Get someone else to do the work for you. Exactly like he was doing now, with those two clowns down the hall. The Sandwich Brothers. It made him laugh to think about it, those two *schmucks* moving pot all over the city. And now Walter could sit back and watch them do it, take his twenty percent without any exposure, any risk, or any effort. Like winning the lottery.

That was the image that came to mind two weeks ago, when that sap Ed had started spilling his guts at the bar. For some reason Walter still didn't understand, Ed sat down next to him and started jabbering away. As if something had happened to him, some personal revelation, like the Virgin Mary appeared in his bathroom mirror and called him a cocksucker. Happened all the time in South America.

Walter didn't care about Ed one way or the other, and he was already half in the bag himself when the guy sat down next to him, ordered drinks for both of them and started whining.

Nobody likes me. That's because you're an asshole, Ed. *It's a thankless job, being a landlord.* Try not being a prick and maybe some of the tenants would say thank you.

Walter gave it to him straight. He never claimed to be Doctor Phil.

It went on like that for an hour before Ed just blurted it out. He caught the brothers moving grass, and now he's on easy street. Walter sobered up real fast, started thinking of angles. If Ed could get a cut, why not Walter? Besides, he needed the money more than Ed. Satellite and digital cable were killing the direct-to-video movie business.

It used to be easy. Think of a few name actors who haven't had a hit movie in a couple of years, then add an actress in the same situation, preferably one with big tits. Casting was everything. Then pick a city to destroy, someplace with some local color. The Southwest was good, because nobody really lived there, but everyone knew where it was. For all the general public knew, the U.S. military was finding aliens and setting off nuclear bombs there all the time. The final step was to run through the list of possible mutations from a nuclear accident, like a house spider becoming a ten-story tarantula or a garden snake growing as long as a sewer pipe. Then you rip-off the plot from the last movie you made, bring in the production for less than you told the investors it would cost, pocket the rest, and clean up at the rental counter.

But now anyone could download a recent movie—a *hit* movie—right from their cable company and watch it whenever they wanted. And the glut of movies from Hollywood made it next to impossible to get any deals with the second tier cable channels. There were too many movies, plain and simple. So the B-movie business was dying, and Walter was feeling the pinch. He was desperate.

But that was two weeks ago, before Walter took control of his destiny. Who knew he could turn things around so soon?

All Walter needed now was to do some homework. Figure how much weed Jerome and Larry were really moving around town. Call around the major office buildings, ask if they use The Sandwich Brothers. Get a head count. Make some assumptions. Walter had no doubt the brothers would try to cheat him out of his share. He could tell by the look in Larry's eyes. Jerome's were so bloodshot, Walter couldn't tell what was going on upstairs. Jerome he wasn't so worried about. But Larry was going to be a problem.

What was he saying? Walter wasn't worried about either one of them. He had them scared shitless because he could drop a dime on them at any sign of trouble. It was just like in the movies. Casting was everything. They were punks, and he was a player.

What were they going to do about it?

Chapter Eight

"We're going to kill him?"

Jerome asked the question as if inquiring about the weather, idle conversation to pass the time while they drove up Mission Street.

Larry sighed. "No, we're not going to kill him. Zorro's going to kill him for us."

Jerome nodded as he pulled a lighter from his pocket. "Cool. When?"

"We haven't asked him yet." Larry heard the scrape of the lighter and whipped his head around. "I told you, don't smoke in the fucking c—" A car horn blared and Larry swerved, narrowly missing a double-parked Honda. Jerome took advantage of the interruption and lit the joint he'd pulled from his other pocket.

"Eyes front, bro," he said calmly, taking his first hit. "You're operating heavy machinery."

Larry's jaw clenched like a fist. "You want to get arrested?"

"Is this a trick question?"

Counting ten-nine-eight. "Fuck it."

"Exactly."

Five minutes later they crossed the imaginary border of the Mission District, storefronts appearing with signs written in Spanish, the streets more crowded, the occasional trendy restaurants interspersed among *taquerias*, groceries, and narrow apartment buildings squeezed together in rows.

Two blocks further down they came to a 76 gas station opposite an auto repair. Next to the pay phone a lone figure paced aimlessly, his head bobbing to rhythms flowing from an iPod hidden in the folds of his baggy clothes, the white earbuds barely visible.

"There's Buster," Larry said, gesturing through the windshield. "Now remember, we don't tell him our plan. We just tell him we need to see Zorro."

"Roger."

"Who the fuck is Roger?"

Jerome gave him a loopy smile, not feeling stoned yet but knowing the look would piss off Larry. "Y'know, like 'Roger, Captain.' I was just being, you know, *gung ho* and shit."

Larry pulled up next to a pump and killed the ignition. "Just stick to the plan, dickhead."

"Aye-aye."

Larry gave the gas station a quick once-over before looking toward Buster, then hopped to catch up with his brother, who was already grabbing Buster's hand and giving him the patented Rasta shake-and-hug move. Larry could never get the hang of the cool handshakes, and as soon as he figured one out, some new twist was added. But Jerome moved into Buster's space like a dancer, the two men jabbering away, Buster somehow understanding Jerome through the audible whine of his headphones.

Larry gave Buster an awkward wave from four feet away. "How's it going, Buster?"

Buster nodded to his internal rhythm. "I go with Jah, mon."

Larry looked to Jerome for translation, but Jerome was busy re-lighting his joint, oblivious to any risks associated with standing in the middle of a gas station, cars cruising by on both sides. For his part, Buster seemed just as carefree, his pale blue eyes shining brightly.

Part Mexican and part African-American, with some Nordic blood coursing through his veins from a forbearer with a fondness for fjords, Buster's skin was more orange than brown, black, or white. Random starbursts of freckles along his face and arms enhanced the illusion, making his skin seem textured, as if Buster had grown on a tree and was ready to be squeezed for juice. He stood just an inch or two over five feet, but his apparent height was closer to five-six because of the mass of dreadlocks sprouting forth in all directions. This week Buster had dyed them shades of blue and green mixed in with his natural black rows. The combination of greenish hair and orange skin reminded Larry of something, but he couldn't put his finger on it.

Jerome beat him to the buzzer.

"An *oompah-loompah!*" he cried, eyes moving up and down Buster admiringly. "You look like a fuckin' oompah-loompah, man."

Buster's eyes narrowed. "What you goin' on about?"

Larry gave Jerome a look and tried to wave him off, but it was no use.

"Willy Wonka," said Jerome. "You know, the guy who ran the chocolate factory?"

Buster took a hit and passed the joint back to Jerome, smoke curling around his lips like whiskers. "Never saw it."

"Really?" Larry couldn't help himself. "It's a classic."

Buster shook his head. "Growing up, no movies in my house. Just video games. There a Wonka-watchucallit video game?"

Jerome pondered the possibility. "Like *Grand Theft Auto*, but with chocolate?"

Buster shrugged. "I guess."

"No," replied Jerome. "But the movie, there's these little guys—they're all orange and shit, with green hair? They work for Wonka, and they sing these songs. It's a fuckin' riot."

Buster's eyes disappeared within folds of skin, which Larry took as a bad sign. "What's that you're saying about *little guys?*"

"Nothing," said Larry, a little too loudly.

Jerome started humming to himself. "*Do-bah-dee-doo.*"

Buster's eyes narrowed again but Larry intervened. "He's just stoned, Buster. You know Jerome…" He let his voice trail off.

Buster nodded and smiled, a quick flash of white teeth, one inset with a diamond. "Sure, Larry. I know Jerome," he said, his voice low and his eyes flat. "I know you, too…how long now?"

Larry tried to sound nonchalant. "Two years, I guess."

"Right!" replied Buster, his eyes suddenly bright again. "And all that time, you boys ever ask to see Zorro when he didn't ask to see you first?"

Larry and Jerome looked at each other, neither one slapping the buzzer this time.

"You don't know?" Buster kept smiling but his voice had changed. "Want me to tell you?"

Larry winced as he forced his gaze toward the mop-headed menace. "Sure, Buster."

"*Jámas*," said Buster emphatically. "Never."

"We've been, uh, busy," said Jerome lamely.

"Yes, very busy," agreed Larry.

Buster shook his head sadly. "No, *amigos*. Never you come visit us."

Larry realized Buster had stopped sounding like a Rastafarian and instead reminded him of a homeboy from The Mission. The carefree Reggae chords of his earlier speech had been replaced by a guttural menace somewhere deep in his throat.

Buster leaned in close and spoke softly. Larry could barely hear him over the white noise of his earphones. "Time to go for a ride, Larry."

Buster waved his right hand, and before either Jerome or Larry could react, an '85 Chevy Impala careened into the parking lot, bouncing drunkenly on worn shock absorbers. The back door on the passenger side swung open as Buster shoved the two brothers toward the car. They had seen Zorro before, so they knew the drill, but it was always at his command, not their request. Somehow initiating contact had triggered an alarm within Zorro's organization, and now there was no way to silence the bell. The two brothers looked at each other before bending to climb into the car, blood rushing through their temples and ringing in their ears. To Larry and Jerome, it sounded a lot like fear.

Buster leaned into the open door and smiled before giving them a quick wave. Then he slammed the door and walked away, his head bobbing to some happy rhythm too faint and too distant for the brothers to hear.

Chapter Nine

"She's got an ass like a ripe apple."

Gail's parting words bounced around Sam's frontal lobe as he waited for someone to answer the door to 21-D. Those were her words of advice on how to recognize one of the "cute young things" down the hall. Unfortunately, she'd neglected to provide Sam any insight on how to recognize his neighbor from the front, but he assumed an equally compelling image would apply.

Sam realized how right he was when the elevator *pinged* down the hall. He turned in time to see two breasts moving languidly toward him, loosely connected to a woman in her midtwenties. They looked like two honeydew melons juggled by invisible hands. Though he had yet to confirm the apple analogy, Sam had to give Gail credit—there was something about this young woman that could only be described using fruit metaphors. She was a cornucopia of eroticism half his age.

Sam wrenched his eyes to her face before she'd closed half the distance, a personal moral victory and the result of being happily married for so many years. Plus all that extensive cop training. She had almond-shaped eyes set wide in a face that was a Eurasian blend of features that made her look terribly exotic and unnaturally friendly at the same time.

"You looking for me?" she asked, coming to a halt right next to him, keys extended in her right hand. "Or Shayla?"

Sam caught his breath and shrugged. "Either," he said. "Or both. I'm—"

"The cop down the hall," she answered, revealing a smile of impossibly white teeth. "I'm Tamara. Gail told us you'd stop by."

"I only talked to her this morning."

Tamara smiled again, making Sam wish he'd worn sunglasses. "She called last night. Once Gail decides something's going to happen, it usually does. Shayla and I think she's a witch." She turned the key in the door. "A good witch, mind you. Wanna come inside?"

She didn't wait for a reply, just pushed the door open and stepped in front of him. Sam saw immediately that Gail was right about the apple.

"Have a seat," Tamara called over her shoulder, gesturing into the living room toward an overstuffed white couch across from a matching loveseat. Moving left into the small kitchen, she tossed her keys on the counter and opened the refrigerator. "Something to drink?"

Sam checked his watch. "Anything with caffeine would be great, thanks."

Tamara brought over a diet soda whose current ad campaign featured an adolescent pop star dry-humping a jukebox to a dance remix of a Beatles' song. Sam took the can without comment and sat down, facing a view through the sliding glass doors very similar to his own.

Tamara sat in the loveseat and cracked open a bottled water, crossing her legs. She was halfway through her first swig when the door swung open.

A tall black woman about Tamara's age glided across the threshold, kicking the door closed with her left leg without breaking stride or dropping the twin bags of groceries. Even with most of her upper body hidden by paper bags, Sam could tell she was as attractive as Tamara, if such a thing were possible. He stood and extended his hand as she dropped the bags.

"You must be Shayla. I'm Sam, your—"

"—friendly neighborhood policeman." She took his hand in a smooth, strong grip.

"Guess my cover is blown." Sam reclaimed his seat.

Tamara spoke from the loveseat. "With Gail as a neighbor, there aren't that many secrets on this floor."

"Except one." Shayla grabbed her own water and plopped down next to her roommate. She turned to Sam. "Guess that's why you're here, huh?"

Sam felt compelled to state the obvious. "You're talking about Ed, I take it."

"*Dead* Ed," said Tamara, nodding.

Shayla turned to face her roommate. "I always told you pigs couldn't fly."

Both women erupted in laughter, then looked at Sam like two schoolgirls caught smoking.

"Guess you both had a motive, then?" Sam asked gently.

The roommates stopped laughing, but their eyes betrayed their amusement. "You probably think we're awful," began Tamara.

Sam shook his head. "Just surprisingly honest. Most people don't speak ill of the dead. At least not when they're talking to a policeman."

"We've got nothing to hide." Shayla spread her arms wide.

"An ironclad alibi," added Tamara.

Shayla nodded. "It's all on tape."

"Tape," Sam repeated. "You went out that night?" He figured they went to an ATM machine that night or a club or convenience store. Walk into any store or restaurant downtown and you were probably on tape for at least half the night. You might have a right to privacy, but the ability to get some was something else entirely.

"No," replied Shayla. "We stayed in."

"C'mon, we'll show you." Tamara uncrossed her legs and stood up in one fluid movement that could have put Viagra out of business. Sam shook his head and followed the roommates across the living room, down a short hallway, and into the first bedroom on the right.

The apartment was a two bedroom, two bath arrangement featuring one bedroom on each side of a short hallway running perpendicular to the living room. The room Sam entered held a bed topped by a down comforter just slightly smaller than Mt. Everest, flanked by a nightstand on the right that held the usual *tchotchke* of reading lamps, tissues, books, and alarm clock. Against the right wall was a couch low enough to trip over, set adjacent to a small desk. On the desk was a computer with a flat screen monitor. Near the left wall was a short dresser pushed up against a princess vanity with enough lights around the mirror to blow a fuse. From bed to carpet, the overall color scheme was pink, with occasional accents of pink against a background of pink, complimented nicely by random touches of pink, just to keep things interesting.

"Go ahead, guess my favorite color," prompted Tamara, launching herself onto the bed.

"That wouldn't be fair," replied Sam. "I am a detective, after all."

Shayla smiled and curled up on the couch. Sam half expected her to start purring.

"You said something about an alibi?" he said hopefully.

Tamara looked over at Shayla and winked, then smiled broadly at Sam and did something that caught him completely by surprise. She curled her arms around her sides and slowly lifted her shirt over her head, revealing a pair of breasts that should have been hanging in the Louvre.

Shayla giggled to fill the silence as Sam was struck speechless. Tamara did her standing-up move and stepped uncomfortably close to him, saying, "Here, check it out." Then she took his right hand in hers and steered him gently over to the computer.

Sam was busy reminding himself to breathe when Tamara released his hand and grabbed the computer mouse, jiggling it back and forth on a pad next to the keyboard. Sam found the jiggling painfully distracting until the screen saver cleared, revealing a new image on the flat screen that explained everything.

Actually it was four images, each in its own quadrant. In the upper left was an aerial shot of the room they were standing in—Sam figured the camera was set somewhere in the corner above the door, based on the view of his own back. The image in the lower left showed a view of the bed from the ceiling. Lower right was a view from behind the vanity, looking directly at anyone sitting there. And in the upper right were Tamara's perfect breasts, warped and magnified in loving detail by a small camera mounted directly above the computer screen.

Sam managed to reverse his blood flow back toward his brain and state the obvious. "You ladies have a web cam."

Shayla giggled again as Tamara theatrically put her arms around him and gave him a peck on the cheek. Then she strolled over to the bed, reclaimed her t-shirt, and hid her twin genetic masterpieces from view. Part of Sam was horribly disappointed, and part of him was relieved. He was suddenly back in the world he understood, the world of vice and human commerce, and no longer in the letters section of a men's magazine.

"It's more than a web cam," said Tamara proudly. "It's the soft-core website of the month, according to Matt."

"Matt?"

"*Masturbation Matt's Reviews*," replied Shayla. "*The* source for quality adult entertainment on the web." Tamara added, "Just go to *masturbationmatt.com*—he gets 80,000 hits a day."

Sam had the sudden need to sit down. "Mind if we go back to the living room?"

When they were back on their respective couches, drinks in hand, Sam put it together. "That's how you pay the rent."

Shayla nodded. "We take turns sleeping in the room with the cameras. Getting undressed, doing our makeup—topless, of course."

"Of course," replied Sam. "You ever vacuum in there?" He had to ask.

Tamara nodded. "Nude."

"Naturally," said Sam. "Who needs lint on their clothes? And how many, um, visitors do you get?"

"We have about two thousand members at any given time," answered Shayla.

"Ten bucks a month," added Tamara.

Sam ran the numbers in his head. "Two hundred and forty thousand dollars a year?"

"Not counting expenses," replied Shayla. "We pay for links to other sites, placement on search engines, that sort of thing."

"I'm going to med school," said Tamara.

"Law school," added Shayla.

"We'd make more if the site was hardcore," said Tamara, frowning. "But a girl's gotta have some privacy, wouldn't you agree?" She adjusted her t-shirt and shifted on the couch.

"Absolutely," replied Sam with a straight face.

"Plus we make some money on the side," added Tamara. "But nothing serious—I'm eye candy."

"I protest," said Shayla.

Sam thought Shayla was jumping to her roommate's defense until he remembered hearing the term before. "Eye candy," he said slowly. "An escort service?"

"Un-nuh." Tamara shook her head empathically. "You're thinking call girls, dressed up like arm jewelry." She turned to face Shayla. "I ain't no 'ho, am I sister?"

Shayla laughed. "She gets paid 500 bucks a night just to go to parties."

Sam nodded. *USA Today* had a feature article about a year ago. He was so accustomed to the underground world of prostitutes that the growing above-ground economy built on sex often eluded him. "Some millionaire is throwing a party or a major celebrity's son is having his eighteenth birthday, they want enough hot girls to fill up the room."

Tamara nodded. "I'm part of the scenery, like wallpaper with tits."

Sam wrestled with the image only for an instant. "No strings attached?"

Tamara shook her head. "Wouldn't do it if there were. Sometimes I even meet someone worth talking to, but most nights it's just boring. Free food and drinks, easy money."

Sam looked at Shayla. "Not you?"

Shayla shook her head. "Don't want to give up my nights. Not enough of a social life as it is."

Tamara nodded ruefully. "San Francisco—half the men married—the other half married to each other."

Sam titled his chin toward Shayla. "And you protest what, exactly?"

Shayla shrugged. "Anything…everything. I get a call, I call some friends, we go to a march."

"You lost me."

Shayla leaned forward. "Remember the antiwar protests last year?"

"Sure," said Sam. "Screwed up traffic downtown for a week."

Shayla smiled, pleased with herself. "I was there. And remember the anti-outsourcing march down Market Street last month?"

"I must've missed that one."

"Didn't get a big turnout," admitted Shayla. "Then there was the bikers' rights ride down Market Street."

"The motorcyclists bitching about having their own lane, like the bicyclists?" asked Sam.

"Yeah, I was on the back of a Harley. It was fun."

Sam drank off the last of his soda. "How does it work?"

Shayla's eyes lit up. "Most people don't know it, but almost all the protests, marches, sit-ins—you name it—are organized by the same four or five guys."

"You're kidding."

"Everything's got a political angle, right?"

"OK."

"Think about it," said Shayla, warming to her topic. "Protest the war, the current administration looks bad. That's worth something to the other party. You don't want outsourcing, well, that's worth something to the unions."

"The guys on the motorcycles?" asked Sam.

Shayla smiled. "Two groups working together. The union guys who paint the lines on the streets and a city councilman who worked the biker clubs to get elected to his district."

Sam nodded. "And wherever there's politics, there's money."

"Exactly." replied Shayla. "So a small group of entrepreneurs got an idea—call yourself a grassroots organization, apply for nonprofit status, and pay yourself outrageous salaries as the organization's executive directors. Then make money by organizing a march or protest for any client—from any political party or cause, in any city—anytime you want the press to cover an issue."

Tamara interjected. "And all you need are a bunch of highly social young people, connected by technology. An instant, mobile army that's highly photogenic."

Shayla pulled a cell phone out of the back pocket of her jeans. "I've got three hundred contacts in this thing—I send an instant message and at least fifty of them show up at any given time, bringing other friends with them. I get paid five hundred for smaller events, a grand for anything that commands national coverage, like CNN."

Sam ran his fingers through his hair, feeling like he was back in school. He should definitely be taking notes. "What are your politics?"

Shayla shrugged. "I'm a libertarian—I think both parties are filled with a bunch of crooks who wake up every day trying to figure out how to take your money and give it to some guy they went to school with—*after* telling you that they truly understand the plight of the black community...or the working family... or the bilingual student...or the ostracized motorcycle gang." Shayla made a face that suggested nausea. "And I don't think a march ever changed a damn thing."

"Then why do it?"

"Because marches make people feel better—like they're doing *something*. And because the money that goes in my pocket comes out of the pockets of those politicians."

"So you're playing the system?"

Shayla raised her eyebrows. "Better than letting the system play me."

Tamara reached across and pinched Shayla's cheek. Her coffee skin turned pale beneath her eye before regaining its luster. "It helps she's a sister—and she's hot."

"That's me," said Shayla. "Tall, black, and nonfat. The politically correct drink of choice for reporters everywhere."

Sam thought of all the college professors and media pundits saying young women were in constant danger of being exploited because of their sex. These two women had turned the tables on everyone, playing off their looks but using their brains to grab the world by the balls. They were going to graduate from med school and law school without an ounce of debt, and they would never look back.

"I'd hate to get on your bad side," he said to both of them.

"You getting back to business, huh?" asked Shayla.

Sam nodded. "You were in the next room, on camera, the night Ed died?"

Tamara nodded. "Yup."

"Both of you?" asked Sam. "I thought you took turns."

"Some nights we hang out together, like normal roomies," said Shayla. "Paint each other's nails." She extended a bare foot, revealing purple toenails.

"Only we sit around with our tops off," added Tamara.

"Gotta pay the rent," said Sam mildly.

"Exactly," replied the roommates in unison.

"Nice alibi."

"You want to see the footage?" asked Tamara helpfully.

"What man wouldn't?" asked Sam, feeling like the straight man in a vaudeville act. "But thanks anyway. How about telling me why neither of you is wearing black to mourn our dear, departed landlord."

Shayla leaned forward. "Easy. He tried to shake us down."

"For money?"

"For sex," replied Tamara.

Shayla lowered her voice and scratched the side of her face as if she had a beard. "*Give me a blowjob and I'll lower your rent.*"

Tamara matched the pitch of her voice and added, "*Fuck me or I'll kick your ass out on the street.*"

Sam shook his head.

Both women nodded. Tamara spoke first. "Ed was a class act, I tell you."

"And that was only the first week we lived here," said Shayla.

"So you did what?" asked Sam, already knowing the answer.

"We invited him upstairs for a drink," said Shayla, smiling at the memory.

"Asshole thought he was going to get lucky." Tamara smirked. "But we asked him to repeat his generous offers."

Sam said, "And you got the whole thing on tape."

"Broadcast live on the web," said Tamara.

"And recorded onto our hard drive," said Shayla.

"Poor Ed," said Sam.

"Poor dumb Ed," said Shayla.

"So the room is miked?"

"Yeah, we have audio," said Tamara, "but we usually deactivate it, so we can talk shit about whatever we want—our members only care about the T&A, not the witty rapport."

Shalya snorted. "Most probably have the sound off on their own computers anyway, so they can beat off while their wives are in the other room."

"How did Ed react?"

"We hit the replay button and all the blood drained from his face," said Tamara.

"It was beautiful," said Shayla.

"Then we made him take his pants off," added Tamara matter-of-factly.

Sam coughed. "You're not serious."

Shayla nodded. "We are *very* serious."

"Very," agreed Tamara. She laughed from deep in her belly. "He was mad as a hornet."

"And limp as a wet fern," added Shayla, laughing just as hard.

"He ever bother you again?"

Tamara stopped laughing. "Would you?"

It was Sam's turn to laugh. "Not a chance."

"So that's our story, Mister Policeman," said Shayla, doing a remarkable Betty Boop impersonation right down to the fluttering lashes.

Sam knew when he was outgunned. "So you settled your score, and you've got the tape to prove it. Gail tells me Ed tried to force her out of the building, too. Anybody else have a reason to dislike our ex-landlord?"

"Can't think of a reason why anyone *would* like him," replied Shayla. "Did you?"

"Nah," said Sam. "I thought Ed was an asshole."

"Did *you* kill him?" asked Tamara playfully.

"I'm a cop, remember?"

"That just makes it easier to cover-up," said Shayla.

"You kill everyone you think is an asshole?"

"No," replied Tamara, still smiling. "We just make them take their pants off."

"Exactly," said Sam. "So how well do you know your— *our*—neighbors?"

"You talk to Gus yet?" asked Tamara.

Sam shook his head. "Is he the old guy, end of the hall?"

"Yeah. Retired, nice as can be—plays tennis at the courts in the park across the street. Says it keeps him young."

"How old is he?"

"I dunno," said Tamara. "Around Gail's age, maybe? He's sweet on her, I think. I've seen them having coffee sometimes— it's cute."

"OK," said Sam, feeling the need to stretch his legs. "Anybody else?"

"Jill," said Shayla. "You know Jill?"

Sam shook his head. "Gail mentioned her, but we've never met."

"Last door on the left," said Tamara. "You'd like Jill."

Shayla looked Sam up and down, like she was weighing him for sale in the produce section. "He *would* like Jill. How old are you?"

Sam told her.

Tamara beamed. "Jill's great, very cool lady. She's a singer—you know the bar on the other side of the park?"

"Yeah."

"Friday nights," said Tamara. "Jazz."

"She's got that husky voice," added Shayla. "You'd *like* Jill."

Sam found himself blushing. "OK—anybody else?"

"How 'bout the crackheads across the hall?" asked Shayla.

Tamara flushed. "They are *not* crackheads. Jerome's cute—he's just…"

"A crackhead," insisted Shayla.

Tamara flared her eyes at her roommate, then smiled at Sam. "Two brothers, Larry and Jerome. They live across the hall. Larry's a little uptight, but Jerome's kinda sweet."

Shayla rolled her eyes. "He holds the elevator door open for her, and the girl swoons."

Tamara smacked Shayla on the leg. "I like men with manners."

Shayla shook her head sadly. "He's a crackhead."

Tamara smacked harder this time. "He's sweet."

Sam interjected. "A sweet crackhead?"

Shayla corrected herself. "I'm just saying that to get under her skin," she said, hitting Tamara in return. "Crack is too old school—and too urban—for these boys. They are white as bread, the both of them. But Jerome wears some powerful cologne that smells a whole lot like reefer."

"So he's a stoner," said Sam simply. No judgment, just matter of fact. With medical marijuana legal in California, he couldn't remember the last time anyone on the force busted someone for pot. The city had bigger problems.

Tamara tried a pout—it didn't suit her. "He just likes to party."

Sam nodded. "And he lives with his brother across the hall?"

"Yeah," said Shayla. "But you probably won't find them there—they go out during the day."

Sam shrugged. "Maybe I'll knock on their door tonight."

"You know where they hang out a lot?" said Shayla. "That Mexican restaurant across the skybridge. We run into them every time we go to the bar."

"Thanks," said Sam, standing up. "This has been, um, enlightening."

Both women stood together. "Stop by anytime," said Tamara.

"Or go to the site," added Shayla. "The URL address is—"

Sam held his hands up to cut her off. "No—thanks. Not sure I could handle it."

"OK, neighbor," said Tamara, sin in her eyes. The more time he spent with these two women, the less real they seemed to Sam. They were fembots from an Austin Powers movie, designed by some evil genius to tease a man to death.

He said, "They sound pretty harmless. Pot smokers aren't known for their tempers."

"Jerome is not a stoner," Tamara repeated defensively.

"Sorry." Sam held up his hands again. "How about his brother?"

"Larry?" said Shayla. "That boy—he's a nervous one."

Tamara nodded. "Nervous. Totally different from Jerome. He's not—"

"Sweet?" offered Sam.

Tamara smiled. "Exactly!" She elbowed Shayla.

"What's Larry nervous about?" asked Sam.

Shayla shrugged.

"Why don't you ask Larry?"

Chapter Ten

Larry was sweating behind the blindfold.

Blindfolds were mandatory accessories for anyone visiting Zorro. The story behind them went something like this:

Once upon a time, there was an informer who once told police where Zorro held all his meetings. The cops tried to bug the place, but Zorro got an inside tip from someone on the force who also happened to be on Zorro's payroll. Zorro cleared out before the cops could even get the warrant, but never again did anyone know where Zorro would be at any given moment.

The other part of the story was that the informer and his entire family had disappeared, leaving behind their clothes, car, cash, and no forwarding address. People in this neighborhood were too smart to believe the witness protection program could move that fast. But they all knew Zorro could.

The interior of the car had been dark when they climbed in, but Larry recognized the hulk in the front passenger seat as it twisted around and tossed two blindfolds at them. Julio, one of Zorro's bodyguards. A man as thick as he was tall, with a face that looked like it was mauled by a pit bull. And now, as Larry tried to visualize anything other than Julio's brutal features, he found himself sweating with the effort. He tried to breathe through his nose.

Jerome's voice was muffled by the vinyl roof over their heads.

"Hey Larry," he said in a forced whisper. "Maybe this wasn't such a good idea."

Larry closed his eyes behind the blindfold and let his head sink into the headrest as they hit their first pothole. He could tell it was going to be a long ride.

"Think maybe we should have killed him ourselves?" asked Jerome.

Larry's eyes snapped open. "*Shut up*, you moron."

Julio's voice rumbled around the interior of the car. "Who you skinny *gringos* going to kill?" Then he waited a full minute before adding, "Zorro, maybe?"

Larry almost shit himself as he lurched forward. "Fuck! Fuck, no! No fucking way, Julio." He started sweating again. "Jesus, man."

"Don't blaspheme, *gilipollas.*" Julio smacked Larry on the forehead with his open palm. Larry's head snapped back as if struck by a cobra.

"Jesus!" Larry repeated, regretting it instantly.

Julio cocked his arm for another smack, but the driver waved him off. Julio grunted and faced forward, crossing his arms as if pouting.

Jerome's stage whisper roared in Larry's left ear. "I think he just called you an asshole, bro."

Larry's head whipped around. "What?"

"He called you *gilipollas,*" said Jerome emphatically. "I'm pretty sure that means asshole."

"So?"

"So?" Jerome was incredulous. "What are you gonna do about it?"

I don't believe this. "I don't think he meant anything by it," he said dismissively.

"You're saying he called you an asshole by *accident?*"

Larry's jaw clenched. "What's your point?"

"That's not cool," said Jerome, his voice getting louder. "We're their *meal ticket,* Larry. You know anyone moving more weed around this city than us? I mean, we probably pay his salary, you know what I'm saying?"

"We're not paying his salary, Jerome," insisted Larry. "Give it a rest."

"What do you think he makes?"

"Are you serious?"

"Sure," said Jerome, leaning sideways on the bench seat. "I mean, you think he's paid a regular salary, by the hour, or…."

"Or *what*?"

"By the *job*," said Jerome dramatically, his voice getting deep. "By the head. By the scalp, you know what—"

"*Shush*," hissed Larry.

"Did you actually tell me to *shush*?" asked Jerome.

"Shush," repeated Larry. "Just be quiet, OK?"

"You're a wreck, Larry, you know that?" Jerome shook his head. "Jesus…"

"Don't hit me!" It was out of his mouth and echoing around the interior before Larry could stop himself.

In the front seat, Julio just shook his head.

"*Gilipollas*," he muttered.

Jerome sat straight up.

"See?" he said triumphantly. "What did I tell you?"

Chapter Eleven

Sam couldn't remember the name of the lesbian bartender.

He knew she was a lesbian because he'd hit on her last year. A moment of weakness during one of his rare nights out, sufficiently lonely to crave companionship and just drunk enough to look past the obvious signs. She'd been clear but kind. Looking at her sober, Sam realized now what a lightweight he'd become. Cues from her wardrobe, hair, and makeup sent signals in all directions that she preferred the company of her own gender.

Some detective he was.

"Sam." Her smile was genuinely warm. "Haven't seen you in a while."

Sam smiled back, relieved this wasn't going to be awkward. Guess there was a difference between being a clod and a jerk. "How you been?"

"Can't complain," she said. "Nobody's hit on me lately."

"Ouch."

A bigger smile as she reached across the bar and gave his hand a quick squeeze. "What'll you have?"

Sam scanned the tap handles. "Boddington's."

A waitress only slightly taller than the Eiffel Tower squeezed next to Sam, tray balanced precariously over his head. "Sadie, I need a Ketel One and tonic." She shifted to a bad Austrian accent, adding, "I'll be back." Without waiting for the drink, she disappeared, weaving between the tables as if she wore roller skates.

"Sadie," said Sam, pleased her name was one less mystery he had to solve, "is Jill singing tonight?"

Sadie set the beer down, the head foaming over the top of the glass. "You bet. End of the bar, to your right."

Sam glanced over as he drank. A woman sat by herself eight stools over, a glass of wine and sheet music in front of her. He recognized her immediately, had seen her around the building, in the coffee shop, the grocery. She'd made an impression.

She wasn't so much beautiful as she was attractive. Auburn hair, gentle curls swept back on one side of her face, falling across the other until she swept the loose strands behind an ear. Smile lines around her eyes, a slender figure, long fingers unadorned with jewelry. Sam guessed she was about his age, but she had aged much better.

She glanced down the bar and caught him looking before he could turn away. She smiled and Sam felt himself pulled across the room, drink in hand and walking before he'd consciously thought to join her. As he got closer, the gravitational pull only increased.

"Hi neighbor," she said, her voice less husky than he'd imagined, maybe sanded smooth by time. "Thanks for coming."

"You're Jill." *Master of the obvious*, thought Sam.

"And you're Sam," she replied. "I knew your wife."

Sam nodded. "Everyone did."

"Great lady."

"Yeah," said Sam.

Jill smiled again. "Sweet of you to come."

Sam shrugged. "I had an ulterior motive."

Jill arched her eyebrows. Her eyes were green. This close, Sam noticed the mote in her left iris, a miniature sunburst of orange, a rogue star about to eclipse her pupil.

"I came to talk to you," said Sam.

"Officially?" Eyebrows headed north again.

"No, no," said Sam, waving his hand. "I'm retired."

Jill gave him a once-over. "You don't look old enough to be retired."

"How much have you had to drink?"

Jill laughed. "Not that much. You look great," she said, adding, "maybe a little wrinkled, that's all."

Sam touched his face and frowned. Jill brushed his hand away. "Not your face. Your *clothes*."

"Oh." Sam looked down—his slacks looked like crepe paper, his shirt like a papîer-mâché project. "Never mastered the iron."

"I'll show you sometime," said Jill, finishing off her glass of wine. "But now I have to go sing for my supper."

"Does that mean I can't buy you dinner afterward?"

Jill stood, gathered up the sheet music. "For a man with so many wrinkles, that was pretty smooth."

"Was that a yes?"

"I'll tell you after my set. Otherwise you might leave early."

Sam watched her move through the crowd, making her way to the small stage at the rear of the bar.

"I'm definitely not leaving early," he said to himself.

You'll like Jill. Isn't that what Tamara and Shayla had said? It made Sam wonder about his neighbor Gail. His ex-partner, Danny. The girls down the hall. For a man who felt disconnected from everyone, shut off from the world, it felt strange to have so many people act like they knew him.

He'd been roused from a coma, amnesia fading with every waking moment, every social interaction. That was it—they were all alive and he'd been damn near dead, trapped between this world and the next, not sure if he should stay among the living or join Marie.

Pretty soon, Sam was going have to choose which side he was on.

Chapter Twelve

"Got any porn?"

The kid behind the counter gave Walter a sullen look in response. He was a study in teen angst, his Blockbuster vest askew over his Limp Bizkit t-shirt as if he didn't give a shit about anything. "What were you looking for?" The punk daring Walter to say a title, trying to embarrass him in front of the rest of the customers.

"*Anal Assassins*," replied Walter, raising his voice. "Volume one or two. Doesn't matter." Walter sensed the girl standing behind him in line move backwards a step.

The kid shook his head. "We only carry soft-core."

"What's the point?"

The kid didn't have an answer to that, just stood there and shrugged. Walter wondered if the kid was grumpy because the store didn't have any porn, or if he was being judgmental. Either way, fuck him.

And fuck this place. Only two of his movies in stock, *The Revenge of the Scorpion* and *Snakes in the Grass 2*. None of the cockroach movies, not a single fungus flick. What kind of a bullshit Blockbuster was this, anyway? Not that he came to rent his own movies, but still, it was the principal of the thing.

As for the porn, it was just as well this dump didn't carry any—Walter had to focus on the job at hand. He dropped his stack of DVDs on the counter, twelve in total.

"Just these."

The kid eyeballed the movies as he scanned them. "You havin' a party?"

"You're not invited."

"I'm crushed," said the kid. "Thirty-two dollars." He crammed the disks into a bag and twisted his sneer into a smile for the girl standing behind Walter.

Twenty minutes later, Walter sat on his couch, the movies spread across his coffee table.

Scarface and *Carlito's Way*, both starring Pacino. *Blow*, the cocaine flick with Johnny Depp. A bunch of other gangster movies with bullshit titles, second-tier actors, but always drugs as the theme. Then some lighter fare, like Cheech and Chong's *Up in Smoke*. He even rented *Dude, Where's My Car*, the stoner classic starring that punk who was boning Demi Moore.

Walter was doing research. He knew he had the Sandwich Brothers by the short hairs, but he also knew the tables could be turned. Happened all the time in the movies. One day you're on top of the world, just like Pacino in *Scarface*, and the next day there's some South American hit squad sent to kill you in your sleep.

Walter had never smoked pot, never used drugs. He came from a different generation, and booze did the trick every time. But now a major source of his income was going to come from a pair of stoners selling pot to a bunch of other dope fiends. Walter needed to understand their psychology, stay one step ahead of them before he got fucked out of his money. And if the movie business had taught Walter anything about life, it was that someone was always trying to fuck you. Walter popped in the DVD of *Dude, Where's My Car* and sat back on the couch, a ruled notebook and pen on his lap.

It was time to get serious.

Chapter Thirteen

"You're serious?"

Julio didn't respond, just looked at Jerome with those dead eyes, his ruined face expressionless. Not satisfied, Jerome turned to his brother.

"He wants us to take off our pants?"

Larry shifted uncomfortably from one foot to the other, his right hand on his belt buckle. He didn't like where this was going—he felt vulnerable enough already. "That's what the driver said, Jerome."

"The guy who left us here with *Telemundo's* answer to the incredible Hulk?"

Larry winced, stealing a glance at Julio, but the ugly giant was immobile. "Yeah, that was our driver. *Just do it, OK?* It must be part of Zorro's security procedure."

Jerome shook his head, dumbfounded. "Bummer, Larry, 'cause I was gonna strangle Zorro with my jeans. Now I guess we'll have to choke him with our socks."

Julio half-smiled like a man about to be issued a license to kill by Her Majesty's Secret Service. As deadly and suave as a rattlesnake.

Larry was up on his tiptoes in supplication. "Ignore him, Julio. He's stoned." Then to his brother, "*What's the big fucking deal?*"

Jerome looked at his feet. "I ain't wearing boxers, bro."

Larry sighed and started to say *Jesus* but caught himself, saying, "Gee, Jerome, I never realized you were so modest."

"Fuck you, Larry."

Larry leaned in close and put a tight squeeze on his brother's shoulder. "Take off your fucking pants, brother. *Now.*"

Jerome did as he was told. He immediately noticed there was a draft coming from outside. Larry followed suit, revealing a pair of boxers with tiny robots on them.

Julio snorted and said something in Spanish. Larry thought he was laughing at his boxers, but Jerome caught the words for *cut* and *short* and got pissed.

"That's right, Julio," Jerome said testily. "No foreskin. I'm a fucking marvel of modern medicine. Welcome to the U.S. of A."

Larry almost cringed in anticipation of a slap, but Julio laughed a deep bark from another dimension. He raised a massive arm and gestured toward the stairs. "*Arriba rápido.*"

The two brothers looked at each other. Now that their moment had come, neither wanted to take the first step.

"Time to see Zorro?" asked Larry, knowing the question served no purpose but to stall.

Julio smiled cruelly. "*El Diablo*," he said, his voice an octave lower than regret. When he shifted to English, it was somehow even more disconcerting.

"It's time for you dumbass gringos to meet the Devil."

Chapter Fourteen

Jill sang like a fallen angel.

Her voice was huskier when she sang, a silky contralto laced with sin. The band was a variation on a jazz quartet—stand-up bass, drums, piano, and alto sax. They opened with the usual standards, then segued into songs Sam couldn't place. The arrangements Jill had been poring over at the bar, songs that Sam felt he must have heard before but somewhere else. Songs from another life.

Half an hour into the set, Sam was having trouble breathing. He had never believed in love at fist sight until he'd met Marie. Now he was wondering if there was such a thing as love at first listen.

You are one lonely bastard, he thought. *You've got to get out more.*

Sam scanned the crowd. Four couples at the bar, five guys clustered at the far end, Sadie working the length of it. Waitresses navigating the crowd, crossing lines of sight but never staying in one place. The tables near the stage full, mostly couples but a few with three or four girls crowded around, heads bobbing whenever Jill started wailing. From his perch at the end of the bar Sam had an unobstructed view to the stage, except for a support beam blocking the guy playing the bass. Sam didn't give a fuck about the bass.

The set lasted an hour, but Sam felt like he'd been listening forever. He could still hear the chords as Jill walked between the tables, nodding her thanks as people clapped, some reaching out to take her hand. She took her seat at the bar, as nonchalant as if she'd just returned from the ladies room. Sadie had a glass of Dewar's already poured and waiting.

Sam nodded toward the whisky. "That explains the voice."

Jill smiled and threw back half the glass, sucking air between her teeth. "I only drink wine before my set," she explained. "This is my drink for winding down." She took another long sip as Sam watched her.

"So what'd you think?" she asked.

Sam shrugged. "It was OK."

Jill studied him for a minute, then burst out laughing, a low throaty chuckle that sounded almost as good as her singing. Maybe better.

"It was incredible," said Sam. "Really great."

Jill's eyes sparkled. "Yeah, I really felt it tonight."

"Me, too." It was out before he could catch it, but once said, it felt surprisingly comfortable. A simple fact, plainly stated.

Jill nodded as if she'd just made a decision, then drained the rest of her drink, catching an ice cube before setting the tumbler down with a thud. Sadie smiled and took the glass away, leaving them alone. Sam hadn't noticed she was there.

"So," Jill said around the ice cube, "What were you saying about dinner?"

Chapter Fifteen

"I eat eyeballs."

To illustrate the point, Zorro reached across his desk and thrust his hand into a jar of blued glass about eighteen inches high, the kind you might see in a candy store filled to the brim with jelly beans. Neither Larry nor Jerome expected to see any jelly beans. Larry grimaced involuntarily while Jerome's eyes went wide in anticipation. But even before Zorro's hand re-emerged, a pickled smell wafted across the room like a sigh from an open grave.

Zorro looked more like an alligator than a fox. His teeth jutted past his lips at odd angles, as if someone had gone to work with a pair of pliers but stopped midway through the torture. When he smiled, it was pure Discovery Channel.

Jerome nudged Larry and managed a stage whisper. "*Bro, I don't think the Mexican mob offers dental as one of their benefits.*"

Larry hissed, which turned into nervous coughing he couldn't control. Soon he was hacking and gasping for air. Everyone in the room watched him with morbid fascination, even Zorro, his hand still submerged in the jar. The seconds ticked by.

Larry pulled it together, his eyes watering. Zorro brought his hand to his lips.

It was an eyeball. Through the tears, Larry noticed it looked too big and suspected it was a sheep's eyeball, considered a delicacy in the Mideast but a disgusting appetizer by any measure.

Still, a great way to scare the shit out of people. Sheep eyeball or not, Larry was definitely creeped out.

Jerome was fascinated. "Does it taste like chicken?"

Zorro's eyes glittered, black as obsidian. His hair matched, slicked back over a high forehead. Deep lines etched his cheeks and made his mouth seem unnaturally wide. Or maybe that was because of the teeth, Larry couldn't tell. He seriously doubted Zorro was going to model for *GQ* anytime soon.

"It tastes like *revenge*, Jerome," said Zorro. "Did you know my victims almost always have their eyes cut out?"

Larry cut in. "No—no, he didn't know that, Zorro. What a great idea."

Jerome gave his brother a petulant look but let it go. He was wearing a towel courtesy of their host, and some of his confidence had returned.

Zorro sucked his fingers for a moment before saying. "So Buster told me you wanted to visit and I was delighted—but *confused*." His voice was pure velvet, his accent barely discernible. "You don't come to my neighborhood, do you?"

"We've been busy," said Larry lamely.

"How busy?" asked Zorro, eyes glowing. Larry met his gaze, only for an instant. Something about the way Zorro asked the question told Larry he'd better come clean before the questions got a lot harder—and the questioning got a lot more insistent. Julio stood behind them, guarding the door, and Larry could sense the giant's hostility rolling across the room in waves.

Larry spilled his guts, talking so fast even Jerome had a hard time keeping up despite already knowing the details. When he had finished, Larry walked over to a big chair on the right side of the room and sat down, uninvited. He was spent. His bare legs bobbed back and forth, banging together at the knees and making the little robots dance.

Zorro steepled his hands in front of him, shook his head sadly.

"You had blackmail problems before and you didn't tell me?"

Larry frowned. "You knew about Ed?"

Zorro didn't answer, which Jerome took as a rebuke.

"We had it handled, Z."

Zorro gave him a look that suggested no one had called him Z before, but Jerome was oblivious. Zorro turned to Larry. Larry was afraid, and fear always pays attention.

"Someone fucks with you, they are fucking with me," said Zorro deliberately.

Larry straightened in his chair. *Now we're talking.*

"This Ed person," continued Zorro. "Did you kill him?"

Jerome pointed at Zorro. "I asked Larry the same thing, Z—but he wouldn't come clean."

Zorro ignored him. "It doesn't matter. What matters is this Walter, *sí?*"

Larry nodded from the chair, forcing himself to look Zorro in the eyes again. "*Sí.*"

"Fuckin-A," said Jerome.

Zorro said something in Spanish, too quickly for Larry to catch—high school Spanish was buried deep in his cerebellum, dormant and irretrievable. Julio grunted, turned, and stepped through the door. Zorro turned back to his guests, gesturing toward one of the chairs in front of his desk.

"Sit down, Jerome," he said. "Relax. I've asked someone to join us."

Jerome took the chair, glanced over at Larry, who looked like he'd just signed a deal with the Devil and was having second thoughts.

"This is going to cost you," said Zorro, his voice a silk tourniquet.

"No problem," said Larry, a little too quickly. "We can pay you tomorrow."

"I don't think so, Larry." The tourniquet tightened immeasurably, cutting off the circulation in the room, making the brothers dizzy.

"Today?" asked Jerome. "You want cash today?"

"Not today," replied Zorro. "And not tomorrow."

The brothers looked at him and waited for the punch line.

"You see, I don't want cash," said Zorro. "I want a percentage."

The remaining blood rushed from Larry's face. "But you get a percentage, Zorro."

Jerome nodded vigorously. "A fuckin' big one, Z."

Larry waved him off. "What did you have in mind?"

"Double," said Zorro simply. It wasn't a question.

"Double?" Jerome's eyes bugged out. "But that's more than fucking Walter is getting."

Zorro nodded in sympathy. "But unlike Walter, I will never threaten to turn you into the police, eh?"

Larry tried to breathe through his nose but sneezed violently. "I dunno, Zorro, I mean—"

"—then it's a deal," said Zorro. "You double my percentage and I kill Walter." He let that hang in the air a moment before adding, "Unless you'd prefer that I kill you."

Larry swallowed. Jerome, for once, had nothing to say.

Zorro looked from Larry to Jerome and laughed, a wicked sound that sent a chill down Larry's spine. He reached into the blue jar and proffered his hand, smiling, his teeth jutting like spikes.

"You guys want an eyeball?"

Chapter Sixteen

"That's disgusting."

"How do you know if you haven't tried one?"

Sam tried to think of a suitable answer. *I tried one before and didn't like it. I hate the French. I'm allergic to things that smell worse than my feet.* But they all sounded like he was chicken, so he reached across the table with his dainty fork and pried a snail free of its shell.

"Tastes like a snail."

Jill laughed. "That's why they call them *escargot*. No one in their right mind would order snails."

"Then why did you order them?"

"I wanted to see how you'd react," she said with a wicked grin. "Besides, how do you know I'm in my right mind?"

"I heard you sing, remember?" Sam smiled briefly, just long enough for the lines around his eyes to make an appearance.

"You really liked it?"

"There's already enough seafood at this table," Sam said, gesturing at the shrimp, snails, and clams scattered before them. "No need for you to go fishing."

"I just like hearing you say it."

"It was incredible," said Sam simply. "How long have you been a singer?"

"Not long enough," said Jill, reaching for her glass.

"What does that mean?"

"Nothing much," said Jill. "I started singing later in life, in my twenties."

"So?"

"So it's a hobby I wish had been a career."

"And you need to start young?"

Jill shrugged. "The odds are against you at any age, but these days it helps if you're video material—you know, sixteen with a perfect midriff."

Sam suspected her midriff looked just fine but didn't say anything.

Jill continued, "Most of the successful acts today are performers, not singers. Their sound comes from a mixing board. I'm just an old-fashioned singer."

"Well, you're a damn good one," said Sam. "What's the day job?"

"Graphic designer. Brochures, business cards, websites. I helped the girls down the hall with their site design—Tamara and Shayla—have you seen it?"

"The website?" Sam blushed despite himself. "No, I haven't."

Jill smiled. "But you've seen the girls?"

"They're hard to miss."

"And what did they have to say for themselves?" asked Jill. "About our late landlord?"

"Not much," admitted Sam. "They thought he was a scumbag."

"They're smart girls."

"That they are."

"That is why we're having dinner, isn't it? To talk about Ed's fall from grace."

"No, that's why we're talking," said Sam. "But that's not why we're having dinner."

"I'll take that as a compliment." Jill held his gaze for an extra beat. "That's why I wanted to eat here—it's quiet."

"So you don't like French food, either?"

Jill chuckled. "I like the atmosphere more than the food, but there's only so many options in the neighborhood. And if we went to the Mexican place, you'd see half the people on our floor there."

Sam nodded. "Tamara and Shayla said the two brothers ate there a lot."

"So does Walter."

"The fat guy?"

"Yes, you could say that," agreed Jill. "Walter could lose a few pounds." The she added, "He tends to leer."

"He's never leered at me."

"No accounting for taste."

"So you know everyone?"

Jill shrugged. "More or less."

"And you knew Ed."

She leaned forward, the mote in her eye electric. "Are we getting down to brass tacks?"

Sam shifted uncomfortably. "There are no brass tacks. If you want, we don't—"

"No, no," said Jill emphatically. "Let's get to it."

"OK."

"I'm *thrilled* Ed bought it," said Jill. "Wish I'd thrown him off the balcony myself."

Sam sat back in his chair. "Jesus."

Jill looked defiant. "Tell me you heard something different from the other tenants, and I'll tell you they were lying."

Sam shook his head. "One thing this case doesn't lack is motive."

The waiter came and cleared their plates. They both ordered coffee and the conversation returned to idle chatter until it arrived. Then Jill said, "Ed tried to rape me."

Sam blinked, not sure he heard her correctly. Her delivery was so flat, so matter-of-fact. But the look in her eyes told him it was no joke. As a cop he'd seen that expression too many times. He gritted his teeth.

"When?"

Jill looked at her hands. "About three months after I moved in. I was recently divorced, not going out much. Wanted to be alone. One night Ed comes to my door, tells me he needs to check a fuse. I go back to the couch, and the next thing I know, he's on top of me." She clenched her fists slowly, then eased the fingers open one at a time, looking up to meet Sam's gaze.

He asked, "What did you do?"

A quick, bitter smile. "Ed didn't realize I studied kick-boxing for fifteen years."

Sam felt a knot in his chest loosen. "But he found out?"

"Got him off me with a shove. He stands up, hands on his hips, starts threatening me. Says I led him on." Jill shook her head in disbelief. "That was the opening I needed…"

"To do what?" asked Sam. "Call the cops?"

"Kick him in the balls," replied Jill.

Sam smiled despite himself. "Nice."

"Figured it was faster than dialing 911."

"What did Ed do?"

"Curled into a ball."

"And then you called the cops?"

Jill shook her head. "Why bother? His word against mine. The kick ended it—I could see it in his eyes. After that, we had…" her voice trailed off, "an *understanding*."

"An understanding," repeated Sam, not sure he understood.

"Ed understood I wasn't interested," said Jill, "and if he ever pressed the point again…"

"Yes?"

"I'd kill him."

Sam watched her eyes but didn't interrupt.

Jill forced a smile. "There, you want to put the cuffs on now?"

Sam shook his head. "Not unless that's something you're into."

"Don't cops think everyone's a suspect?"

"If this were a real case, *everyone* would be a suspect," replied Sam. "But I'm not a cop, just a neighbor."

Jill gave him a look that said she didn't believe that any more than he did, but she let it pass.

"OK neighbor," she said. "Let's go home."

Chapter Seventeen

"Where do you live?"

Larry didn't want to answer. The little guy asking the question was decidedly creepy, not someone you'd give your home address to, even if he was a cab driver and you were drunk. Zorro with his carnivorous smile and the jolly Mexican giant, Julio, looked normal by comparison.

Not that the guy had any noticeable scars, birthmarks, or tattoos. In fact he was amazingly average, forgettable in every way. A little short, maybe, but dressed in simple chinos and plain white shirt, clothes you could buy at any Gap. A typical hair cut for a guy his age, which Larry guessed around thirty-five. A bland expression on an unlined face.

But his eyes were something else entirely. Zorro might be a scary fucker, but when this guy locked eyes with you, you practically shit yourself. At least that's what Larry almost did until he blinked.

Zorro had the temperament of Beelzebub, but he wasn't the Devil. Not even close. This short fucker won that contest hands down. He had the eyes of Satan, two black pools of pure sadism poured into his skull and left there to cool.

"Tell Carlos the address," prompted Zorro, his fingers tapping idly on his desk.

Larry mumbled the street name, keeping his eyes fixed on Zorro. Jerome shifted from one foot to the other but remained silent.

"*Bueno.*" Zorro clapped, once, and the driver came through the door. He nodded at Julio, then turned his attention to Zorro, who said, "Hernando will take you and your brother home, then he will watch your building until this *pajero* Walter shows his face. Then Carlos will decide what to do."

Out of the corner of his eye, Larry could see Carlos nodding eagerly and felt the excitement pour off him in waves. There was a twisted, erotic energy around him, as if he were getting aroused in anticipation of the kill. Larry tasted bile but fought the urge to gag.

Zorro must have noticed because his tone became almost soothing. "You OK, Larry?"

Larry nodded but couldn't speak. *Walter was a dead man the moment we came here.* Suddenly Larry missed making sandwiches for a living.

Zorro swiveled in his chair. "Jerome?"

Jerome shrugged but avoided eye contact with everyone, even Larry. "Whatever you say, Z."

"*Amigos,* go home and relax. It is out of your hands." Zorro stood up, smiled. "From now on, there is no reason to worry."

Chapter Eighteen

"I'm worried."

Walter said it out loud, feeling the need to keep himself company.

"This is bad," he added, grabbing the TV remote and thumbing the off button.

"I'm fucked."

He threw the remote onto the couch and began pacing from the living room to the kitchen. Crumbs from popcorn, chips and Cheez-its fell off his shirt and chin with every step, crunched softly into the carpet, but Walter didn't notice. He was replaying movies in his head, looking for some flaw in his logic but finding no escape.

He'd discovered a dangerous pattern in the drug business: Things ended badly for the drug dealers.

Not sometimes. *Always.*

Not for some of the drug dealers. *All of them.*

Not just the big fish. *Every fucking fish in the pool.*

Walter had seen these movies more than once, like everybody else. In the theater when they came out, then on cable again and again. He knew the top guys always got greedy, took a fall. But Walter wasn't planning on becoming the top dog. He wasn't Tony Soprano or Tony Montana or any other fucking Tony who wanted to be on top of the world.

Walter wanted to be a tapeworm.

He wanted to live off the inside of the drug trade, invisible and unnoticed, sucking away enough sustenance to keep him swimming in greenbacks during his twilight years. No ego, no hubris. No risk of ending up dead like the movie kingpins. He wanted to be a character actor, part of the story but quickly forgotten when the movie ends, until the name comes up in some Trivial Pursuit question and someone says *I remember that guy... he didn't get killed in that movie...he must've skipped town with the cash, got the girl after the boss died, outlasted them all...at least that's what I think would happen if they ever made a sequel.*

Walter wanted to be the one that got away, so he searched the rented DVDs for one that did. He wanted to find just one happy ending for some bit-player he could relate to.

But there were no happy endings. Even in the comedies, no one got away unless they got out of the business. And in the dramas? Everybody got killed or went to jail. No exceptions. No happy ever after for the drug lords.

Walter had rented this one flick, *Layer Cake*, an English crime drama by one of the guys that made *Lock, Stock and Two Smoking Barrels*. The lead actor was the blond guy playing James Bond. Totally smooth, always one step ahead of the competition. Ready to bail at the first sign of trouble. A middleman who outlasts them all. Walter's kind of criminal.

After ten depressing movies, Walter was rooting for this guy, and sure enough, he gets away with it—keeps the drugs and the money, even gets the girl. Walter practically fell off the couch with relief.

But then, in the final scene, right before the credits roll, the guy gets capped. Out of nowhere, some minor character from earlier in the movie, somebody Walter had forgotten all about, comes up and shoots the drug dealer right in the chest. *Boom.* Then the movie ends, just like that. Walter couldn't fucking believe it.

No one got away with it. Even Johnny Depp went to jail for life, fucked over by his own wife. So even if you get the girl, the bitch is your undoing.

More worrisome for Walter, the middleman actually got the worst of it. Funny how you forgot those parts until you saw them again. No matter how many times you'd seen the movie before, you only remembered what happened to the main guy. But long before the drug dealers went down, and way before the kingpin met his grim fate, somebody cut out the middleman. Sometimes the guys dealing on the street wanted to move up in the food chain. Other times the Mob boss needed a scapegoat. No matter how much money there was in the drug business, the margins weren't big enough for the guy in the middle.

And Walter was the guy in the middle. Hell, he'd put himself there.

Might as well paint a target on my back.

Walter looked at the DVDs scattered across his living room and felt the sweat under his arms. Easy money was one thing, but getting killed was another. He had to figure out a way to stay off the radar.

He thought of the two brothers, how they'd backed into this drug business. Maybe there was an angle there. Walter knew people, places. Maybe he could supplement their distribution. He worked with all the edit bays in town, the recording studios. Production companies. They weren't office buildings, but the people working there ate lunch, didn't they? And they smoked pot, almost to a person, except for dinosaurs like Walter.

Maybe if he helped the brothers expand their distribution, he'd become an active partner instead of a silent one. Get on the front lines, away from the middle. Become the third leg of their stool. Then, when trouble came knocking, as it surely would, he would run out the back door and let those *schmucks* down the hall take the rap.

It just might work, if he didn't get too greedy. The middle was the killing ground. He had to change positions.

Walter went over it in his mind until he was satisfied. *From now on boys, we work together.* Sound confident, tell them how it is. *You are the puppeteer.* Set them up now, before they see it coming. Then get out when the heat arrives. He recited these principals like a series of mantras until he was calm again.

Piece of cake.

Walter snatched his keys off the counter and stepped into the hallway, barefoot and covered with crumbs. In ten strides he had reached the brothers' apartment.

Taking a deep breath, Walter raised his right hand and knocked on the door.

No one answered.

Walter put his ear to the door, heard nothing. Knocked again, loudly. Felt the adrenaline rush fade. Standing there in the hallway barefoot, he felt exposed. Vulnerable.

Fuck. He was getting paranoid. Walter checked his watch. Still early. They were probably having dinner, maybe at the Mexican place. He returned to his apartment and sat down heavily on the couch. Looked at the clock on the wall, just to see if it contradicted his watch. Still early.

Grunting with the effort, Walter pulled on his shoes. If he hurried he could make it to the grocery store before they closed, buy a six pack. Then he'd sit on his couch and wait them out. When he heard them walking down the hall, he'd give them five minutes to get settled.

Then he'd knock on their door and they'd invite him in.

Piece of cake.

Chapter Nineteen

"Piece of cake?"

Jill stood in her doorway, her russet hair backlit by the light from the foyer. From where Sam was standing, it looked like she had a halo.

"It's angel cake," she added.

"Naturally."

"What's that supposed to mean?"

Sam shook his head, recovered. "You bake?"

Jill gave him a warning look. "I cook," she said with just a hint of pride. "But I rarely bake. When you live alone…" She let that sit before adding, "Gail made it for me."

"Birthday?"

Jill shook her head. "No, she was just being neighborly." She said the last word slowly, as if she realized it might sound foreign to him. When he didn't bite, she asked, "Want to come in for a cup of coffee?"

Yes. Absolutely. That would be great. Sam stood rooted to the spot, his shoes leaking glue into the floorboards, his soul nailed down like a tarp.

"No, thanks," he said half-heartedly. "Maybe another night."

"I don't bite, you know," said Jill gently. "At least not on the first date."

Sam's right eye twitched at the word *date*. "Dinner was great."

Jill looked him up and down. "It won't get any easier, you know."

"What?"

"Joining the human race," she said with a sad smile. "The longer you wait, the harder it is."

"You talking about you now," said Sam, "or me?"

"Maybe both of us."

Sam nodded but stayed on his side of the door. "I like the way you sing."

Jill answered with a smile that dimmed the lights in the hallway.

"So do I," she said, leaning forward and kissing him gently on the cheek.

"Why—," Sam began but stopped before the question could sound anything but lame.

"Sometimes you just get a feeling for someone," replied Jill.

"I figured you were just being neighborly."

Jill smiled ruefully. "I haven't met many good men in my time—probably my fault as much as theirs." She raised her right hand, jabbed her index finger against his chest. "I think there's a good man buried somewhere underneath all that scar tissue. Maybe next time we get together, you'll introduce me."

Before Sam could respond, she took a step back and closed the door. He stood looking at her door for a minute, remembering the sensation of her finger tapping, putting pressure on his heart. Somewhere deep inside his chest, ice was breaking apart in silent agony, drifting toward an empty horizon.

But Sam could feel a part of him grasping—reaching out to savor the cold—as if the ice were the only life raft he had. Taking a deep breath, he turned and walked toward his apartment, thinking that the hallway had never seemed so long.

Chapter Twenty

"So long…*so long!*"

Jerome waved like a drunken idiot, a sneer on his face as he added, "*Adios,* motherfuckers." The taillights of the Chevy had disappeared around the corner before Jerome gave the middle finger, but Larry grabbed his arm with a fevered hiss.

"You want to get us killed?"

"That a trick question, Larry?"

"We're fucked."

"What are you talking about?" demanded Jerome. "The Z-man just told us our problems were as good as solved."

Larry looked around for a sharp object to stab his brother, but they were standing at the corner of Davis and Jackson streets, the only things nearby a grocery store, their apartment building, and a row of newspaper kiosks. He unclenched his fists and breathed through his nose.

"Zorro is going to charge us more than Walter would have," said Larry. "We would have been better off paying our fat-assed neighbor."

"I told you, Larry. Math's not my thing."

Larry lunged, ready to choke the life out of his younger brother, their mother be damned. His clawed hands had just made contact when he caught sight of Barney, the building's security guard. Larry crumpled into his brother, transforming his abortive assault into an awkward hug. Before Jerome could react, Larry started sobbing uncontrollably. Larry was unstable on the best of days, and today was definitely one of the worst in recent memory.

Jerome smiled sheepishly at the aptly named Barney, who was shaped like a purple dinosaur and acted like Barney Fife from the Andy Griffith show. He was a threat deterrent on par with Inspector Clouseau.

"Hey Barney," said Jerome.

"You guys OK?"

"Our hamster died," replied Jerome, patting Larry on the back. "Larry's kind of torn up about it."

Barney nodded sympathetically but kept walking, smelling trouble just around the corner.

Larry wiped his nose on Jerome's shoulder and tried to pull himself together before saying, "Sorry…I'm…I'm just a little stressed about all this."

"You're wound too tight," said Jerome with surprising tenderness.

"Maybe you're right." Larry took a deep breath, blew out his cheeks. "It's not our problem, right?"

"Not anymore," replied Jerome. "Besides, it could be worse."

Larry blinked. "How?"

"We could be Walter."

Larry felt faint. "Don't you feel guilty?"

Jerome tapped his forehead. "No room for guilt up here, big brother."

Larry wanted to ask what there was room for, but he said nothing.

"Did we force Walter to blackmail our asses?" asked Jerome.

"No…no, we didn't." The observation caught Larry by surprise—the brutal simplicity of it all. Larry marveled at the wisdom of his younger brother when he wasn't stoned. An innate, naïve logic that kept the real world at a manageable distance. He wondered if Buddhist monks were all stoners.

Jerome slapped Larry on the back. "Let's go have a drink at the Mexican place—we'll make a toast."

"To what?"

"A life without guilt."

Chapter Twenty-one

Sam felt guilty for being alive.

He'd been a cop in the line of fire every day. Earned a few scars and a wound to the leg trying to do more good than harm, but only succeeding on rare occasions. Marie had been a civilian, a prosecuting attorney, doing more good in a day than most people did in a lifetime. But she got sick, suffered, and died, while Sam's only lasting injury was her loss.

The guilt grew in the space she left behind. A warm, dark place deep inside his heart where the light of logic and reason couldn't penetrate. A chamber full of longing for things that might have been.

Sam shook his head to clear it, leaned against his kitchen counter as he opened the refrigerator. You didn't have to be a police detective to guess he was a bachelor. The beer was gone, which meant the fridge was half-empty. The random assortment of foodstuffs looked suspiciously pale and faded, a sure sign of expiration dates long gone.

Running his hands through his hair, he walked disconsolately down the hall to his bedroom, kicking off his shoes as he crossed the threshold. The cloying guilt was fueling an undercurrent of depression, dragging him down. The bed was telling him to sleep, his brain saying *not a chance*.

The bed was winning the argument until he saw the message light on his answering machine.

"Hey partner, call me." Danny Rodriguez' voice bounced off the walls of his bedroom, shaking Sam out of his funk.

The pressure on his balls had returned.

Sam bent down and pulled on his shoes, walked down the hall, and grabbed his keys. He'd call Danny back later.

Right now, he needed a drink.

Chapter Twenty-two

"I'll have a mojito."

The bartender nodded, pulled a frosted glass and dropped in some mint.

Larry shook his head. "How can you drink those things?"

"I just like saying it," replied Jerome. "Go ahead, try."

"No, I just want a beer."

"It'll make you happy."

"No, it won't."

"*Mo—heeeet—ooh!*"

Larry clamped his hand around Jerome's mouth. "Cut it out."

"Mmm…hhmmm…uuh."

"What?" Larry lifted the lower half of his right hand, giving Jerome just enough clearance to work his mouth.

"I said…*mojito*!" Jerome got it out before the hand could slam into position. "There, doesn't it make you want to smile?"

The bartender, a good-looking guy in his twenties, chuckled as he mixed the drink. The guy looked carefree, relaxed, content—everything Larry wasn't. He turned to his brother and took a deep breath.

"I think you're bipolar."

Jerome slurped his drink. "Have you been reading again, Larry?"

"Never mind," said Larry, realizing he was wasting his breath. "We need a plan."

Jerome caught an ice cube and started sucking on it. "I thought we had a plan. I thought Z was—"

"Shhhhhhhhhh!" snapped Larry, almost coming off the bar stool. The bartender had moved about ten feet away, serving two girls who looked barely out of college.

"Did you just shush me again?" Jerome sounded deeply wounded.

"Don't say his name, for Chrissakes."

"That's why I used the letter, Larry. It's like a secret code."

"Don't even use the letter," Larry insisted, looking right and left. He realized they were sitting in a Mexican restaurant. Who knew how many spies Zorro employed in the quick service restaurant industry? "Someone might guess."

"OK," Jerome shrugged. "How about Q? It could be like James Bond."

"No."

"X?"

"Drop it."

"Fine," said Jerome, taking another long pull on his drink. "So the drug lord we're not talking about? I thought he had our back…"

Larry leaned close to his brother. "What if something goes wrong?" he asked. "Who do you think is going to take the fall for…" He paused, looked around before adding, "Walter?"

"You mean W?" Jerome said in a stage whisper.

"You know who I mean, you retard."

"That's *whom*, Larry. Gotta watch your grammar, bro."

After a deep breath through his nose, Larry tried again. "We need a plan."

Jerome crunched his ice and reached for the basket of chips on the bar. Music blared from cheap speakers overhead, all the lyrics in Spanish. This entire place was designed to give you a headache unless you drank heavily. Jerome swiveled on his stool to look Larry in the eye.

"You think we need a plan," he said. "In case Z fucks us over."

Larry let the use of the alphabet slide, relieved Jerome had tuned into reality. "Exactly."

"You think he will?"

Larry shrugged. "If you asked me a week ago, I would have said he needed us."

"We move a lot of pot for that guy."

"Now I'm not so sure," replied Larry. "It's a lot of pot for *us*—but what about all the runners he has, working the streets in the Mission, the Tenderloin district, Polk street? All those guys feed back into—" Larry stopped before he said the name.

Jerome finished the thought. "Back into Z."

"Yeah," said Larry. "You add all those runners up, moving all those bags around the city, now *that's* a lot of pot."

"So maybe we're expendable."

Larry nodded and reached for his beer. "If anything goes wrong, we take the fall."

"How tough can it be to kill Walter?" Jerome palmed a stack of chips. "I mean, the fat fuck is halfway to a coronary."

"Accidents happen," said Larry simply. "Mistakes get made."

"That dude Carlos doesn't look like he makes too many mistakes."

Larry shivered at the memory of those eyes but didn't say anything.

"I guess the cops could take an interest," said Jerome. "You know, after the deed is done."

Larry caught his reflection in the mirror behind the bar. Drawn face, tired eyes. *Shake it off.* He shook his head and took a swig of his beer. *Optimists win, pessimists go to jail.*

"We're not on their radar," he said with forced bravado. "The cops don't know we exist." He turned to face Jerome, noticed a man moving toward them. An older guy, a little rumpled. Walked right up and stood between them, an easy smile on his face. He looked familiar, but Larry was having a hard time placing him.

"You must be Larry," the man said, nodding. He shifted his gaze. "And you're Jerome."

"And you are?" Larry spoke up before Jerome picked another fight with the wrong guy.

"Sam," came the reply. "I'm the cop who lives down the hall."

Larry looked at himself in the mirror, saw his eyes bugging out of his head.

Be cool.

"Mind if I ask you a few questions?" asked Sam.

"Sure, have a seat." Larry shifted over one stool, making a space between him and Jerome. Kept his eyes off the mirror. "Want a drink?"

"I'll buy," said Sam. "What're you having?"

"You're a cop?" asked Jerome.

"Yeah." Sam had an instinct to leave out the part about his retirement.

Jerome held up his glass, crushed ice and mint languishing at the bottom. He seemed unfazed, had his mojo working. *Chilled.* Not for the first time that day, Larry considered switching to Jerome's drug and alcohol regimen.

"Another mojito would be great right about now," said Jerome. "You should try one."

"No thanks." Sam shook his head, caught a whiff of something that wasn't cologne. *Eau de cannabis* saturated Jerome's clothes.

"I just like saying it," said Jerome.

"What's that?"

"*Mojito,*" said Jerome. "Sort of makes you happy, doesn't it?"

Sam looked into Jerome's eyes and smiled.

"Sure does," he said.

Chapter Twenty-three

Carlos decided to shoot Walter in the head.

He'd considered using the plastic explosive C-4, which was easy enough to obtain, but Zorro said no collateral damage. Innocent bystanders getting hurt would bring too much heat. A murder investigation he could handle, but the FBI analyzing bomb fragments was not a good idea. This homeland security thing had made his job challenging, but Carlos still loved his work.

He offered to get his hands dirty, kill Walter with a knife or an axe. Make it bloody, send a signal to anyone thinking about stealing from Zorro, but again the boss said no. The apartment complex was too small, the people too gentile. The brutality would overwhelm the message. That sort of killing was fine among the gangs or their families—for those who knew of Zorro—when cutting a man's heart out or taking his eyes sent a warning in a common language of violence. But in downtown San Francisco the murder should be sudden, dramatic. Like something out of movie.

An assassination.

Carlos knew all about assassinations. He wasn't Mexican like the others but hailed from the Basque region of Spain, an area known for its beautiful landscapes, unique culture and a rich history of terrorism. Carlos' father had been a member of the ETA, a separatist group committed to forming an autonomous Basque state. Over long nights at the kitchen table, he taught Carlos how to mold plastic explosive into a shaped charge that could adhere to the underside of a man's car. After they had finished, his father would look at him with unvarnished pride, tousle his hair. Then he would throw his hands in the air and shout *Boom!*—they would both laugh till they cried.

Carlos blinked and ran a finger under his eyes. He was getting sentimental.

Carefully, he opened the long box before him, scooting forward in his seat to set the styrofoam packing materials on the back half of the kitchen table. He smiled as the gun was revealed.

It was a Browning hunting rifle with a magazine capable of holding five 7mm bullets, though Carlos only needed one. He was going to use 175-grain cartridges, standard for hunting elk or deer. One of Zorro's young recruits without a criminal record named Alberto had purchased the gun and bullets at an outdoor supply store in San Leandro, so the gun was clean. For now.

After the killing, the gun would be destroyed. If something went wrong and the gun was captured by the police, Alberto would say that it had been stolen. If that didn't work, then young Alberto would be on his way to having a criminal record like everyone else, his first step toward becoming a man.

The rifle could be fitted with one of the Leupold scopes that Carlos owned and was accurate to well over 300 yards. But Carlos had decided to go with the fixed sights, use the gun right out of the box. Based on the layout of the kill zone, he would be close to the target. So close he couldn't miss.

One shot to the head in broad daylight.

Simple. Bold. Daring. A message no one could ignore.

There would be no eyeballs taken this time. Carlos regretted the missed opportunity, but he admired Zorro's restraint. Maybe they would steal the eyeballs from the morgue.

Carlos checked the action on the gun, savoring the sound as the bolt slid into place. He felt himself stir, aroused by the sensuality of the metal, the deadly precision of the rifle. Taking a deep breath, he carefully set the gun back in the box and checked his watch.

It was almost time.

Chapter Twenty-four

"Young man, get your ass in here."

Gail gave Sam the come-hither motion with her hand, then disappeared inside her apartment. He'd barely made it halfway down the hall before her door had snapped open.

He stepped across the threshold, shut the door, and made his way to the living room, taking the seat he'd occupied the day before.

"Shouldn't you be asleep?" he asked. "It's late."

"Sleep is for babies and drunks."

"How'd you know I was coming?" asked Sam, wondering if maybe the girls down the hall were right, and Gail really was a witch.

"These walls are tissue paper." Gail gestured vaguely toward the front door, the age spots on her hand making Sam think of a leopard. Fortunately her claws seemed to be retracted. "Besides, you have a very distinctive walk."

Sam unconsciously rubbed his left leg where the bullet fragments had lodged so many years ago. He'd walked with a limp so long, he was the only one who didn't notice it.

"What's on your mind, Gail?" Sam tried to fight a yawn, lost, and gave into it.

"I figured you'd need some coffee." She gestured at the service on the coffee table, surrounded by carefully arranged cookies and chocolates.

"Martha Stewart's got nothing on you," said Sam as he poured himself a cup.

"You want an almond cookie?" asked Gail, gesturing at a cluster of pale ovals to her right. "They're to die for."

Sam shook his head. "I'm good, thanks."

"Are you?" Gail leaned forward, her eyes bright.

"Am I what?"

"Good," said Gail. "Are you good, Sam?"

"I try to be."

"Good answer, young man." Gail nodded, satisfied for the moment. "Most people would say *yes, of course. Me, absolutely. I always do the right thing.* Let me tell you something—no one *always* does the right thing."

"You going somewhere with this, Gail?" Sam leaned forward and refilled his cup.

"I don't like bullshitters."

"Me neither," said Sam. "Who knew we had so much in common?"

Gail barked a laugh. "You're waking up—I can tell from that smart mouth of yours."

"The coffee is working."

"That's not what I meant," replied Gail. "I can see it in your eyes. This case has you hooked."

Sam put his cup down. "I'm not a cop anymore, Gail. There is no case."

"Now who's bullshitting?"

"You want to know if I talked to our neighbors." Sam smiled despite himself.

"I'm not stupid, young man. I know you talked to our neighbors. I want to know what they said."

"Shayla and Tamara, the "sexy young things," think you're a witch."

Gail cackled. "I do like them," she said. "But I called them pretty, not—"

Sam held up a hand. "Trust me, Gail, they're sexy...and dangerous."

Gail's eyes were backlit. "How dangerous?"

"That's not what I meant," said Sam. "Dangerous to unsuspecting young men. But they didn't kill our landlord."

"How can you be so sure?"

"Let's just say they had him on a short leash."

"He killed their dog," said Gail.

"What?"

"I just remembered that," said Gail, "when you said leash. They had a cute little thing, white and fluffy. A Coton, at least I think that's the breed."

"And Ed killed it?"

Gail nodded. "He told them to get rid of the dog, even though our rental agreements clearly state pets are permitted. So naturally they refused."

Sam thought of Shayla and Tamara, their *fuck authority* attitude. "Naturally."

"A week later, the doggie was run over by a car, right in the courtyard. Behind the penguins, in fact."

"Ed's car?"

Gail shook her head dismissively. "Hit and run, so of course they couldn't prove anything."

Sam sighed. "But you know it was Ed."

Gail clenched her jaw. "You should've seen the look on that bastard's face the next time he saw those girls. I was there, sitting in the lobby waiting for a friend."

"And this happened when?"

"About a month ago."

Sam shrugged. "They didn't mention it. Must have been more traumatic for you than them."

Gail arched her eyebrows but didn't say anything.

Sam took the bait. "I thought you liked them."

"I do!" Gail leaned forward, put a hand on his knee. "They're a couple of spitfires. They remind me of me."

"But you just established a motive."

"I'm just trying to help with the investigation."

"*There is no investigation.*"

"Besides, I'm not suggesting you turn them in or anything."

Sam laughed. "Even if they did it?"

"Nonsense. I'm just saying…"

"What are you saying, Gail?"

"I'm just saying that whoever killed out landlord did this community a great service."

Sam shook his head but remained silent.

"What?" demanded Gail.

"Let's just say, I've never seen an investigation like this, that's all."

Gail arched an eyebrow. "I thought you said there wasn't an investigation?"

Sam turned his hands palms up. "You got me." He put both hands on his knees and stood up.

"Time for me to go to bed," he said.

"What about the others?" asked Gail, almost coming out her seat. "Those two suspicious-looking boys down the hall."

"Who do you think I was having drinks with?"

Gail's eyes went wide. "And…what do you think of them?"

"I think they are suspicious." Sam moved toward the door. "But for a different reason."

"Why?"

Sam ignored the question. He had reached the threshold, the door knob in his hand. "I also spoke with Jill."

A deep smile as Gail said, "I like Jill."

"So do I. Good night, Gail."

Before she could say anything, Sam was out the door, leaving the interrogation room behind.

He was almost to his apartment when he heard the footsteps. Before he could turn, a hand seized his elbow with an iron grip. Sam started to pivot, his right hand cocked for a roundhouse punch, but he caught sight of his assailant before he finished the move.

A man of at least seventy stood before Sam, bright blue eyes fixed beneath a headband, the terrycloth kind worn on tennis courts in the 1970s. Glancing down, Sam noticed the rest of the outfit matched: a Fila shirt over white shorts, banded socks, and tennis shoes. He checked the guy's other hand for a racket but only found a wristband, also terrycloth.

"Guess how old I am," said the man.

"You want to let go of my elbow?"

The man complied. "How old?"

Sam shrugged. "Seventy?"

"Hah!" said the man. "Try 84, junior."

Sam was genuinely impressed and said as much. "You look good."

"You got that right," replied the man, sticking his hand out. "I'm Gus."

Sam nodded, remembering the name from his earlier conversations. He shook, reclaimed his hand. "Sam."

"The cop down the hall."

"I'm retired."

Gus waved a hand. "You retire, you die. You want my advice?"

"Does it matter?"

"Get back on the job," snapped Gus. "Work keeps you young."

"Work," said Sam. "And tennis?"

Gus gestured toward his clothes. "More time on the courts, less time at the Doc's. You play?"

Sam shook his head. "Got a bad knee."

"Want me to pick you up?"

"Excuse me?"

"Lift you in the air," replied Gus. "Show you how strong I am."

"Please don't."

"Don't think I can, do you?" Gus shifted sideways like a crab, started to bend into position.

Sam held out a restraining hand. "I'm sure you can, Gus. You're a regular Jack Lalane. Now, if you don't mind, I was just—"

"—just leaving *my girl's* apartment."

Sam smiled. "Gail."

"You don't deny it?" Gus reared up on the balls of his feet.

"She invited me in for a cup of coffee."

Gus gave him a hard look. "That's your story?"

"Yeah." Sam fought back a smile. "She was just being neighborly."

"Neighborly." The word seemed to have a soothing effect on Gus.

"She thinks the world of you," added Sam, unable to resist.

Gus lit up. "She say that?"

"Not in so many words," said Sam. *She was too busy accusing your neighbors of murder.* "You know how women are."

Gus gave him a sly look. "Do I ever."

"She wanted to talk about—" He caught himself before he said *murder*. "About Ed dying. She's a bit torn up over it."

"*Fah,*" spat Gus. "Now you're yanking my chain."

"What do you mean?"

"Gail torn up?" Gus was incredulous. "She hated that bastard."

Sam chuckled. "I guess you two are close, after all."

"Told you," said Gus. "I'd kill for that woman."

"I didn't want you to get the wrong idea," said Sam. "You know, that I was giving Gail a hard time."

"The day anybody gives my girl a hard time, that'll be the sorriest day of their life."

Sam held up a hand, started toward his doorway. "Nice meeting you, Gus."

Gus shuffled his feet as if he might give chase.

"Wait a minute, don't you want me to answer any questions?"

Sam shook his head. "You just did."

Chapter Twenty-five

Walter awoke to find a hand on his crotch.

It took a moment to realize the hand was his, shoved down the front of his pants while he slept. Lord knows what it had accomplished while he lay snoring on the couch. No matter how or where he fell asleep, he always woke up in this position. He'd considered setting a video camera on a tripod to record himself, see what the Hell was going on, but decided that would be too kinky. Besides, these days his right hand was the only action he was likely to get.

Morning already. He stood and made his way to the kitchen, scratching himself every step of the way. Checked the clock on the stove. Rush hour, people headed to work. Walter sighed, relieved he didn't have a nine-to-five job, almost felt sorry for the dumb saps who did.

He yawned, tasted beer on his breath as he surveyed the wreckage of his living room. Empty bags of chips, crumbs on the couch. Twelve beer bottles lined up like toy soldiers. It was only when he saw the DVDs scattered across the coffee table that last night's revelation returned, rushing back on him like a cold shower.

So much for talking to the brothers. He'd managed to pass out on the couch avoiding his big confrontation with his erstwhile partners. After trying their door that first time, Walter had come home and waited for them, keeping one ear cocked to the door.

But he was jumpy from the movies, needing to wind down, so he turned on last night's baseball game, which he had recorded on his Tivo. Then he started drinking, because everybody knew you couldn't watch baseball without drinking beer.

Opening the refrigerator, Walter saw a barren wasteland of half-eaten Chinese and stale milk. Not breakfast material, even with his stomach. And no delivery scheduled until Monday. Walter could feel the hangover headache working its way across the front of his skull. He patted his pockets, found his wallet still in place. Much as he hated to do his own shopping, Walter had to get some food and coffee into his gut before he did anything else. Brushing his teeth and taking a shower could wait. It's not like he had a date.

The elevator ride was mildly suspenseful, his stomach rolling with the motion. His legs buckled slightly as he stepped from the lobby, the fresh air a slap across his face. Good thing the grocery store was just on the other side of the courtyard. He walked with his head down, unsteady on his feet, watching the cobblestones warily.

He didn't notice the Dodge wagon parked at the far end of the courtyard, its rear hatch ajar.

There were always cars parked there—people visiting the rental office, guests of other tenants. But in this town most of those cars were Japanese or German sedans, SUVs, or roadsters. Wagons were a rarity, and American wagons several years old even more uncommon.

But Hernando had stolen the car from a parking lot on 25th Street the night before, following Carlos' instructions very carefully. They needed a car with a long cargo area in which Carlos could spread out, pointing the rifle through the rear hatch, which Hernando would raise at the last minute. That way someone would have to be directly in the line of fire to see Carlos or the gun, and by then it would be too late.

"*Todavía no.*" Carlos spoke in a raspy whisper, his face barely visible over the edge of the rear window. "Wait until he returns from the grocery store."

"How do you know he's going to the grocery store?" asked Hernando, tracking Walter's progress in the rearview mirror.

"Look at the belly on that guy," replied Carlos. "A man like that, he only walks somewhere if there is food at the other end."

Hernando shrugged. He would've shot the guy. *Get it over with.* But he kept his mouth shut, even though he couldn't stand Carlos. *Fucking Basque.* Hernando thought Carlos was a fucking terrorist asshole. A sociopath. Shitheads like Carlos gave professionals like Hernando a bad rap.

But today Hernando was just the driver, so he kept his mouth shut and the motor running.

Walter typed his PIN into the keypad and waited for his groceries to be bagged. The young Asian woman at the checkout smiled so brightly he wished he'd worn his sunglasses.

"You got miles!" she exclaimed happily.

Walter frowned. "Miles?"

"Frequent flier miles, from your club card." She beamed proudly.

"Hoop-de-do," said Walter acidly, grabbing the bag.

"You want your receipt?"

"Why?"

The enthusiastic checker didn't have a ready answer, and Walter showed her his back before she could reply. She gave his back her middle finger as he left, then turned and beamed at the next customer.

As Walter stepped onto the first cobblestone, Carlos licked his lips and pressed his cheek against the stock of the rifle.

"Open the hatch, *amigo.*"

I'm not you're fucking amigo, thought Hernando as he pushed the button. The hatch opened silently on pneumatic hinges. Carlos worked the action and slid the bolt into place, ramming a 7mm cartridge into the chamber and cocking the gun. He sighted along the barrel, keeping both eyes open and fixed on Walter.

Walter eyed his groceries as he made his way back from the store. Bagels, orange juice, a box of powdered donuts, and a six-pack of beer—just in case he didn't make it out again for a few hours. He'd stop at the coffee shop in the ground floor of his building, then take the elevator upstairs and crank up his blood sugar, start the day off on the right foot.

But Walter's right foot turned out to be the wrong foot as he took his eye off the cobblestones and twisted his ankle, falling to the pavement at the precise moment Carlos pulled the trigger.

Before the sonic boom reached anyone's ears, the bullet had scorched a path through the air, speeding over Walter's head and ricocheting off the stone pillar supporting the corner of the building. The angle of deflection caused the bullet to bounce against the cobblestones and rocket back the way it had come at an oblique angle.

By the time the bullet hit the underside of the Dodge wagon, it was moving close to the speed of sound and had achieved a surface temperature as hot as the sun. The *crack* of the rifle finally caught up with the bullet, but nobody heard it—the sharp sound was muffled by the *whump* of the gas tank exploding. The Dodge leapt three feet into the air.

It landed in a heap of twisted metal, shattered glass, and melting Mexican mobsters.

Chapter Twenty-six

The explosion almost woke Jerome.

His eyes fluttered and he smacked his lips, unconsciously trying to relieve the cotton mouth building in his sleep. The mojitos had taken their toll.

He rolled over and hugged his pillow, dreaming that somewhere close, an orchestra of car alarms was serenading a crowd of screaming fans.

Sam ran to the window and saw the flames, smoke billowing around the penguin statue in the courtyard, obscuring people running in all directions. Grabbing his keys, he ran down the hallway to the fire exit and took the stairs two at a time.

Walter lay sprawled on the cobblestones, his head twisted toward the burning car. His first instinct was that some dipshit drove a Pinto into the lot and backed into a fire hydrant. He'd used plenty of Pintos in his B-movies, always good for a cheap explosion.

But as he raised up on one knee, Walter glanced at the pillar to his left and saw the gouge at eye level, a deep scar in the stone. He followed an invisible line from the indentation to the melting car, and suddenly Walter connected the dots. Master Ling would have been pleased.

Walter felt his stool soften.

Chapter Twenty-seven

"Something smells funny."

Jill wrinkled her nose as Sam held his right arm up to his face and sniffed.

"I think it's me," he said.

"You smell like smoke."

"Could be worse," he said. Sam didn't want to ruin the moment, but he had smelled something other than gasoline and oil in the wreckage. A smell any homicide cop would recognize, the unmistakable stench of burning flesh.

"What do you think happened?"

Sam shrugged. The fire department had come and the crowds had dispersed, onlookers kept at bay by the intense heat. Most people assumed the car was empty, a freak accident. A ruptured gas tank, a discarded cigarette. In this town where four out of five cars were imports, no one trusted American cars anyway. Surely they exploded in the streets of Detroit every day, an occurrence so common it didn't even make the national news.

Only a few people got very close to the wreckage, and Sam couldn't be sure of what he'd seen in that inferno.

"I think a car blew up," he said noncommittally.

"You must be a detective."

"I'm retired, remember?"

Jill smiled. "Is that why you asked me out for coffee? Too much time on your hands?"

They'd walked two blocks in a comfortable silence. He'd suggested coffee and she chose Peet's, a short stroll from their apartments but with an advantage over the coffee shop located in the ground floor of their building. "I like that you can order a small, medium, or large coffee at Peet's by saying *small, medium,* or *large,*" she had said. "You don't have to speak Italian or learn any bullshit phrases to order a cup of coffee."

Sam almost fell in love right then and there.

Now, having regained his composure, he sat across from her at a small table outside, the foot traffic slow around them.

"When I invited you for coffee," he said, "I was just being neighborly."

Jill looked at him over the rim of her cup. "And how do you like our neighbors so far?"

"An interesting bunch."

"Aren't they?"

"Everybody likes you."

"You've been checking up on me? I'm flattered."

"You keep coming up in conversation."

"You always tell murder suspects how your investigation is going?"

Sam made a face. "You always this paranoid?"

"Doesn't Columbo take the murderer out for coffee?" asked Jill. "Visit their apartment, slowly wear them down until they confess?"

"Do I look like Columbo?"

"Well, your clothes are a little wrinkled."

Sam sighed. "I thought you wanted me to join the human race."

Jill reached out and squeezed his right hand briefly, then wrapped hers around her coffee. "I'm being a bitch, aren't I?"

"If I answer that honestly, you might not say yes to dinner."

Jill arched her eyebrows. "Was that an invitation?"

Sam shrugged again. "Maybe I'm just being neighborly."

"Depends on which neighbors you're talking about," said Jill. "Who have you been talking to?"

"I've met everybody so far," said Sam. "Except Walter."

Jill shook her head. "*Walter.*"

"Yeah, I was going to try him later. But I met the brothers, Jerome and Larry."

"I almost never see them," said Jill. "I think we're on different schedules. I'd find it hard to believe they mentioned me."

"I brought you up," admitted Sam. "I wanted to see who they knew on the floor."

"And?"

"Jerome thinks you're hot."

Jill laughed. "I think he's a little young for me."

"You don't know them all that well?"

"No," said Jill. "Why?"

Sam watched an older couple pass by pushing a stroller, wondered if they were grandparents. He waited until they had cleared their table. "They're jumpy, but they seem harmless."

"Jerome's a major stoner," said Jill.

"You think?"

Jill finished off her coffee. "You'd have to be deaf, dumb, and blind to miss the signs. I have plenty of friends who still smoke grass, but he *reeks* of pot. You ever stand in the elevator next to him?"

"Haven't had the pleasure," said Sam, "but he is pretty obvious."

"And you're a cop," said Jill. "Maybe he was worried you'd bust him."

Sam shook his head. "That's not what I meant—Jerome's not the jumpy one—Larry is. Without thinking, tell me the first word that comes to mind when you visualize Larry."

"*Serious,*" replied Jill. "Earnest. Tightly wound."

"That's four words."

"But you get the idea."

"I do."

"Maybe he's stressed out at work?"

"Uh-uh," said Sam. "You know what they do for a living?"

"Nope."

"They make sandwiches," replied Sam.

"They make sandwiches?" repeated Jill. "That's their job?"

"Yeah," said Sam. "To sell at office buildings."

Jill frowned.

"How stressful can that be?"

Chapter Twenty-eight

Larry was chewing Rolaids two at a time by the time he hung up the phone.

"That was Buster," he said miserably.

Jerome yawned. "I didn't know he had our number."

"He's got our number," said Larry feverishly. "And he's got our address, remember? Zorro's thugs drove us home."

"My bad."

Jerome leaned his elbows on the bar that fronted the kitchen. Larry was directly across from him, back against the kitchen counter, his left hand next to the toaster, his right popping antacids into his mouth.

"Don't you want to know why he called?" asked Larry. "Aren't you wondering why I'm chewing these?" He held up the Rolaids as if they were exhibit one in a murder trial.

Jerome shrugged. "I know they're an excellent source of calcium."

"Buster was calling about Zorro's hit man."

"That Carlos dude with the spooky eyes?"

Larry took a deep breath. "Exactly."

"What about him?"

"He's gone missing," said Larry. "So Buster wanted to know if anything happened. Anything out of the ordinary."

Jerome frowned. "Like what?"

"Oh, *I don't know*," said Larry in an exaggerated voice. "Like maybe a car exploding?"

"That's what that was?" said Jerome. "Can't believe I slept through it."

"I can," scoffed Larry. "It was horrible. I can still smell the smoke."

"That's my toast, Larry." Jerome pointed to the counter behind his brother where a small fire had erupted. "Hit the button—*quick!*"

Larry spun and jabbed at the button but missed. By the time he made contact, the toast that emerged looked like it had been in a car fire. Smoke wafted toward the fluorescent light overhead.

"Shit," said Jerome.

Larry grabbed a fork and snagged the edge of the toast, dropped it into the sink, scowling at the toaster as if it had just pissed on the rug. The front was dented, the power cord frayed, copper wire showing through tears in the insulation.

"I told you to throw that piece of shit away," he said. "That thing is a fire hazard."

"It's my lucky toaster," protested Jerome.

"I could've been electrocuted!"

"I've had it since college."

"People don't get emotionally attached to appliances, Jerome."

"But I really like toast."

"Aren't you fucking listening?" demanded Larry. "Carlos is missing...a car blew up."

Jerome blinked, focused. "Carlos was in the car?"

"What if he was?" asked Larry.

"You think he was?"

"It doesn't matter what I think," said Larry. "What matters is what Zorro thinks."

"What did Buster say?"

"He said Zorro might want to see us."

"Might?"

Larry nodded. "I didn't like the sound of that, either. Like he's waiting to hear from Carlos..."

"...and if he doesn't," finished Jerome.

"We take another ride."

"Or we get visitors," suggested Jerome.

The idea panicked Larry. "You think they'd come here?" he asked. "To the apartment?"

Jerome shrugged. "Why not?"

Larry was about to answer when someone knocked loudly on the door. The brothers looked at each other, eyes wide.

The knocking continued.

"Let's pretend we're not here," said Jerome, realizing too late he'd raised his voice instead of whispering. *Damn, he needed coffee*. Larry looked apoplectic.

"Open up, guys," came a muffled voice. "I can hear you in there. C'mon, we need to talk."

"Walter?" said Larry.

"The fat guy?" asked Jerome.

"Open up." The pounding continued. "I have a proposition for you."

Jerome raised his hands, palms up. Larry took a deep breath and stalked across the living room, turned the latch on the deadbolt and returned to the kitchen. He wanted to be near the telephone. He sat on the stool next to Jerome and watched the door.

Walter bellied his way through the door and shut it behind him. He looked rumpled, unshaven, and paler than Larry remembered. Shaken up, even. Larry felt his hands start to sweat, wondering if Walter had any clue about what was going on.

"You look like shit," said Jerome. Larry tried to elbow him but caught his arm on the counter.

Walter took Larry's old spot against the kitchen counter and faced the two brothers. He braced his hands behind him, breathing heavily.

"You're right," he said to Jerome. "That's because someone just tried to kill me."

Larry started laughing, a forced laugh at first, long *ha-ha-has* to show how ridiculous Walter sounded, but it degenerated into uncontrollable giggling, then hyperventilating. Soon Larry had his head on the counter, gasping as Jerome patted his back.

Jerome pulled it together. He began, "What my brother meant to say—"

"Yeah?" asked Walter.

"Was...*HA!*"

"Ha?" repeated Walter.

"Ridiculous," said Jerome, nodding. "Utterly ridiculous."

Walter fidgeted against the counter, sweat on his brow, staining the underarms of his shirt. At first he didn't say anything.

The sight of Walter so distraught calmed Larry, making him realize Walter was just as out of his depth as they were. He felt himself breathing more easily. *Relax, he's the one with the price on his head.*

"Look," said Walter. "I know how this works. I watched *Scarface*."

The brothers frowned simultaneously, brows furrowed. Larry regained his breath enough to say, "With Pacino?"

"Yeah," said Walter. "And I watched a bunch of other movies, too, so I know what happens to the middleman."

"The middleman..." repeated Jerome thickly.

"Me," replied Walter. "I'm overhead, right?" He unconsciously slid his hands back and forth across the counter, trying to erase the mistakes of his past. Jerome watched him with a sense of foreboding. This guy was wound even tighter than Larry.

"Guys like you don't need overhead," continued Walter. Now he was bouncing against the counter. "So I want to change our arrangement."

Larry leaned forward, his breathing almost back to normal. "Change it how?"

"I want to carry my weight," said Walter.

"That's a lot of weight," said Jerome. It was such a lay-up, he almost regretted saying it.

Almost.

Walter slid his hands behind him again, the change in motion causing his gut to undulate with seismic intensity. "I deserved that," he said. "But I'm serious—we can work this out."

"OK…" began Larry, but Jerome's eyes went wide and he said, "That's a bad idea."

Larry turned toward his brother, annoyed at being interrupted. "What are you—"

"*Bad idea!*" shouted Jerome as he started to climb off his stool, but he was too late.

The toaster's power cord caught between the middle and index fingers of Walter's right hand as it slid across the counter, the exposed copper wires pressing hard into the soft flesh at the top of his palm. He jerked forward as if shot from behind, then began vibrating so rapidly his skin became a blur. He was a cartoon character getting erased and redrawn at the speed of thought.

A buzzing in the overhead lights was the only sound as Walter's mouth stretched open in silent agony, his eyes bulging. By the time Jerome's feet touched the ground and Larry blinked, Walter had collapsed, face down on the floor of the kitchen. A caustic smell assailed the room, and this time it wasn't the smell of burnt toast.

Larry turned to Jerome, who smiled sheepishly.

"I told you it was my lucky toaster."

Chapter Twenty-nine

"Well, that went well."

Sam said the words aloud despite being alone in his apartment. The row of photographs along the fireplace mantle returned his gaze, but no advice was forthcoming.

"Coffee, I mean—with Jill," he added. "I kind of like her."

Sam looked to the closest picture for a reaction. Marie stood on the beach at Crissie Field, squinting into the sun, the Golden Gate Bridge behind her. Her expression was relaxed, happy; not forced or posed in any way. A woman comfortable with herself, in love with the man taking her photograph.

"You OK with this?" he asked.

Sam looked at the adjacent picture, Marie caught sitting in a chair, reading. Looking up at the camera at the last minute. The look on her face was almost identical—content. She was a woman with no regrets.

She looked the way Sam wanted to feel.

"I know, take it slow," he said. "You don't want to see me get hurt."

Sam let his eyes roam across the uneven row of frames, skipping past family and friends, always searching for Marie. Still thinking she might sneak into the apartment while he stood there, put her hands over his eyes. *You've already been hurt*, he told himself. *But at least you felt alive.*

A bitter thought he wouldn't dare speak aloud.

"Remember that Pink Floyd song we listened to in college, 'Comfortably Numb'?" His eyes shifted to a younger Marie. Longer hair, gingham dress. "Well, I've decided that was bullshit—there's nothing comfortable about it."

Marie's eyes lit up the frame.

"Yeah," said Sam softly, "I thought you'd like to hear that." He ran his hands through his hair and forced a tired smile. "Thanks for listening, babe."

He headed toward the bedroom, thinking a shower might be just the thing. Halfway across the living room, the phone rang. Sam cut across to the kitchen and grabbed it on the third ring. Danny Rodriguez practically jumped out of the handset.

"Get down here!"

Sam gave his ex-partner a few seconds before stating the obvious. "Where is *here*, Danny?"

"Shit. Sorry, Sam—the morgue."

Sam didn't say anything.

"You too busy?" asked Danny, the stress in his voice making the phone vibrate.

"Not me," said Sam. "I'm retired, remember?"

"You got a problem with dead people?"

Sam glanced at the photographs on the mantle.

"Some of my favorite people are dead, Danny."

"These guys won't make that list," replied Danny. "We got IDs on the bodies in the station wagon."

"You got dental already?"

"Amazing what survives a fire and what doesn't," mused Danny. "Laminated driver's license, for example, might just curl around the edges while the wallet gets incinerated, along with the guy's pants, butt, and scrotum."

"That's a lovely mental picture."

Danny continued undaunted. "Or another guy's skin might spontaneously combust on contact with the burning gasoline, leaving behind only those body parts not covered by the fuel as it erupted like a geyser from the exploding gas tank."

Sam didn't want to, but he took the bait.

"*Only those body parts,*" he said deliberately. "Such as?"

"His legs."

"Just a pair of legs?" asked Sam. "That's all that's left?"

"Get down here," said Danny. "I need your help."

"With a pair of legs?"

"Get down here," repeated Danny.

"What do you want me to do?" asked Sam, but there was no answer.

Danny had hung up.

Chapter Thirty

"Grab his legs."

Jerome grunted from the effort. "Why do I get the heavy end?"

Larry dropped Walter's flaccid arms unceremoniously to the floor but kept his eyes on his younger brother.

"It was *your* toaster."

Jerome gave that some thought. When a rebuttal didn't surface, he shrugged and tightened his grasp on Walter's slacks.

"How much does this guy weigh?" he asked.

"There's a reason they call it *dead weight*," snapped Larry. "It's not like Walter can help us, can he?"

Jerome kept his mouth shut and grunted as Larry found his grip on Walter's forearms. They only managed to lift Walter a few inches off the floor, but that was enough to swing him three feet closer to the door, drop him, then do it all over again. They had tried dragging him but gave up when one of his arms took down a floor lamp.

Almost there. Just one more lift, swing, drop.

Walter wasn't complaining. His face was locked in a rictus of shock, eyes bulging like a goldfish in desperate need of the Heimlich maneuver. His skin had turned a mottled shade of gray.

After Walter had first hit the floor, they turned him over to see if they could find a pulse. Jerome tried to find the carotid artery while Larry held Walter's wrist as the body cooled. You didn't have to be a doctor to know Walter was dead before he hit the floor, his heart shocked into silence. After five futile minutes, Jerome shook his head and Larry ran to the bathroom to throw up.

Larry figured they had a choice: either call 911 or leave the apartment immediately and never come back, flee to Mexico or Canada and change their names. Both plans seemed equally sound to him until Jerome made a suggestion.

"Why don't we just take him home?"

Jerome found Walter's keys in his pants pocket, stepped into the hall, and unlocked the door to Walter's apartment. He left the door ajar and returned to their place.

Now they had Walter to the edge of their front door and Jerome was peering into the hallway.

"Clear."

Larry listened carefully for any movement, human or mechanical. Someone next door grabbing their keys and preparing to go out. The elevator on its way up. A tabloid photographer lurking on the fire escape.

Nothing.

"OK," he said. "On three, we pick him up, run down the hall, and drag him inside his apartment."

Jerome let go of Walter's right leg and gave Larry a big thumbs-up.

"Cut it out, Jerome."

"Okey-dokey."

"Do you want to get arrested?"

Jerome rolled his eyes. "One…"

"*Two*."

"Three," they said in unison.

Jerome had to shuffle backwards on his heels as Larry short-stepped on his toes, but they made it. Larry kicked Walter's door shut once they were inside and they both sat down heavily, Walter's bulbous corpse between them.

Jerome twisted his head around to look at the living room where movies and empty food containers littered the coffee table, crumbs decorated the sofa.

"This guy needs a maid."

Larry was panting from the exertion, wondering why his brother wasn't out of breath. He made a mental note to contact the AMA about which had a more deleterious effect on lung capacity, smoking five joints a day or stress. He suspected stress would prove to be much, much worse.

He surveyed the living room. "The couch?"

Jerome nodded. "Why not?"

"Maybe he had a heart attack while watching a movie."

"An *action* movie…all the excitement…"

"…the noise…"

"…the late fees."

"Exactly," said Larry. "It was a tense situation."

Jerome nodded. "Stress is a killer."

"Tell me about it."

"Ready?" asked Jerome.

"Let's get it over with."

After three tries they got it right. Walter slouched on the sofa, his crooked fingers wrapped around the remote. *That was a nice touch*, thought Larry. Attention to detail might make all the difference. Jerome stepped forward and sprinkled some broken chips across Walter's chest.

Larry took a step back, nodded his approval.

Jerome brushed crumbs off his hands. "Our work here is done."

"What do you think," asked Larry. "Leave the keys?"

Jerome nodded. "I put 'em back in his pocket."

"OK," said Larry. "But let's leave the door unlocked, just in case we need to come back.""

Jerome frowned. "Why would we need to come back?"

"We might have forgotten something," said Larry.

"Like what?"

"If I knew, then we wouldn't have forgotten it."

"Well, try to remember," insisted Jerome. "It might be important."

"There is no '*it*', you moron—I just made it up to make a point."

"This isn't a game, Larry."

"You're unbelievable."

Jerome looked bemused. "Can we go now?"

Neither one of them said goodbye to Walter. For his part, Walter didn't seem to give a shit.

Larry went first. He had just reached their apartment when he heard one of the elevators *ping*. Whipping around, he saw Jerome pull Walter's door shut as the elevator doors began to open.

Jerome stood, transfixed, as Tamara jiggled her way down the hall. She held a coffee cup in each hand, a pose that forced her shoulders back and her breasts forward. Only the radiance of her smile had enough magnetic pull to wrench Jerome's eyes to her face as she said, "Good morning!"

"Hey Tamara," he replied.

Tamara glanced past him down the hall. "Hi Larry."

"Tamara." Larry half-nodded and half-bowed, one leg already inside their apartment.

Tamara turned her gaze to Jerome, who had to quickly readjust his line of sight.

"I just got coffee," she said. "And Shayla's making breakfast. You guys want to join us?"

"N-no," said Larry, a little too quickly. "Thanks—thanks, but we've got a lot of work to do."

Jerome made a face. "We do?"

"Well, *I do*," said Larry, sliding his other foot into their apartment. Now only his head and torso were visible. "See you, Tamara." Then he closed the door.

Tamara tilted her head to one side.

"What about you, Jerome?" she asked. "We're making eggs, bacon, toast—"

"Toast?"

"Wheat bread," she said. "Interested?"

Jerome nodded like a lost puppy.

"I love toast," he said.

Chapter Thirty-one

"You want to shove this up your nose?"

Danny Rodriguez held the middle and index fingers of his right hand close enough for Sam to examine the Vicks Vapo-Rub he had smelled the moment Danny opened the jar. Sam already knew what Vicks looked like and wondered if his former partner was offering to shove it up his nose for him, a surprisingly intimate gesture even between friends. When Sam shook his head, Danny shrugged and jammed the two fingers up his own nose in one fluid motion.

"Hate the smell of dead people," said Danny.

"I hate the sight of them," replied Sam. He pulled a pair of Ray-Bans from his jacket pocket and slipped them on. Danny scowled.

"I never understood that," he said. "It's not like you're not looking at 'em."

"Helps me keep some distance."

"Whatever you say, *ese.*" Danny took a deep breath through his freshly greased nostrils, making sure he couldn't smell anything but the cold medicine. He pulled his coat on and eyed Sam's light jacket. "You gonna be alright? It's as cold as a meat locker in there."

"It *is* a meat locker in there," replied Sam. "I'm fine—but you're starting to sound like an old woman."

Danny made a face and pushed through the door.

Fluorescent lights ricocheted off stainless steel tables, making Sam glad he wore the glasses. Six tables ran along the left side of the room, each with a suspended microphone overhead, a scale, an adjoining rolling cart, and a drainage system. To the right were metal drawers set into the wall, three high and twelve across. Sam wondered how many had occupants.

A lone figure wearing a white lab coat stood next to the last table, his black hair disheveled, gray eyes magnified by Coke-bottle glasses, hands covered in rubber gloves. He had looked up when they arrived but immediately turned his attention back to the misshapen mound on the table in front of him.

The man spoke without raising his head. "Rodriguez, you said you'd be right back."

"I am back," replied Danny.

"*Right* back implies *alacrity*, Detective Rodriguez."

Danny turned to Sam with a sad expression. "Alacrity."

"It means fast," said Sam.

"*Mamame la verga*," said Danny. "I *know* what it means— was just remarking on the man's tone of voice toward an officer of the law."

Sam smiled. "I doubt he meant any disrespect—did you, Oliver?"

The man in the lab coat seemed to register Sam for the first time. "Hello, Sam," he said, watery eyes blinking behind the glasses. "I thought you retired."

Sam nodded. "I'm here as—"

"—a material witness." Danny cut in, adding his own spin in the event anyone asked questions later. Sam didn't contradict him.

"You saw this go down?" asked Oliver, his voice showing the first sign of warmth since they'd arrived. Sam must have met with Oliver more than a hundred times over the years, and his normal disposition was as chilly as the room in which they were standing. But mention murder and he'd light up. Get into the gruesome details of a crime and a light sweat would break across his brow. Help him understand the motive, and he'd start rubbing his hands together like a man warming himself by an open flame. That's why all the cops called him Twisted Oliver.

Danny said it to his face, which is one of the reasons they didn't get along.

"A car blew up," said Sam noncommittally.

Oliver's face betrayed his disappointment.

"You could smell the burning flesh," added Sam.

Oliver licked his lips.

Danny cut in. "Show him, Twist."

Oliver narrowed his eyes, making it clear Danny had ruined the moment. He sighed before yanking the sheet off the table with a theatrical flourish.

Sam blinked behind his sunglasses, waiting for his brain to catch up with his eyes. It took a moment.

"You found them like that?" he finally asked.

Oliver nodded, a small smile at the corners of his mouth. "Apparently the gentleman's pants were made of some synthetic material—"

"—fake leather," said Danny. "Cheap-ass, fake leather pants."

Oliver continued as if the interruption never occurred. "Which was surprisingly flame retardant. But his undergarments—"

"—cheap-ass, cotton briefs," said Danny. "Picked up the flame from his shirt and roasted his balls."

"Indeed." Oliver clenched his jaw. "Which is why you see a blackened, carbonized area here." He paused, waving his hand like a magician. "But below the groin you see the legs are unscathed."

Sam blinked again. The legs had separated from the torso, burned free of sinew and bone. He assumed the upper half of the deceased lay in one of the metal drawers, since only the lower half was on display. Where the legs conjoined, in place of the body's private parts, a molten terrain of charred flesh obscured any sign of gender. But once the legs took their separate paths the skin became pristine, unscarred save for the tattoos encircling both thighs.

The blue-black ink of prison tattoos covered the upper thigh of each leg, teardrop flames carved with surprising detail, the tip of each pointing toward the crotch. As Sam studied the tattoo, he noticed the fire pattern was layered, as if individual flames had been added at different times. Some of the ink was faded and gray, lighter than the copper-colored flesh, while other sections were deep blue. The net impression was that of a real inferno, exploding from the knees and burning its way upwards.

"Given how the guy died," said Sam. "That's kind of an ironic tattoo, don't you think?"

Danny chuckled. "Each flame tattoo represents a kill. By my count, this pair of legs killed over twenty-seven men."

Sam gave a low whistle. "And you know the guy?"

Oliver pursed his lips. "At this point we don't have all the tests which positively—"

Danny raised a heavy hand. "Scumbag's name was Carlos. He did contract work for Zorro."

Sam raised his eyebrows. "Zorro?"

Danny nodded. "The fox himself," he said, adding, "Your old friend."

"Friends, my ass," replied Sam. "I don't think we're exactly on speaking terms."

Danny chuckled. "You think he'd hold a grudge against the only cop to ever bring him in?"

Sam shrugged. "The charges didn't stick."

"But you had the balls to bring him downtown."

Sam let it go, but now he understood why Danny wanted him to see this for himself. "Why would Zorro's men be hanging around in that neighborhood?"

Danny glanced at Oliver. "Why, *indeed*?"

Sam looked at the medical examiner. "When will you have positive IDs?"

Oliver shrugged. "Another day, max."

Danny jutted his chin at the table. "You can put your toys away, Twist." Then he added, "And thanks."

Oliver let the nickname and the *thanks* cancel each other out. He pulled the sheet over the severed legs as Danny led Sam away from the cold light into the hallway.

When they stood just outside the door, Sam leaned against the wall and pushed his sunglasses back on his head. "Things are heating up."

"That some kind of joke?" asked Danny.

Sam shrugged. "Might not have anything to do with the jumper."

"Now you're saying the guy jumped?"

"Aren't you?" demanded Sam. "That is the official department line, isn't it? My landlord got depressed, took a long walk off the balcony."

Danny chewed his lower lip. "Yeah, until we have reason to open an investigation."

"But?"

"You gonna make me say it?"

Sam smiled. "Yeah, partner, I am."

Danny pushed himself off the wall. "*But*—three deaths within three days in the same zip code is quite a coincidence."

"Zip code, shit." Sam snorted. "How about the same fifty-foot radius?"

"How about it?"

"Cops don't believe in coincidences," said Sam matter-of-factly.

"And I'm still a cop," replied Danny.

"But I'm not," said Sam. "Wait here." Without waiting for a response, he dropped his sunglasses into place and pushed through the double doors.

Oliver was straightening some equipment near the same spot Sam had seen him last, but the legs were gone from the table.

"Hello again, Sam." Oliver scanned his immediate surroundings. "You forget something?"

Sam jammed his hands into his jacket pockets. "Yeah, Oliver, I did."

Oliver's eyes swam behind his thick glasses but he didn't say anything.

"Do you still have the—" Sam hesitated. "The remains of the guy who jumped off my building?"

Oliver's eyes stopped swimming and locked in place. "That was your building?" he asked, as if Sam were the luckiest man in the world.

Sam nodded.

"Do you see it?" asked Oliver, his voice quavering. "The impact?"

Sam shook his head. "Sorry, Ollie. Just the aftermath."

Oliver took a deep breath through his nose, braving his disappointment. "That's too bad."

"But even that was pretty gruesome," said Sam. "Clumps of flesh on tree branches. Blood everywhere."

Oliver took another breath, this one more shallow. "Everywhere?"

Sam nodded. "You couldn't get the stench out of your nose for hours, even after you left the scene."

Oliver sighed like a man who'd just eaten too much dessert. "Thank you, Sam."

Sam shifted from one foot to the other, letting Oliver have his moment. It took a while before the M.E. focused again.

"Did you *want* something, Sam? Is there something I can do for you?"

"Yeah," replied Sam. "Are you gonna run the usual battery of tests on the body?"

"There wasn't much left of the body to work with."

"But you did the blood work?"

Oliver shook his head. "Not unless someone tells me to. It's a suicide, right?"

"Absolutely," said Sam, too quickly. "So, no tests?"

"Not the full run," replied Oliver. "I just hold the corpse until the police give the final word, suicide or murder. Should come down in another day or two. Why?"

Sam rolled his shoulders. "He was a neighbor, Ollie. And a lot of the other neighbors, they knew him, you know, and were just wondering—"

Oliver nodded his understanding. "Was he on drugs? Or drunk. Some outside agent to explain his behavior, a focus for their anger and grief."

Sam was glad he wore the dark glasses. "Something like that."

Oliver leaned in close and spoke in a conspiratorially whisper. "For you, Sam, I'll run the tests. A-to-Z."

Sam held out his hand. "Thanks, Ollie. And you won't tell anyone? Not even Danny?"

Oliver spared a caustic look toward the door. "Especially not Rodriguez."

Sam squeezed the other man's hand, noticing how cold and clammy it was. "Thanks, Oliver." He pulled a card from his wallet. "That's my home phone, ok?"

Sam pushed through the doors to find Danny looking at him suspiciously as he jammed a Kleenex into his right nostril. With a nasally twang he demanded, "What was that about?"

Sam shrugged. "A hunch."

Danny switched to the other nostril, using a backwards twisting motion.

"I thought you didn't believe in hunches?"

Sam smiled. "I usually don't," he said. "But cops do."

"You ain't a cop no more," replied Danny. "That's what you told me. You're retired."

"You got me into this," said Sam.

"So?"

"Maybe it's time for me to go back to work."

Chapter Thirty-two

Jerome was high on life.

That bullshit expression had never rung so true. Jerome sat next to Tamara at her kitchen counter, finishing his breakfast. Shayla was in the bedroom, getting ready for their next webcam broadcast. Two beautiful women, a home-cooked meal. Jerome smiled shyly as he took another bite of his toast.

It was perfect.

Tamara had made the toast herself, wearing an apron over a t-shirt and shorts, the perfect curve of her breasts visible on either side of the shoulder straps. As she spread the butter lovingly across the finely browned surface of the bread, Jerome made a mental note to mark this as the most erotic moment of his life.

Jerome had always done well with the ladies. They liked his laid-back style, his loopy grin. Most didn't even mind that he was stoned most of the time, treating him like a wayward pet in need of their care and affection. For his part, Jerome fed their need to be needed, playing up his hapless role for all it was worth.

But with Tamara, it was different. It had been several hours since Jerome's last hit, but he wasn't missing the *ganja* one bit. He wasn't tense at all—in fact, he felt more relaxed than when he was high. He took a deep breath, his eyes bright. There was definitely more oxygen in the air when Tamara was in the room.

"So what's keeping Larry so busy?" she asked. "He seemed… tense."

Jerome felt a twinge at the sound of his brother's name, an electric jolt across his temple. A sharp pain that was here and gone as quickly as the mental image of Larry's scowling face, replaced by Tamara's beatific smile.

"You OK?" she asked. "Jerome?"

He blinked. "Sure, why?"

"Thought I'd lost you there for a second—I'm not boring you?"

"No, not at all," Jerome shook his head emphatically. "I've just got a lot on my mind."

Like my obsessive-compulsive brother, he thought.

In a rare moment of mental clarity, Jerome realized why he smoked such epic amounts of weed. Sure, he liked the high and the perspective it gave you, but after so many years that was getting harder to sustain. It was wearing thin. Even though he was on track to be nominated to the Bob Marley Hall of Fame, lately he was just getting by, the clouds of smoke barely managing to obscure the details of his maddening existence.

His brother was driving him crazy. Subconsciously Jerome knew his incessant smoking was designed to return the favor and *annoy the living shit* out of Larry. Keep Jerome too fuzzy for a serious conversation. Too stoned to be an equal partner in Larry's codependent enterprise of angst.

"Busy at work, huh?" Tamara nudged him back into the moment.

Jerome shrugged. "Makin' sandwiches." And selling weed to every middle manager in San Francisco. The thought used to give him a thrill, but now it seemed so...mundane. Make the sandwiches, sell the pot. Day in, day out. Larry ran their operation like a coal mine, never a break in the routine. It was another epiphany for Jerome, finding the cause for his cancer if not the cure. He was feeling more enlightened by the minute—just sitting next to this babe was elevating his IQ.

"That must keep you busy," said Tamara. "Doesn't it get boring?"

He and Larry might not be stuck in cubicles anymore, but Jerome was bored out of his mind. He shrugged again, saying, "All those mouths to feed."

"What about *your* mouth, Jerome—still hungry?" Tamara stood up as if to move around the counter.

Jerome looked at his plate, clean except for a handful of crumbs. "No, I'm good." And he was good, and getting better. He thought of Larry, but this time the image didn't stress him out. He imagined his brother back in their apartment, vomiting from the stress. Jerome had just polished off a huge breakfast without a hint of a stomachache. Walter was dead, and Jerome was OK with that.

He had assumed Larry killed their landlord, got into some scuffle with Ed over their deal and the asshole fell off the balcony. Maybe, maybe not. *But Jerome didn't really care.* It was his third revelation of this remarkable breakfast. Eat some toast and discover your moral compass.

Those guys were assholes. Crooks. Stealing from two hardworking boys. Well, sometimes there is justice in the world.

Fuck them.

Jerome felt suddenly light-headed, emboldened by this new moral treatise. He was one of the good guys.

Tamara had moved to the kitchen and was washing dishes, her hips doing a silent samba as she soaped the plates. Jerome breathed through his nose and nodded his head. Life was good, too good to waste in a cloud of smoke. His puppy dog days were over. Time to act like a man.

"Hey," he said. "Tamara."

She turned at the waist, looking like a sculpture of the letter *S*. "Yeah?"

"You want to go to dinner with me sometime?"

Tamara turned completely around, hands braced against the counter. Her smile almost blinded him.

"*Damn*, Jerome."

"What?" he asked, momentary panic on his face.

"I thought you'd never ask."

Chapter Thirty-three

Sam made a U-turn when he spotted Buster on the corner of 29th and Mission.

The best thing about driving a vintage Mustang convertible was it made Sam feel younger, if not young. But the worst was the turning radius. Buster was stepping out of a bodega onto the sidewalk when Sam jumped the curb and almost took his foot off.

"*Maricon!*" Buster leapt backwards, hands raised in panic as Sam punched the brakes, rocking the car. He took off his sunglasses so Buster could see his face.

"Sorry Buster."

Buster squinted, flipping through his mental Rolodex until he landed on Sam's card.

"*Hola*, officer Sam," he said with forced joviality. "What brings you to my neighborhood?"

"Can I give you a ride somewhere?"

Buster shook his head. "I got nowhere to go, thanks."

"Good." Sam killed the ignition, leaving the car on the sidewalk. He slid across the front seat and climbed out the passenger side before Buster could bolt.

Buster's dreadlocks shifted nervously, but he kept his eyes focused on Sam, his expression one of studied calm. "Been a long time since I seen you in this part of town."

Sam ran a hand through his hair.

"You kill anybody lately Buster?"

Buster chuckled. "Not me."

"Maybe that's why you haven't seen me," said Sam. "I work for the dead."

Buster didn't say anything but smiled. Gold and silver light shot from his mouth like darts, revealing a custom grill over his top row of teeth. The *gangsta* prosthetic of choice.

"How about you," prompted Sam. "You still work for Zorro?"

Buster was shaking his head before Sam finished saying the name, his hair catching the light and shifting from blue to green. The hoops in his left ear jingled softly.

"I don't believe I know this person," he said.

Sam nodded his understanding as he leaned in close, careful not to touch Buster but intimate enough to make things uncomfortable.

"We're on the street, Buster," he said quietly. "In broad daylight. I can understand that's awkward for a man in your position. But this is off the record."

Buster's eyes narrowed as a cruel smile flashed across his lips. "Sure it is, amigo."

Sam had backed Buster against the storefront, with no room to reestablish his personal space. "Want me to let you in on a little secret?"

Buster's eyes shifted right and left, but he kept quiet.

"I'm not a cop anymore," said Sam deliberately. "I retired."

Buster straightened. "No shit?"

"The truth."

Buster pushed off the wall, brushing past Sam as he made to leave. "Then why the fuck am I talking to you?"

Sam caught Buster's shoulder with his right hand, exerting just enough force to spin him around. He wrapped his arm around Buster's neck, two old friends getting reacquainted. With Buster's neck in the crook of his elbow, he squeezed just hard enough to make a point.

"Tell Zorro his soldiers are marshmallows now."

Buster raised his eyebrows.

"Carlos got cooked," said Sam. "Along with his driver."

"You saw this?" Buster asked the question as Sam eased up on his neck.

"I thought you didn't know these people."

Buster shrugged. "What people? I'm just making conversation."

"I saw it."

Buster waited for the rest.

"It wasn't pretty," added Sam.

Buster whistled through his teeth. "That's too bad, Sam."

"You ever smell burning flesh, Buster?"

"I got a barbecue at home."

"You're missing the point."

"Must have been very upsetting…" Buster's eyes clocked the street before turning back to Sam.

"I'll get over it."

"…but why tell me?"

"That's the thing," said Sam. "I thought *you* might tell *me* why two of your crew were hanging around *my* apartment building."

"You live there?" Buster seemed genuinely surprised. "It's a small fuckin' world, no?"

"You know where Zorro is right now?"

Buster reached into his pockets and pulled out his headphones, carefully placing a small white ball into each ear. Sam could hear the whine of the music coursing through the thin wire that ran from Buster's jacket.

Sam shrugged and took a card from his pocket, jammed it into the front of Buster's jacket. "That's my number, in case you get the sudden urge to confess." Buster didn't react, just left the card there.

Sam walked around the front of his car. He climbed behind the wheel as Buster took a step back, head bobbing with the music. Sam raised his voice only slightly, keeping eye contact the entire time.

"Tell Zorro to stay in his hole like a good fox," said Sam, "because the cops won't be a polite as I am."

Buster's eyes narrowed again, his skin creasing like a desiccated orange.

Sam knew Buster could hear every word, so he added, "Stay the fuck away from my neighborhood. We clear on that, *ese?*" Sam spun the wheel as he threw the car in reverse, forcing Buster to jump backwards again.

Glancing in his rearview mirror, Sam caught the expression on Buster's face and knew he'd just started another fire. He prayed he'd see the smoke before the flames crept under his door.

Chapter Thirty-four

"Stay cool."

Larry ignored his brother's advice and grabbed the phone on the first ring. He'd been standing next to the counter all morning, staring at the handset as if it were a cobra and he couldn't tear his gaze away for fear it would strike.

Jerome had not succumbed to its spell. He had taken a shower, gone out for a haircut, and now lay on the couch watching his brother spasm with anxiety.

Larry's skin stretched across his knuckles as he gripped the phone. "Yeah, Buster, is that you?"

Jerome waved from the couch. "Tell him I said hi."

Larry ignored his brother. "Yeah, tonight. I understand. Sure, we can—" He startled as Jerome leapt from the couch and grabbed the phone away from him.

"Hey," barked Jerome. "*Hey, Buster*, it's me, Jerome. Yeah, I heard Larry saying something about tonight? Yeah, well—" He cut himself off and listened, nodding.

Larry leaned against the kitchen counter and stared at his brother, eyes wide with disbelief as Buster's disembodied voice rattled the plastic handset.

Jerome cut in again. "Yeah, well, that's not gonna work, Buster."

Larry heard the buzzing of Buster's voice grow louder, a hive of angry hornets about to spew from the phone.

Jerome continued unabated. "You see, Buster, I got a date tonight."

Buzz, buzz, buzz.

"Yeah, a date."

Larry dry swallowed.

"So tell Zorro we'll meet with him another time," said Jerome pleasantly. "How about tomorrow, say about noon?"

BUZZ, BUZZ, BUZZ.

"Hey, Buster," said Jerome. "Get fucked."

BUZZZZZZZZZZ.

Jerome held up a hand for silence, as if Buster was in the room with them. Amazingly, it worked, causing Larry to wonder if his brother had mastered The Force.

"Tell Zorro his guys were a pair of fuckups," said Jerome, "so me and Larry, we did the job ourselves."

Dead silence. The buzzing had suddenly stopped.

"You still there, *amigo?*" sneered Jerome.

Larry heard a slight rattle through the plastic casing of the phone. Barely a whisper.

"Tell Zorro that whatever he was paying spooky Carlos, now he's gotta pay us."

Silence.

"*Comprendé?*" Before waiting for an answer, Jerome added. "See you tomorrow at noon." Then he punched *off* on the handset and handed the phone back to Larry, who clutched it to his chest and slid slowly down the wall as if he'd been punched in the gut.

Larry's mouth opened and closed several times before any sound came out, a fish out of water. "What," he began. "What the fuck? *What the fuck did you just do?*"

Jerome rocked his neck back and forth until it cracked, then let his eyes settle on his brother. "Nut up, Larry."

"What?"

"Grow a sac, bro," replied Jerome without malice. He reached down and squeezed Larry's shoulder. Larry noticed for the first time how clear Jerome's eyes looked, deep brown and placid.

Larry realized he hadn't seen his younger brother smoke all day. He considered the possibility that he'd been teleported to another dimension, where Mister Spock had a goatee, Captain Kirk was a scumbag, and his brother Jerome was the responsible one.

He shook his head to clear it. "What on Earth did you just do?"

"Relax, Larry," said Jerome. "Zorro thought he was driving this situation? Well, I just put us behind the steering wheel."

Larry stared at his brother.

"We're behind the steering wheel?" he repeated lamely.

"Abso-fuckin-lutely," replied Jerome.

"And what do you expect me to do?" Larry asked.

Jerome smiled his big loopy grin.

"That's easy, Larry," he replied. "Get in the back seat where you belong."

Chapter Thirty-five

"You mind sitting there?"

Jill shook her head. "Not at all."

The Tadich Grill was packed, a common occurrence this time of night, couples stacked two or three deep at the bar. The restaurant didn't take reservations, so Sam and Jill could either wait an hour for a table or take two of the stools at the bar reserved for people who wanted to eat and not just drink.

"Some women don't like sitting at the bar."

"You've brought a lot of women here?"

Sam flushed red. "That's not what I—"

Jill put her hand on his shoulder. "Kidding."

Sam nodded. "But I'm not. There's a reason so many people are waiting for tables. A lot of people don't like it. You're looking across the bar, not facing each other. Rubbing shoulders, bumping into each other, depending on which hand you eat with."

"I'm right-handed."

"Me, too."

"I'm so relieved."

Sam turned to face her, caught the grin. "You enjoy fucking with me, don't you?"

Jill laughed, smooth velvet somehow cutting through the din of the restaurant. "It's just…you're so—"

"Neurotic?"

She laughed again. "*Thoughtful.* That's the word. You're always asking me how I am." She held his eyes for a moment before adding, "It's nice."

Sam studied her for a minute. "How long were you married?"

Jill sat back on the stool, her eyebrows revealing her surprise. "I don't think I mentioned being married. Or divorced."

Sam flushed again. "Sorry, that was abrupt. I was suddenly curious."

"But…"

Sam ticked off the fingers on his left hand as he broke eye contact. "You're smart, talented, and very attractive…" He let his voice trail off as he gathered his thoughts.

"Keep going," chided Jill. "You're doing great so far."

Sam swung his eyes around to meet her. "You seem to like men."

Jill flashed a smile.

"And men seem to like you," said Sam. "If our stoner friend Jerome and I agree on something, it must be true."

"If you say so."

"And you notice things," continued Sam. "Like manners. I'm not the most socially graceful guy, but I guess I'm polite."

"Manners are important," said Jill simply, her smile still there but tucked into the corners of her mouth.

"I think they're more important to you. I think maybe you were married and you got taken for granted."

The orange mote in Jill's left eye seemed to darken. "That's it?" she asked. "That's how you figured I was married once?"

Sam shook his head. *In for a dime, in for a dollar.*

"You seem sad, like something was taken from you."

A flash of something in her eyes, just this side of anger. "I seem *sad* to you?"

Sam shook his head. "Only when you sing."

Her expression softened and the smile returned to her eyes, if not her mouth.

"You must have been a great cop."

Sam shook his head. "I was married, too, remember."

"And something was taken from you."

"Yeah." Sam shifted his eyes to the menu as he visualized Marie. "Yeah, it was."

"But?"

"But I couldn't sing like that."

Jill smiled broadly this time. "I'd say you were more of a baritone."

"You know what I meant." Sam paused, then his tone softened. "That pain had to come from somewhere."

"Like a man?"

Sam shrugged. "Men are good at causing pain. It's in our DNA."

Jill didn't comment.

"And I figured if you were a widow, like me," said Sam, "you would've told me when we first met. People tend to do that."

"The same people who don't like to sit at bars?"

Sam chuckled. "Yeah, them."

"Maybe they think the pain will go away if it's shared."

"They're wrong."

"I was married ten years," said Jill. "He was a jerk."

"For ten years?"

"No, he was just a jerk the last two years, though I didn't know it at the time."

"Know what?"

"That he was banging someone else behind my back."

Sam winced. "How'd you find out?"

"I walked in on them," Jill said matter-of-factly. "In our bed."

Sam let out a low whistle but didn't say anything.

"He thought I was at a concert, but I came home early."

"What did you do?"

A bitter but not unhappy smile spread across Jill's face. "Remember I told you I studied kick-boxing?"

"Yeah."

"He ran," she said. "Grabbed his pants and ran. I changed the locks the next day."

Sam felt suddenly embarrassed. "I'm sorry I brought this up. That was rude to drag—"

Jill cut him off with a wave of her right hand, which landed gently on his left. She curled her fingers around his and squeezed until their knuckles changed color.

"Know what the worst thing was?" she asked.

"No."

"He ran away," she scoffed. "What kind of man does that, runs away from a woman because she might kick his ass?"

"He was naked," offered Sam.

"He was a pussy."

Sam coughed at the word but managed not to laugh.

Jill shook her head in disgust. "How could I have married a pussy?"

"I don't know what to tell you."

Jill squeezed his hand. "Tell me a story," she said. "I wasted enough time with that asshole. Let's talk about something else, OK?"

"OK."

"So tell me a story."

So Sam told her about being a cop. He talked about walking the streets, being surrounded by people but feeling cut off from all of them. Spending so much time around scam artists and deadbeats you started to feel like one yourself, cutting deals with assholes in hopes of catching a bigger one. He talked about his early years working robbery, before he started handling homicides. Most of the stories ended with someone going to jail or worse, but for some reason they made Jill laugh, maybe because of the colorful characters, or maybe because of the way he told them. Sam didn't care; he just liked the sound of it.

Sometime between the story about a burglar who got caught asleep in the apartment he was supposed to be robbing and the transsexual con artist who liked to dress like a nun, Jill and Sam finished their dinner.

Sam signed the bill as Jill asked, "Are all criminals really that stupid?"

"Not all of them, no. But a lot of these guys, they're not that bright, and to tell you the truth, they're not even that bad."

"Not that bad?"

"I'm not defending them. And I'm not talking about stone killers, either." Sam blinked as an image of severed legs flashed behind his eyes, flame tattoos encircling the thighs. "I'm talking about regular people, like you and me."

"Am I being insulted?" asked Jill playfully.

"That's up to you," replied Sam. "But most murders are not committed by serial killers or professional hitmen. Hannibal Lecter isn't eating one of your neighbors."

"I thought I saw him waiting for a table."

"Funny." Sam gestured across the restaurant. "You take any of these people and put them under tremendous pressure, you never know how they're going to react. You want to find a killer, nine out of ten times it's a friend of the victim. A colleague. A family member."

"Really?"

"Yeah," said Sam. "Nine times out of ten, it's someone the victim knew."

Chapter Thirty-six

"Do I know you?"

Jerome didn't understand the question, so he responded by staring into Tamara's eyes. He wasn't sure if she was hypnotizing him or the other way around, and he didn't care. This girl was awesome.

But she wasn't letting him off the hook. "You planning on answering my question?"

Jerome frowned. "Not sure what you mean, babe."

"I mean you're different," she said simply.

"Since when?" he asked. "This morning?"

Tamara studied him for a minute. They sat in a corner booth in the Mexican place, not exactly intimate, but when Tamara asked where he liked to eat, Jerome drew a blank. This was the only place he could think of, being so preoccupied with a single, burning thought.

This girl is awesome.

The waiter did a fly-by but kept walking when he saw their drinks had barely been touched. Tamara seemed to make up her mind. "Yeah, since this morning. When I first saw you in the hallway you seemed like the Jerome I knew and—" She stopped just this side of embarrassment.

"—liked?" Jerome suggested. "The Jerome you knew and liked?"

Tamara blushed only for an instant. "Yeah, you could say that. But yesterday I thought you were cute…" Again her voice trailed off. "I don't know, like—"

"—a puppy dog?" Jerome said hopefully.

Laughing, she said, "Maybe."

Jerome smiled knowingly. "Yeah, that was the *old me*."

"The old you?"

"The stoner—Jerome the lovable stoner."

Tamara watched him for another minute, took a sip of her marguerita. "You make it sound like you were a character in a movie."

Jerome shrugged. "I was definitely acting. Playing a part in my brother's play."

Tamara's forehead creased, but she still looked totally hot. She asked, "Larry wanted you to be a stoner?"

Jerome shook his head. "It's a long story, but I was acting out my frustrations, trying to get under Larry's skin. A classic case of passive-aggressive displacement. Very common among siblings close in age."

Tamara took another sip. "Come again?"

"Larry was getting on my nerves, so I subconsciously decided to drive him nuts by becoming someone he couldn't control."

Tamara gave him that studied look again. "Jerome, what did you study in college?"

"Psychology."

"Uh-huh." Tamara shifted in her chair and leaned in closer. "And when did you decide to get off the grass?"

Jerome screwed up his face. "This morning, I guess."

"Just like that," she said.

"Gimme a break, Tamara. We're not talking crystal meth here."

"Sorry," replied Tamara. "I'm just…curious. I mean, you smoked *a lot*, right?"

"*Jah, mon.*"

"No cravings?"

"Not since you made me breakfast."

Tamara looked like she might cry. That's when Jerome knew.

He was in love.

Grab the bull by the horns. You're in the driver's seat. Put the pedal to the metal. Strike while the iron is hot. Fish or cut bait. Every bullshit motivational cliché Jerome had ever heard ricocheted around his brain. All day he'd felt guided by an invisible hand, and so far it hadn't steered him in the wrong direction.

Shit or get off the pot.

Tamara was watching him over her drink, as if she expected him to make the next move. This was destiny calling. Jerome took a deep breath and gave her his trademark lopsided grin, which he could now summon at will.

The Force was with him.

"Hey, Tamara, let's say you and me get married?"

Chapter Thirty-seven

"I said, *do you want to get married?*"

Gail reached across the loveseat and jammed her index finger into Gus' right ear. Finding the little dial on his hearing aid, she spun it like a roulette wheel till he winced from the feedback.

"What did you say?" His voice was unnaturally loud, as if Gail had turned up the volume on his vocal chords by accident.

"Don't pull that selective hearing shit with me, you old bastard," said Gail, her tone more playful than angry. "And don't make me ask you again."

Gus looked sheepish but scooted closer until their hips touched. "Gee, Gail, I dunno. I mean, what we've got is sure nice, but this is kinda sudden, and—"

Gail leaned in close and barked directly into the hearing aid. "Sudden? *Jesus-H-Christ* Gus, we've known each other fifteen years!"

Gus worked his jaw, trying to ascertain if Gail had rattled his dentures. "When you put it like that, I guess—"

"I guess you could make an honest woman of me."

Gus put a dry right hand on Gail's lap, waiting for her left to join it, which it did. Their parchment fingers intertwined for a long moment before Gail untangled herself and moved his hand away.

"OK, enough of that, you old rogue."

Gus looked wounded. "Enough of what?"

"No more free lunch for you."

"Free lunch?" Gus tried not to sound indignant. "That wasn't even a snack, Gail."

Gail smiled, but her eyes went supernova.

"Do you love me, Gus?"

"Of course," he replied without hesitation. "You know how I feel."

"And do we not have a bond, Gus?"

"A bond?" Gus tried the word on for size. "I never thought of—"

"It's time, Gus."

"Time for what?"

"Time to shit or get off the pot."

Gus smiled wanly. "My mother used to say—"

"I'm not your mother, Gus."

"I wasn't saying—"

"Just wanted to be clear on that. A lot of men want to marry their mothers."

"My mother's been dead fifty y—"

"I'm just saying."

"*Jesus.*" Gus stood up. "Is this how it's gonna be?"

Gail blinked. "What do you mean?"

"You didn't even let me finish a sentence till I took the Lord's name in vain, for Chrissakes."

"You're not religious."

"That's not the point, Gail."

Gail looked him up and down, then smiled gently. "No, it's not, is it? Sit down next to me." She patted the sofa, then gestured toward the tray of cookies on the coffee table. "You want an almond cookie? They're to die for."

Gus shook his head and sat down heavily. He ran his hands through his thinning hair and smiled. "You want me to eat one of your cookies, Gail? Is that what you want?"

"What do you think I want, Gus?"

Gus shook his head as if to clear it, and Gail thought he might bolt. Instead he dropped to one knee with surprising grace. All those years on the tennis court had paid off.

"I want to marry you, Gail," said Gus, taking her hand in his.

Gail blinked, and for a moment Gus thought she was going to cry, but then he came to his senses. She did manage to look surprised, which was no small trick. Gus felt like a marionette that had been forced to dance a polka.

What a woman.

"So?" he asked, maybe sounding a little too eager, but what the hell—he was on his knees.

Gail scooted to the edge of the couch and leaned forward to give Gus a slow, dry kiss.

Gus thought she tasted like almonds.

Chapter Thirty-eight

They kissed for a long time.

Sam felt the heat from her lips radiate across his nerve endings. The block of ice in his chest fractured slowly, shards of despair melting into his bloodstream like dying icebergs.

Jill was a great kisser.

She fumbled for her keys as she pulled away, her right hand resting gently on the back of his neck.

"I feel like a kid in high school."

Sam didn't answer as she worked the lock. Grabbing his right hand in hers, she pulled him across the threshold and kicked off her shoes, but she lost her grip when he hesitated just inside the door. When she turned around she caught his gaze, one eye on her but the other somewhere else. Another time and place.

Slowly, and not without a hint of sadness, Jill took both of his hands in hers and pulled him close.

"Am I going too fast?"

Sam shook his head but said, "Yeah," but then added, "No—not at all."

"You sound so certain," she said playfully.

"Maybe."

Jill's eyes sparkled. "It's OK, you know."

"What's OK?"

"That you're alive," replied Jill. "You know that, don't you? It's OK."

Sam frowned but stayed close. "Yeah, I get that. But thanks for pointing it out. I still forget sometimes."

"Well," said Jill. "If it's alright that you're alive, then…" She let her voice fade.

"What?" Sam squeezed her hands.

"Then you're supposed to *live*," said Jill.

"Live a little?" chided Sam. "Is that a come-on or something?"

Jill smiled and said gently, "It's only going to get harder."

Sam let his eyes dart to the front of his pants before they rejoined hers. "Now that was definitely a come-on…or maybe you were boasting."

Jill blushed. "That's not what I meant, and you know it."

Sam pulled her closer and let his hands slip around her waist. "Sure," he said. "Whatever you say."

Their lips met and they half-slid, half-shuffled across the foyer into the living room. Somehow they made it to the couch without breaking their embrace. Sam liked how she kept her eyes open while they kissed.

"Thanks." Sam pulled back only slightly.

Jill blinked, his face almost too close for her to focus. "For what?"

"For thawing me out."

She smiled but didn't say anything, tilting her head so she could kiss him on the neck. He felt her tongue tickle the edge of his left ear, her hands warm against his chest. Slowly, almost reluctantly, he took her hands in his and maneuvered them so she sat on the edge of the couch and he was on his knees in front of her. Holding her gaze, Sam slipped his fingers inside the waistband of her skirt and pulled it gently down her legs. The panties had caught on the inseam and came along for the ride.

"Hey." It was more a plea than a protest, her voice dropping an octave, reminding Sam of her singing. Without a word he took her right foot in his hands and started kissing her toes, starting with the pinky and working his way across. By the time he reached her calf, she'd wrapped her left leg around his back, letting him know escape was no longer an option. She need not have bothered.

Somewhere deep inside, Sam felt the last vestiges of ice turning to water and then to steam. Her heat enveloped him, and he forgot entirely the circumstances under which they had met.

Chapter Thirty-nine

Sam could still taste her as he padded quietly down the hall toward his apartment.

Jill lay asleep in her bed, which is where they had ended up after the couch led to the shower, followed by a short interlude in the kitchen. He was buzzing with an afterglow of lust and surprise—at himself, more than anything else. He was out of practice and not getting any younger, but that didn't seem to matter. Jill triggered something deep inside him, a chain reaction that unleashed the lost vitality of his youth. Fuck the fountain of youth. Sam suspected Ponce de Leon would still be around today if he'd known Jill.

He'd left after watching her sleep for an hour. He was too jacked too sleep. His heart hadn't worked this hard in a long time, either physically or emotionally. The note he left told her where he kept his spare key—under the mat in front of his door—and asked her to call him or stop by later.

As he passed their neighbors' doors he noted the sounds of stillness. It was too early for civilians to be awake. Only the homicide cop coming home after his night shift would recognize these sounds. The throbbing of the truck engines as garbage was collected before dawn. The distant but shrill cries of the parrots on Telegraph Hill. The clockwork ticking of the building's ventilation system, counting off the seconds until the next heating bill arrived under your door.

Sam was mentally counting off the names of his neighbors as he passed their doors when a thought occurred to him.

I haven't talked to Walter.

Walter's door was across the hall from Sam's to the right. Directly in front of where Sam stood, this instant. Walter never seemed to be home, and if this were a normal homicide investigation, he'd be on the witness list. Sam knew exactly what he'd do if he was still a cop.

Wake him up. At least you know he's going to be home.

Sam hesitated for an instant, wondering how neighborly it was to knock on someone's door when even the pigeons weren't awake. But he remembered someone—Gail or Jill—saying Walter and Ed, the landlord, had been friends. Sam shrugged, raised his right fist and knocked on the door.

Nothing.

In for a dime, in for a dollar. Sam knocked again, harder this time, knuckles prominent.

The door slid open a crack, the latch slipping across the strikeplate. The door had either been kicked shut or pulled closed by someone in a hurry. *Who doesn't turn their deadbolt when they sleep?*

Sam knocked again, even harder.

The door creaked open just enough for Sam to peer across the foyer into the living room. From the hallway, Sam could see Walter sprawled on the couch, the remote clutched in his hand, his chin on his chest.

Sam took a deep breath and stepped inside the apartment.

Chapter Forty

They were inside the apartment and tangled in the pink sheets before Jerome could pull his socks off.

Tamara's clothes had already vanished, so he left them on. At least he wouldn't have to worry about having cold feet and ruining the moment, even if he did look like a dork.

Tamara made some kind of *ninja* move, twisting her bodacious hips and pulling one of his arms across her body, which planted him flat on his back. Before he could respond with a stunt of his own, Jerome was pinned—she had one hand on his chest, the other pressing down on his thighs. Tamara aligned herself perpendicular to him, lowered her head and began kissing his chest. He could feel her perfect breasts brush against his side as she worked her way across his stomach. Jerome was so hard, he was lightheaded.

This girl is awesome.

The thought had become a mantra, a rhythmic chanting inside his head. His life's new digital soundtrack. *Who needed Bob Marley when you had Tamara?*

Jerome gasped as Tamara worked her magic. He twisted his head sideways, his hair mashed against her perfectly pink pillow, which matched the painfully pink bedspread they'd knocked to the floor. He stole a glance at Tamara to capture a freeze frame of the most erotic moment of his life (since breakfast). He looked away almost immediately, afraid the excitement of bearing witness to his own ecstasy might finish things before they got started.

A sudden movement in the corner of his eye pulled Jerome's gaze to the desk, where he saw something that changed the course of his life forever.

Jerome saw himself, getting the most amazing blow job in the history of recorded civilization. In all the excitement, Tamara had left the computer and the webcam turned on.

Not sure what else to do, Jerome smiled at the camera and waved.

Chapter Forty-one

Sam sat down across from Walter, wishing he had brought his sunglasses.

Walter looked like shit, his face an ashen gray, chin melting into his chest like Play-Doh. Sam suspected Walter hadn't looked much healthier in life, but in death he made you want to go on a diet and start exercising. Sam figured a photo of Walter dead on his couch would raise more money for the American Heart Association than any celebrity endorsement.

Sam stood and touched Walter's neck, careful not to disturb the corpse or its surroundings. The body practically radiated cold, and Sam felt the chill in his fingers long after he broke contact. Walter had been sitting here for at least twelve hours.

Sam walked around the apartment, not touching anything but taking in every detail. The place looked better than its occupant, but not by much. You didn't need to be a detective to guess Walter had been a bachelor living alone. There wasn't much to see, and nothing looked out of place.

Sam returned to the living room and stood behind Walter, looking over his drooping head toward the television. He followed Walter's line of sight toward the screen, gauged his reach to the bowl of chips, his position on the couch. After a while Sam circumnavigated the couch and studied Walter from the other direction, blocking the dead man's view of the TV. Walter didn't complain.

Sam noticed a bulge in Walter's pants, north of the crotch on the right side. Stepping closer he saw Walter's slacks had pockets on either side, cut vertically as you'd expect with khakis, not the wide horizontal pockets of jeans. Sam pressed against the bulge from the outside, not wanting to put his fingers into the pocket and get his prints on anything. The contours were obvious as soon as his fingers rubbed against the teeth: it was a set of keys.

Not a gun or a knife. Not a crack pipe or bong. And definitely not a suicide note or a confession. Just a set of house keys.

Sam took a deep breath and regretted it instantly. All sense-memory of Jill was expunged as he forced himself to exhale, but the cloying smell of Walter had found purchase. It was going to take a lot of coffee and a long shower to chase it away.

Sam took a lingering look at Walter, then turned and walked across the living room to the door. Pulling a handkerchief from his pocket, he gingerly pulled the door open, then used the same motion to pull it closed once he was in the hallway. He was careful to make sure the door didn't latch, but Sam pulled it closed far enough to look shut.

Exhaustion hit as he turned his key in his apartment door, the adrenaline rush of sex dissipated by the sudden chill of finding a corpse. He shook his head to clear it and focused on the tasks at hand. *Get to the phone and call Danny. Tell him about Walter. Only then do you get to take a shower and go to bed.*

As the door opened, he said in a tired voice, "Honey, I'm home."

He greeted Marie each time he stepped through the door, every day since she left him alone among the living. Then he might tell her about his day, or sometimes he asked for advice, but it always started with a simple greeting, a hopeful glance at the mantle. Sam knew that no matter what he had done, good or bad, she'd be there watching over him. After the ups and downs of the past twenty-four hours, he needed that right now.

But as Sam looked across the kitchen into the living room, he knew he wasn't going to get what he needed. Not now, and maybe not ever again.

Someone had been in his apartment.

A chill ran down his spine as Sam looked at the photographs of his beloved wife, ageless in her perfect silver frames. She wasn't looking at him with unconditional love in her eyes. She wasn't looking at him at all.

In every picture, in every frame all the eyes had been cut out.

Chapter Forty-two

Larry gripped the edge of the kitchen counter until his knuckles turned white.

Where the fuck was Jerome? He'd been gone most of the day and stayed out all night. They were due to meet Buster in an hour, and this time of day it would take at least twenty minutes to drive uptown to the Mission District. Larry thought they should just pack their bags and head to Mexico with the cash they'd squirreled away. Instead Jerome got a haircut and went on a date, leaving Larry at home to sweat. Larry had half a mind to skip town and leave his brother behind.

But the thought of running was terrifying. Actually it was the prospect of being chased that paralyzed him with fear. A sudden image flashed across Larry's brain. He was running in the desert, Mexican gangsters chasing him in Jeeps, agents of Zorro who followed their trail across the border. They were hunting him like an animal. As he collapsed in the dirt they drew their guns from their *bandileros* and took aim…

Bandileros? Maybe he was being chased by *gauchos*, Mexican cowboys on horseback. Or *banditos*, fierce men with big moustaches and even bigger hats, firing into the air like Yosemite Sam chasing Speedy Gonzalez.

Wait a minute—wasn't it Sylvester the cat who chased Speedy Gonzalez, and didn't Speedy always get away? Larry nodded to himself, satisfied. Maybe he was just like Speedy

Gonzalez—small and weak, but fast and clever. Always one step ahead of his larger, more savage nemesis.

Larry smiled grimly. Things were going to work out. His mental tour of racial stereotypes had given him perspective. Fuck Zorro, they were in charge of the situation.

But the fact remained, Jerome was late.

Larry tapped his right foot on the tile floor until the sound started driving him crazy. He released the counter, fingers numb. His stomach lurched and made a sound like mating call of a major appliance. Jerome was right, stress was a killer.

Jerome.

Stress.

For the longest time, two sides of the same coin. But now it occurred to Larry he was just as tense without Jerome in the room. Maybe he was going crazy, and Jerome was a mere catalyst, not the cause. Like his brother, Larry had studied psychology in college, and lately he was beginning to suspect he suffered from one of the more obscure obsessive-compulsive disorders. He hadn't told anyone, but last week he pulled an old textbook out of storage to refresh his memory.

Hyperscrupulosity. Also called "responsibility OCD." The feeling that you are responsible for everything. It's your fault, no matter what happens. Someone drops dead, you probably could have prevented it. A cat falls out of a tree, you should have been there to catch it.

Because no one else will. No one is as responsible like you are.

Living with Jerome, that's how Larry felt most of the time. If I don't do it, no one else will, certainly not my brother. I'm the only responsible one in this room, maybe in any room. Maybe on the whole damn planet. Without me, the whole world goes to shit. Just look at the news—no one takes responsibility for anything.

Larry took a deep breath, tried to visualize himself as Speedy Gonzalez running happily through a drainpipe. He closed his eyes and counted to ten, in Spanish.

Uno, dos, tres…

When he reached *diez*, Larry opened his eyes. His gaze landed on the kitchen counter, where Jerome's stash sat undisturbed. *Stash* was probably the wrong term for a gallon ziplock overflowing with pot intermixed with eight or ten joints the size of Roman candles, but there it was.

Larry was stunned Jerome had left the bag at home. His brother was more likely to forget his wallet or keys. Or his underwear. Larry rubbed his temples, conscious of the headache he'd had all morning. It was a headache he normally blamed on Jerome and the smoke he generated, the constant marijuana haze that followed him everywhere, but today it was worse. Much worse.

Larry was still staring at the bag when an insidious thought crawled into his brain like an earwig.

I felt better when Jerome was here, smoking. I actually felt better.

Today he felt more anxious than he had in weeks. True, they had contracted to kill a man and ended up doing the job themselves. And a Mexican drug lord with horrible teeth was threatening to eat their eyeballs. But that was true yesterday, yet this morning Larry felt like his skull was going to implode from the pressure. Their criminal enterprise and the very real threat of getting killed were constants in this equation. The *only* difference in his situation, really, was no Jerome.

And no pot.

Larry studied the bag. It didn't move, and neither did he. He just stared, as if trying to make a decision, predict an outcome. After a long moment, he licked his lips and opened the bag. He selected a joint slightly smaller than a fountain pen but larger than a cigarette, hefted its weight in his hand. It felt good, reassuring. It felt…*relaxed* in his palm.

It felt the way he wanted to feel.

Larry fumbled in the kitchen drawer until he found a lighter. Sparks flew. He lit up and took a deep, long pull, a soothing moment that ended abruptly when he started coughing. He felt his eyes water as he gasped and hacked, holding on to the counter for support. After a minute he took a deep breath and tried again. This time he got the timing right. He felt the smoke fill his lungs, held it, and released in a long, slow exhale that filled the small kitchen with a billowing cloud of calm. Larry felt his blood pressure drop and the pounding in his temples fade.

He made his way over the couch and put his feet on the coffee table. Jerome would get here when he got here. Then they could figure out what to do. Jerome said he wanted to drive, fine. Larry took another heroic hit.

They were two speedy fucking rodents, he and Jerome, smart enough to outfox Zorro and his crew. Everything was going to be OK.

Larry exhaled and nodded in satisfaction. It's all good, he told himself.

It's all good.

Chapter Forty-three

"This is bad."

Sam didn't respond. He watched his former partner move along the mantle, careful not to touch the frames but standing close. Danny Rodriguez was in some of those pictures. The muscles in his jaw worked overtime as he scanned from right to left, taking in the ruined faces, the missing eyes.

"Really bad."

Sam remained mute, his own jaw clenched.

"You want me to get the tech guys down here?"

Sam shook his head. "Don't bother."

"You sure, partner?"

"It's not like we don't know who did this."

"Might get some prints off the frames," said Danny half-heartedly.

"Yeah, you might," said Sam. "But you get the techs involved, that makes it official."

"Breaking and entering not official enough for you?"

"This isn't official, Danny." Sam stood up. "It's personal."

Danny took a deep breath, looked Sam in the eye. "You know how I felt about Marie, Sam, and you—"

Sam held up a hand. "I'm not asking you to do anything, Danny. Either as a cop or a friend."

Danny shifted his weight, watching Sam carefully. "Then why did you ask me to come here?"

"I wanted you to know," said Sam.

Danny felt his eyebrows jump involuntarily. "Wanted me to know? Like, just in case anything happens to you?"

Sam shrugged but didn't answer.

"Don't do anything stupid, Sam."

Sam managed to twist his mouth into some semblance of a smile. "What would you do?"

Danny looked away, toward the picture frames. "That's different, *hombre*. I'm a cop."

Sam nodded. "You didn't answer the question."

"You mean, what would I do, as a man?" said Danny. "Someone did this to my home?"

Sam smiled, seeing the look in his friend's eyes. "I thought so."

"*Chocho*," said Danny. "That's what you are—you know that, don't you?"

"I've been called a cunt before," replied Sam. "But you make it sound so...romantic."

"Fuck you," said Danny. "Just don't kill anybody, OK?"

Sam bowed his head. "Yes, officer."

Danny made a face as he crossed to the kitchen. Opening cabinets, he located some instant coffee and a mug. "You want any?"

Sam took his seat on the couch. "Help yourself."

Danny said, "You told me there were two things you wanted to talk about."

Sam put his feet on the coffee table. "Remember the guy lives across the hall? Heavy set, in his fifties. You talk to him when you first canvassed the building?"

Danny nodded and took a sip of coffee, made another face. "This coffee is *nasty*."

"He's dead."

Danny almost dropped his mug, recovered at the last minute. He put it down very deliberately before asking, "You got any beer?"

While Danny twisted the top off his beer, Sam told him about Walter. He sketched the scene, giving the layout of the apartment and condition of the body. He described Walter's position on the couch in great detail. When he had finished, Danny said, "You could've mentioned this when you called."

Sam's eyes flicked to the mantle. "I had other things on my mind."

Danny blew out his cheeks. "This guy was overweight. A train wreck."

"So?"

"You think *gordo* had a heart attack?"

Sam knew that in a city the size of San Francisco, there were approximately two thousand heart attacks occurring over any given year, maybe a third of those fatal. Cops knew that sort of thing, so did firefighters. So did Danny. Sam watched his former partner's eyes as he calculated the odds of Walter going into cardiac arrest in the same building that three men—one landlord and two gang-bangers—had already died. Not only in the same building, but within the same week.

"He had his keys in his pocket," said Sam.

Danny worked his tongue around the inside of his right cheek. "You mentioned that."

"Take a look when you go in there," said Sam. "They make quite a bulge."

"Uncomfortable."

"What's the first thing you do, Danny, when you walk through your front door?"

"Kick the dog, yell at my wife, and then…" He let his voice trail off.

"Throw your keys on the counter," said Sam.

"Yeah," said Danny, "but we got this little basket my wife bought—she loves baskets, got 'em for everything—I throw my keys and wallet in there."

Sam jutted his chin toward his own kitchen counter, to the left of Danny's beer. "What do you see there?"

Danny spared a glance at the ring of keys and rapped his hands on the counter like a drummer. "You sit down to eat chips and watch movies—"

"—and you're overweight—," added Sam.

"—you probably don't keep your keys jammed in your front pants pocket."

"There goes the fucking camel's back," Danny sighed. "Looks like I gotta open an investigation."

"Not yet," replied Sam, standing. "You leave, I'll call the ambulance. But when they bring the body to the morgue, make sure Oliver runs all the tests. Bloodwork, everything."

Danny studied his friend before asking the obvious. "Why wait, Sam? I should've started a case file when Ed jumped, we both know that."

"It *could* have been a heart attack," replied Sam. "The guy was fat, maybe under a lot of stress."

"Now you're arguing the other side?" Danny scowled. "What is this, the fucking debating club?"

Sam held up his hands. "Oliver's gonna tell us if it was a heart attack, Danny. You can open the case then."

"Yeah, but why wait?"

"Because I want a headstart on the cops," replied Sam, his gaze back on the mantle, searching for the loving gaze that had been taken from him, twice. He could feel the glacial retreat of the last forty-eight hours reverse itself, ice encroaching once more upon his heart.

"A headstart," said Danny. "To do what, exactly?"

"Relax, Danny." Sam smiled, all the warmth gone from his face. "I'm just going to visit an old friend."

Chapter Forty-four

Jerome woke with a start to find himself flanked by two pairs of perfect breasts.

On his right was Tamara, arms crossed demurely beneath her perfect pair. She was propped against two enormous pink pillows, the sheet covering her legs. To Jerome's left was Shalya, sitting on the desk next to the computer with her legs crossed, right foot tapping in mid-air to some unheard beat. She wore a pair of tights—electric blue—and ankle-length socks, but what struck Jerome most about her appearance was that she was topless.

Her mahogany skin looked like it had been carved lovingly by angels. Pleased with the metaphor, Jerome decided her areolas were halos poised above nipples that could only be described as *epic*. The thought sent a shudder down Jerome's spine as he looked from the goddess on his left to the one lying next to him in bed. He had always wondered what Heaven looked like.

"Am I dead?" he asked.

Shayla seemed to notice him for the first time, her eyes swiveling his way like a gun turret, daring him to break eye contact.

"Not yet, crackhead."

Tamara squeezed his right arm. "Don't mind her, sweetie. She's just jealous."

Shayla lifted a corner of the sheet to reveal Jerome's manhood and said, "*Puh—leeeze.*"

"*Hey!*" said Jerome, pulling the sheet back into place.

"Jerome's kicked the habit," said Tamara defensively.

Shayla snorted but leaned forward to peer into Jerome's eyes. The move brought to mind an introductory physics course during his first year at college as her breasts performed a near perfect demonstration of Brownian motion, the highly random but excited motion of particles suspended in liquid. Even when he wasn't stoned, Jerome marveled at the brain's knack for free association.

"Clear," Shayla announced, looking across Jerome toward Tamara. "But he snores like bear."

"Allergies," said Jerome.

Shayla brought her gaze back to Jerome, caught him looking south, and gave him a stern glance. "When did you quit?"

"After breakfast." Jerome stopped, trying to remember what day it was. Shit, today was the day he and Larry were meeting Zorro.

"Breakfast when?" asked Shayla. "Your ass is still in bed."

"Yesterday." Jerome blinked himself back to the here and now. "After breakfast yesterday, I kinda…lost interest."

Tamara gave him another squeeze. "The power of love."

Shalya pointed her index finger toward her open mouth and made a gagging noise. "You two deserve each other."

Tamara beamed and jiggled. "Exactly."

Shayla shook her head but smiled. "So you want to stay with this thing?"

Jerome started to object. First she calls him *crackhead* and now *thing*, until he realized Shayla was gesturing toward the computer when she said it. The previous night's acrobatics came to him in a torrent of freeze-frames, each orgasmic moment made all the more memorable because he had watched himself, live, on the computer screen.

He looked from Shayla to Tamara and back again, half-remembering they'd been in the middle of a conversation when he first woke.

"What'd I miss?" he asked.

Shayla shifted sideways on the desk, revealing the computer screen. At first Jerome saw the screen divided into four windows, each with a different view of the room, all revealing their exposed chests, his included. He suddenly felt self-conscious but more than a little titillated at the prospect the performance of a lifetime had been recorded. Before he could comment, Shalya starting typing commands and the screen changed, the four images replaced by a green and blue bar chart, the kind you'd see at an annual sales conference.

"The green bars are visits to our homepage," explained Shalya. "Where we have random low-resolution images from these cameras." She slid the nail of her index finger across the screen, left to right. "The blue bars represents registered members, people who have signed up and paid for unlimited access to the site. As you can see…" Her finger stopped midway across the screen at two bars that were five times the size of the bars preceding them. "…our membership skyrocketed last night during your, um, *festivities*."

Jerome squinted at the screen. Maybe math was cool, after all. "How many people we talking about?"

"We're gonna be rich," said Tamara, leaning over to give him a kiss. Jerome felt himself stir beneath the sheet and started to get embarrassed, but Shayla was still looking at the screen. She mumbled something.

"What's the problem?" asked Tamara.

"I supposed we'll have to cut *him* in on the action," Shayla sighed.

"The name's Jerome."

Shayla ignored him and jutted her chin toward Tamara. "Three ways?"

Jerome slid closer to Tamara to make room. "Hey, whatever you girls are into, I'll do my best to accommodate—"

Tamara put a hand over his mouth. "She means splitting the money three ways, honey."

As soon as she removed her hand, Jerome said, "Right, of course," doing his best to not sound disappointed. He studiously avoided eye contact with Shayla as he asked, "So how much money will be coming in?"

Shayla frowned, scanning the numbers on the screen. "Depends on whether or not you two disappoint our new customers," she said dryly. "But since they're obligated to pay three months in advance, I'd say it's safe to quit your day job if you want."

The mention of his day job hit Jerome like a bucket of cold water. "What time is it?"

"Almost eleven," replied Shayla. "Why?"

Jerome jumped out of bed, realizing he didn't care if someone sitting behind a computer screen in some other state saw him naked. He had bigger things to worry about than his newfound lack of modesty.

"Gotta go," he said, jumping back in bed long enough to kiss Tamara lightly on the lips. He stood and half-bowed to Shayla, not sure of the proper etiquette when your girlfriend's roommate was topless and you were buck naked. Shayla didn't move, just arched her eyebrows.

"Where're you off to in such a hurry?" she asked.

Jerome got his pants on, grabbed his shirt in one hand and his shoes in the other. He called over his shoulder as he dashed through the door.

"Going to quit my day job."

Chapter Forty-five

Jerome still had his pants on, which he took as a good sign.

He and Larry stood in Zorro's office, waiting for the drug lord to arrive. Julio had left them alone five minutes ago, locking them inside the windowless room with the plain oak desk and folding chairs. They'd made the trip to the building blindfolded again, but this was clearly the same room as before, so Zorro had not moved his headquarters since their last meeting. And this time they got to keep their pants. Things were looking up, despite the stress of getting here on time.

Jerome had returned to their apartment to find Larry sprawled on the couch, a miasma of smoke spreading across the ceiling like the ash cloud from Mount St. Helens. One look at his brother told him all he needed to know. It was like looking in a mirror. Jerome grabbed the keys from the counter and told Larry he was driving today. Larry didn't object.

Now Jerome was pacing Zorro's office, wondering if it was bugged. He wrinkled his nose when his gaze fell upon the jar of pickled eyeballs. "Let me do the talking, Larry."

"OK by me. I'll just do color commentary."

Jerome started to object but caught himself. It sounded like something he would have said to Larry the day before. Instead he thought of Tamara sitting in bed, her beatific smile blinding in his mind's eye. *Don't let him push your buttons.* Jerome rubbed his hands together and watched the door as he pulled his thoughts together. Zorro would be here any minute.

As if on cue, the door swung open. Julio came first, Zorro invisible behind his bulk until he took position next to the door. Behind Zorro was another man, short with a wispy mustache and wire-frame glasses. He nodded at the two brothers, then took a seat against the wall to the right side of the desk. He held a small notebook and pen in his lap. Jerome thought he looked like an accountant.

Zorro waited until he was seated behind the desk before he made eye contact with the two brothers. His gaze lingered on Larry for a minute before shifting back to Jerome. Whether by body language or expression, Zorro somehow sensed the role reversal that was going on between them.

"That took *cajones*," he said slowly, "to reschedule our meeting. You are too busy to meet with Zorro?"

"I had a date," said Jerome.

Zorro repeated dumbly, "A date?"

Jerome nodded. "With a girl."

Zorro waited for more of an explanation but got nothing. Nonplussed, he went on the offensive.

"She must have beautiful eyes," he said, reaching for his jar of sclerotic horror.

Jerome made a face but didn't take the bait, instead jerking his chin toward the man with the glasses. "Who's the new guy?"

Zorro gulped down an eyeball and answered with his mouth full. "This is Ramon," he said, gesturing. "He handles my finances."

"Central casting," said Jerome.

"No shit," said Larry.

Zorro's mouth twitched but he kept his eyes on Jerome.

"You came to me for help," he said. "Because you had a problem with your friend Walter."

Jerome shook his head. "Wasn't our friend Z, and he's not a problem any more." He smiled and added, "No thanks to you."

Zorro's right eye twitched. Jerome heard Julio's feet shuffle on the hardwood floor behind them but stop when Zorro gave a quick shake of the head. He stared at Jerome for a full minute before speaking again.

"You are a new man, Jerome," he said. "You have found your balls." He moved his eyes to Larry. "And you, Larry, what happened to you? Are you now your brother's bitch—eh, *puta*?"

Larry started to rise from his chair but sat down again as if he'd slipped. Jerome worried Larry was going to either jump across the desk or wet himself, depending on his current state of mind, but before Jerome could read the expression on his brother's face, Larry started giggling uncontrollably.

Jerome and Zorro stared at Larry until his fit subsided. By way of explanation, Jerome said, "My brother's totally baked, Z."

"*Hic!*" Larry had given himself the hiccups.

Zorro scowled and Jerome decided to jump in headfirst. *Time to quit my day job.*

"Look, Z," he said. "We had a deal. You get rid of Walter and we pay, right?"

"*Hic!*" added Larry.

Zorro ignored him. "*Sí*, Jerome. You double my percentage."

"I don't think so."

"You don't think so?" Zorro blinked slowly, reminding Jerome of an iguana his best friend in high school had as a pet. Jerome wondered if Zorro was really as cold-blooded as he wanted to appear.

"Walter's dead," said Jerome. "Because me and Larry took him out."

"*Hic-hic-hic.*"

"How?" said Zorro.

Jerome shook his head. "That's on a need-to-know basis, Z. All you need to know is we did your job for you."

Zorro sucked his teeth, half of them protruding beyond his lips. "I lost two men."

Jerome frowned. "So we're even."

Zorro tapped his fingers on the desk. "I made an investment on your behalf."

"How much of an investment?"

Zorro spread his hands. "Can you really put a price on human life?"

"Sure," replied Jerome, confident that Zorro did it all the time. "How about five percent?"

"Twenty."

"Ten."

"Deal," said Zorro.

Off to the side, Ramon made a notation.

Jerome held up his right hand, index finger extended. "*Here's the deal*—we pay you another ten percent each month, but in return you do us a favor."

Zorro's eyebrows met in an angry black line across his forehead. "What favor?"

"You sent guys to kill Walter," said Jerome. "But we killed him instead."

Zorro looked impatient. "Did we not talk of this already? You want a medal? A hug, perhaps?"

Jerome raised his hand again. "You have guys on your payroll who do bad things to nice people." He turned and made a theatrical gesture toward Julio.

"I'm a drug dealer," said Zorro defensively. "What do you expect?"

"It wasn't a criticism, Z—it was an observation. You have guys who can take the heat when cops knock on your door. Dudes who can disappear, run for the border."

Zorro nodded his understanding. "Perhaps."

"Or guys who can take a fall," added Jerome.

Zorro's eyes flicked to Julio before landing on Jerome again. "What are you asking, Jerome?"

"When the cops come looking for Walter's killer, I don't want them looking at me or Larry."

Zorro steepled his hands and smiled, revealing his full array of ruined orthodontics.

"I think I am going to like working with you, Jerome." He turned to Larry briefly. "No offense to your brother, of course."

"Why?" asked Jerome.

"Because we think alike, you and I."

Jerome frowned, worried he'd lost control of the conversation. "You understand what I'm saying? *I want the cops coming to you.*"

"Relax, Jerome." Zorro's impossible smile grew even wider. "There is a cop coming to me."

"There is?"

"Oh, yes." Zorro plucked another eyeball from the jar and took a bite. "I invited him yesterday—I think you know him."

"We do?"

Zorro chewed slowly. "He is your neighbor."

Chapter Forty-six

Sam pressed his ear to the door and heard singing.

He listened to Jill for another minute, her husky voice distorted by the door. He was about to knock when the door to the neighboring apartment opened and Shayla stepped into the hall. Sam started to straighten up, but Shayla smiled wickedly as he blushed.

"We *told* you that you'd like Jill."

Shayla looked stunning, as always, but her hair was now shaped into matching spheres on either side of her head, more like orbs than ponytails, the jet black hair tinted electric blue.

"Nice hair."

Shayla beamed. "Gotta mix it up. Never went blue before."

"Got a date?"

"Gotta protest," replied Shayla.

"Global warming?"

"That was last week," she said. "Besides, we could use a little warming in this city, don't you think? Too fucking chilly for my taste."

Sam shrugged. "It's the fog. Maybe you should protest that."

"Not until there's a budget," said Shayla. "Today it's drivers who want cyclists to stick to the bike paths. Next week the cyclists are staging a protest to get the cars off the streets."

"And onto the bike paths?"

Shayla shook her head. "Don't think they figured that out yet."

"Be careful out there," said Sam, adding, "I like the blue, by the way. Suits you."

Shayla's smile lit up the hall. "Say hi to Jill for me." She turned and sauntered over to the elevator, which arrived almost immediately. Even an elevator wouldn't keep Shayla waiting.

Behind the door Jill's voice continued to soar. Sam knocked reluctantly and was surprised when she opened the door right away and the singing continued from somewhere inside the apartment. Jill stood on her toes and kissed him lightly on the cheek. She was wearing sweat pants and an oversized t-shirt. Sam thought she looked amazing.

"Are you a ventriloquist?" he asked.

Jill led him through the living room, down the hall and into the guest bedroom. Instead of a home office, she had a recording studio. On a plain oak desk sat a computer with a widescreen monitor, a keyboard, and the kind of mixing board typically found in professional studios. Four speakers occupied the corners of the room, and Sam found himself surrounded by Jill's voice.

"This is quite a setup."

Jill nodded and gestured at the computer. "The software is cheap, and I can do all my mixing right on the Mac. Here, check this out." She moved close to the desk and traced a series of rows running across the screen. At first it had looked like a spreadsheet but Sam noticed the rows were moving, spreading across the screen as the song played. Jill's index finger danced lightly from one to another. "These are the different instruments, which I can adjust up or down, and this purple bar here is my voice." She clicked on the mouse and dragged it across two of the bars, causing the singing to shudder and jump as if a record had skipped, then resume. Sam noticed the bass notes had become more pronounced.

"I knew you designed websites," he said, "but I had no idea you were so technically proficient."

"This is simple compared to building and maintaining a site, especially a big one like Tamara and Shayla's."

"All that video," mused Sam.

Jill smiled. "Have you checked it out yet? It really is a great site."

"I've had all the excitement I can handle."

Jill pulled him close with her right hand. "Was that a compliment?"

"Absolutely."

Jill began to wrap her left arm around him but stopped when it brushed against something hard. She gingerly felt the contours through his jacket and frowned.

"Is that a gun in you pocket, or are you just happy to see me?"

"Both." Sam held her at arms length and met her gaze.

Jill's eyes flicked to his side. "Something you want to tell me?"

"I had a great time last night."

"Me, too," replied Jill. "But that's not what I meant."

"I'm going to be working late. Otherwise I'd ask you to dinner."

Jill waited for the other shoe to drop. "I thought you were retired."

"So did I."

Jill looked at him carefully. "You didn't strike me as the strong, silent type."

"No?"

"Doesn't suit you." Jill's eyebrows collided in a frown. "The past few days, you've said more to me than my ex-husband did our entire marriage."

"Guess I was trying to decide whether or not to tell you anything. Didn't want you to worry."

"Then you should've left the gun at home, cowboy."

"Fair enough." Sam took her by the hand and led her back into the living room, where they sat on the couch while he told her about Zorro and the photographs in his apartment. He left out the part where he found Walter's corpse and his conversation with Danny. In fact, he left out a lot of things. He had always talked to Marie about his cases after they were closed but never during an investigation. Some habits die hard.

"You said you arrested Zorro before, but you didn't say why."

"He beat up a girl," said Sam. "A prostitute."

Jill winced. "Badly?"

"Very."

"But you had to let him go."

"The girl dropped the charges, then claimed I'd harassed her into making a complaint. Threatened to sue the city. Out of nowhere she's got a high-priced lawyer making calls to the mayor's office."

"What happened?"

"I was put on forced leave of absence until the matter was resolved," said Sam, sounding like he was repeating the exact words said to him at the time. "The charges were dropped," he added.

"That's it?"

Sam hesitated before answering. "The girl wound up dead in a dumpster three weeks later. She'd had both her eyes cut out."

Jill gasped and put a hand to her mouth. Sam watched her begin to stand, then sit down heavily, as if she'd been contemplating a run to the bathroom. He waited until her breathing returned to normal before saying, "I can be the strong, silent type."

Jill took a deep breath. "No, I wanted to know. I do want to know...really."

"OK."

"But did you tell the police about what happened in your apartment?"

"The police can't do anything," replied Sam. "This is personal. And that's not me being macho—that's just the way it is."

"But shouldn't you ask for their help?"

"The police can't even find Zorro."

"But you can?"

"I know someone who can."

"Can he be trusted?"

Sam smiled, but there wasn't any warmth in it. "Absolutely not."

Chapter Forty-seven

"Why don't you trust him?"

Tamara disappeared as she asked the question, her face covered by the camisole slipping over her shoulders. The white silk flowed across her almond skin like milk as it settled on her torso, the fabric straining just enough to reveal the promised land that lay within her divine cleavage.

Shayla sat in the corner of the small dressing room and nodded her approval. As Tamara pulled the top off and grabbed the next one off its hanger, Shayla took the approved lingerie item and tossed it into a bulging Victoria's Secret shopping bag. Next to it on the floor lay an equally large pile of rejects, a graveyard of silk and polyester.

"He's a man," said Shayla. "Why should you trust him?"

"Jerome is a honey."

"Honey's something you put on pancakes."

"I prefer syrup."

"See?" said Shayla. "Already there's conflict in this relationship."

Tamara blew out her cheeks. "You saying you don't like the company of men?"

Shayla sat up straighter on the seat. "I never said *that*."

"I'm pretty sure you did."

"I *like* men just fine," said Shayla. "But liking and trusting are two different things."

"I think you don't respect men."

Shayla considered that for a minute. "Maybe you're right, but that doesn't mean—"

"Didn't you give me a little tongue last time we kissed on camera?"

"That was business." Shayla shot a warning glance, but it bounced off the smirk on Tamara's face. "And so is this, miss. Get back to work."

"Yes, ma'am." Tamara shrugged into the next item, a bra that seemed to lift, separate and enhance all at the same time. "How's this?"

Shayla frowned judiciously. "Not enough nipple action."

Tamara ran her index fingers across the front of the bra in little counter-clockwise twists. "How about now?"

Shayla made a face. "Cameras will never pick it up."

Tamara snapped the bra open and let it drop. "I'm tired."

"That's why they call it work."

"Your turn. I need a break."

Shayla stood. The two women shimmied past each other in the enclosed space and Tamara sat down as Shayla began to undress in front of the mirror. When she undid the last button on her blouse, Shayla asked, "Besides, how well do you know him—I mean, really?"

Tamara shrugged. "I'll get to know him. That's part of the fun of it. But finding out where he grew up or went to school is different. There's a difference between knowing and trusting. One happens in your head, the other in your heart."

"He could be a criminal."

Tamara made a face, perfect features contorted in mock anger. "We're not the most respectable girls on the block, you know."

"You having pangs of guilt?" Shayla raised her eyebrows. "Qualms about our arrangement?"

"I don't have qualms," replied Tamara. "I'm going to med school."

"And I'm going to law school."

"I'm *qualm-less*."

"Me, too."

"No qualms here."

"You already said that."

"Then why did you bring it up?" Tamara dropped her smile, held her roommate's eyes until Shayla broke contact and sighed deeply.

"I just don't want you to get hurt."

Tamara stood up and kissed Shayla gently on the cheek.

Shayla scowled. "Hey."

"What?"

"Save that for the cameras, girlfriend."

Tamara grinned. "You're such a romantic."

"Know where you're gonna have the wedding?"

Tamara looked at her like she was an idiot.

Shayla asked, "What?"

"Where do you *think* we'll have it?"

Shayla started to say something when it hit her. "You're going to get married on camera."

"Guess what I'll be wearing?" Tamara waved her hands in front of her, the gesture sweeping past her naked breasts to her panties.

Shayla shook her head and started laughing.

"What?"

"And you called me a romantic," Shayla said. "You're incredible."

"Does that mean you'll be my maid of honor?"

Shayla held her hands out from her sides and stood there, topless.

"Absolutely," she said. "Hell, I already know what I'm gonna wear."

Chapter Forty-eight

Danny Rodriguez wasn't wearing any pants.

He sat in his boxers and a plain white t-shirt at his kitchen table, his toes drumming the linoleum floor as he doodled on the notepad. His keys were in the basket on the counter with his wallet and badge. His gun was in the cabinet directly above the counter, safely out of his daughter's reach but within his own should anything happen.

The thought of something happening at home involving his gun sent a chill down Danny's spine. He worked hard—and so did his wife—so they could afford to live on a decent block, send their daughter to a good school in a city where public schools were hit or miss. Not easy on a cop's salary. His wife was a teacher, a damn good one, but she got paid a lot less than he did.

He looked around their small apartment, listened for the sound of his daughter's breathing, his wife's snoring. His wife claimed she never snored but sometimes that was the first sound that welcomed Danny home when he worked the night shift. It used to keep him awake, but now he found it soothing. It was there, just beyond the hum of the refrigerator. Danny began to smile but gritted his teeth as he thought about what had gone down in Sam's apartment. The ruined pictures. The violation. Almost twenty years on the force dealing with every kind of scumbag produced by humanity's inbred gene pool and he'd never had so much as a knock on his door. He'd never realized how lucky he was until tonight.

Danny looked at his crude drawing, the outline of Sam's apartment building, rectangles marking the entrances and exits, a crooked line indicating the fire escape. On the roof, a lone X led to a series of dashes arcing across the page toward a lopsided oval meant to represent the penguins. A series of squares along the top of the building, one for each apartment. He'd drawn an X through Walter's square marking the dead body. In the space where the courtyard would be were two more Xs, drawn within the crooked outline of a car.

On an adjacent sheet of paper he'd written all the names of the tenants with their corresponding apartment numbers. If this were a homicide investigation, every one of them would be a suspect. Even Walter. But this was a mess. A twisted tangle of strings that led to nowhere. For a cop, a no-win situation.

Danny had too many real cases. Open homicides he knew he could close. A dead pimp. A drug deal gone sour. A mugged tourist who died from a fractured skull. He had witnesses. Evidence. Motive. Even a suspect or two. Real *Law & Order* shit, maybe even some *CSI* crap if Twisted Oliver came through. Plenty of opportunity to improve the department's closure rate.

Danny stood and stepped over to the refrigerator, pulled out a beer, sat back down. He looked at his list of names and resumed his stoic tap-dance on the tiles. Muttered under his breath as he reluctantly added Sam's name to the list.

Every one of them a suspect.

Danny drew a line directly below Sam's name and scribbled *Zorro* along with the names of some of his crew, at least the ones Danny was familiar with. He scanned the list and shook his head in disbelief. Zorro had no business in that neighborhood. None at all.

Or did he? Danny drank the rest of his beer and crumpled the can in frustration. Zorro was a barracuda, teeth and all, and the people in that building were easy prey.

If Zorro was really involved with these people, they should all be dead by now.

Chapter Forty-nine

"They should be dead by now," said Julio.

Zorro nodded patiently from behind his desk, his eyelids drooping enough to make him look like a crocodile trying to lure its prey closer to the banks. Julio had seen that look before.

"Dead," Julio repeated the word, hoping to rouse Zorro out of his reptilian slumber. Actually the word Julio used was *muerto*, since they were speaking Spanish. A close relative to *muerte*, or Death, a word that carried far greater menace in his native tongue than in English. Every word in Spanish had a gender, and *muerte* was female. Julio liked to think of Death as a vengeful bitch, showing no mercy or remorse, a constant presence in his life much like his beloved wife.

"Perhaps," said Zorro.

"They put us at risk."

Zorro nodded absently. "They have been useful, Julio. They can go places closed to people like you and me. Office buildings, banks, small companies."

"There must be other gringos in this town who can make sandwiches."

Zorro chewed on his lower lip as he considered the argument. "But these brothers, they make us a lot of money."

"But at what cost?" said Julio, careful not to raise his voice. "They attract too much attention, Zorro. Two of our men, *dead*. The fat gringo who was blackmailing them, *dead*. The police will have to do something."

Zorro put his feet on the desk, closed his eyes and nodded. He had to remind himself Julio was smarter than he looked. Just because a man weighed as much as an orca and had an unnatural proclivity for violence didn't mean he was stupid.

"And what would you suggest, Julio?"

Julio thought he'd already made a perfectly good suggestion, so he repeated it slowly.

"We…should…kill…them."

"Ah," said Zorro, "but won't that make the police even more suspicious?"

Julio hesitated. He knew how cautious Zorro could be, but he also knew the two brothers were looking for a fall guy, and Julio had no intention of taking the fall. Let Zorro think of him as the loyal bodyguard—it paid well. But when the police came, Julio was going to be the first one out the back door. The last time he was in prison, he'd promised himself it would be his last, ever. He'd kill himself before he went back behind bars.

The thought gave him an idea.

"What if they killed each other?" he asked.

Zorro opened his eyes. "Killed each other?"

"Why not?"

"You mean they have an argument…"

"…over a woman…"

"…or a double-suicide?"

Julio shrugged. "Must happen all the time in this fucking city, no?"

Zorro brought his hands together. "Maybe they were depressed."

"You could plant some evidence—"

"—linking them to the other killings."

Zorro took his feet off the desk. "This is a great plan."

"It is a *great* plan, Zorro." Julio emphasized the words carefully so it sounded like it had been Zorro's idea in the first place.

"Yes," agreed Zorro, "it is."

Chapter Fifty

It was a great plan.

That's what Buster thought when Zorro first told him how they were going to get rid of that *hijo de puta* cop who almost drove over his foot. Zorro had designed an elaborate mouse trap for Sam, and Buster was going to be the cheese.

The big cheese. That's how Buster had been thinking of himself all day. *El queso grande*. The bait that would lure that meddling *guardia* to his grave. And that was only the beginning.

The plan had three parts. First, eliminate anyone nosy, which meant Officer Sam. Normally they couldn't touch a guy like that. But now that he wasn't a cop, he was fair game. Buster had even called the precinct house to make sure Sam wasn't bullshitting about being retired.

After what they did to Sam's apartment, it was only a matter of time before he came to them. He might act tough, but guys like that never followed through. Even the baddest cops had rules of conduct, their own code that let them think they were better than the people they arrested. Buster would act stubborn at first, then play the part of the two-faced informant, which came naturally. Then he'd give Sam an address where he could find Zorro.

Except Zorro wouldn't be there when Sam arrived.

Julio and one of Zorro's other soldiers, some dude named Rafael, would be waiting for Sam with a chainsaw and a box of industrial strength garbage bags. Officer Sam would be shark chum before the next high tide.

Part two of the plan involved tying up loose ends. After they had taken care of Officer Sam, there was no one to stop Zorro from cutting those two fuckups Larry and Jerome out of the picture.

Buster had frowned when he'd first heard the second part. He'd always liked Jerome, but Larry was an asshole. Typical privileged white boy, thinks he's better than anyone with an accent, anyone who didn't go to college. You could see it in his eyes. Even when he was so scared he was practically pissing himself, Larry managed to look down his nose at you. Too bad for Jerome his brother was such a *pijo*.

The third and final stage was to find two new lunch monkeys who could front Zorro's distribution network of San Francisco office buildings. Buster figured he could hang around near The Metreon, the big movie complex on Mission and 5th, and approach preppy *gringos* until someone took the bait. Sell them a dime bag, start a conversation, see where it leads.

Yes, it was a great plan, thought Buster, not realizing that it contained one fatal flaw. It was a mistake so fundamental that Buster wouldn't appreciate the irony until much later, when he was writhing on the sidewalk in agony.

Chapter Fifty-one

"Well, this is ironic."

"Fuck you, Larry."

Jerome tried to get his bearings but was too agitated. Zorro's driver had dropped them off at the usual corner, next to the gas station, and Jerome remembered parking only two blocks away. But where was their fucking car?

"No, really—*hic*—I mean it," said Larry. "You never lost the car when you were stoned."

"That's because you always drove."

"Oh," said Larry. "I hadn't thought of—*hic!*"

"Hold your breath."

"Why? Am I waiting for something?"

"Two reasons, nimrod," said Jerome. "First, to stop those annoying hiccups. Second, to get you to *shut the fuck up* so I can find our car."

Larry took a deep breath, held it, and mumbled something through his bull-frogged cheeks that sounded a lot like, "*Mmm-hmmm-mmm-aaa.*"

"What?" Jerome asked.

Larry exhaled loudly, his bloodshot eyes watering. "It's one block over."

Jerome stopped dead in his tracks.

"You knew where our car was?"

Larry took in another lungful of air and said, "*Mmm-hmm.*" Cheeks bulging, he pointed with his right hand.

"Why didn't you say anything?"

"You didn't ask."

Jerome put his hands on his hips and turned slowly. *Don't take the bait.* He moved stiffly to the corner and waited for the light to change.

Traffic was light in the Mission District this time of day. Some kids on their way home from school moved in small clusters along the sidewalks. Old women carried their groceries. Some teenagers were hanging outside a bodega, talking trash and making each other laugh. Just the normal comings and goings of a neighborhood where families tried to make ends meet, and where those that made it knew which corners to avoid, when to look the other way, and what time of night the streets belonged to someone else.

Larry took a shallow breath, followed by another, then smiled. He was about to say something when a hiccup interrupted him. *So close.* He drew as much oxygen into his lungs as a free-diver and followed his brother across the street. Jerome took advantage of the silence to think aloud.

"I think that went OK, considering."

Larry raised his eyebrows theatrically and spread his hands in a gesture that implied, *if you say so.*

"What are you, a fucking mime?"

Larry didn't say anything.

"I hate mimes, Larry," snapped Jerome. "Everybody hates mimes."

Larry exhaled. "Not the French."

Jerome scowled as Larry took a breath, released. Another, in and out. *So far so good.*

Their car was untouched, a few minutes left on the meter. Jerome fished the keys from his pocket and hit the button to unlock the doors. Sliding behind the wheel, he started the engine as Larry got in the car.

"Maybe it didn't go well," said Jerome cautiously. "Hard to tell with a sociopath."

Larry nodded, suddenly sober at the thought of Zorro. "Maybe we should talk to the cop."

"Are you crazy?" Jerome flexed his fingers around the steering wheel but left the car in park. "We just talked to Z about making sure the cop isn't our problem."

"Do you trust Zorro, Jerome?"

"We're criminals, Larry. Cops don't talk to criminals—they *arrest* them."

Larry shifted in his seat like a fidgety kid. "I don't want to be a criminal."

"I don't want to get arrested."

"Maybe he'll let us off with a warning."

"We didn't get a fucking parking ticket, Larry. We moved pot for the Mexican mob, killed a guy and then covered it up."

"It was an accident."

"Which part?" Jerome swiveled on the seat, then turned and faced the windshield. His brother's restlessness was contagious.

Larry sighed. "OK, not all of it was an accident. Only the big stuff."

"By *stuff*, you mean the part where Walter fried himself on our toaster."

"Yeah, that. That was an accident. It's not like it was murder or anything."

Jerome chewed on that for a minute. "But it was premeditated."

"Because we *thought* about killing him. That's not against the law. Married couples do it all the time—it's only murder if you turn those thoughts into action."

"So we got lucky," said Jerome. "That's our defense?"

"Works for me."

"But you're stoned."

Larry shook his head. "Not so much. It's wearing off... mostly."

"Mostly." Jerome chuckled. "I know that feeling."

"What a surprise."

Jerome didn't say anything, just gripped the steering wheel as he watched pedestrians and cars flow past, oblivious to the brothers' dilemma.

Larry cleared his throat, fought a hiccup, and said, "Hey Jerome."

Jerome turned to face him. "Yeah?"

"You did good back there."

Jerome looked for some hint of sarcasm or irony in his brother's expression but found none. Larry was as limpid as a pool.

"Thanks, Larry."

"I couldn't have done that."

"I was scared shitless."

"Didn't show."

Jerome pushed a smile forward but couldn't hold it. "You really think we should talk to the cop?"

"I was just thinking out loud."

"We talked to him before," mused Jerome, "and we're still free men. Maybe we could do it again."

"Might learn something."

"Without giving anything away?"

"You never know till you try."

"We'd have to find him first."

"That's easy," said Larry. "We know where he lives."

"True," said Jerome. "But we don't have a lot of time, do we?"

Larry frowned. "Not if what Zorro said was true. He said Sam was coming to him."

"Then we do have to find him," said Jerome. "Unless we want to get caught in the middle."

"We're already in the middle."

"It's the *caught* part I want to avoid."

Finally the brothers agreed. Jerome asked the question on the tip of both their tongues.

"I wonder where Sam is now?"

Chapter Fifty-two

Sam spotted Buster on his usual corner, adjacent to the gas station. Spinning the wheel, he bounced the convertible across oncoming traffic and coasted to a stop in front of a closed service door of the garage, watching out of the corner of his eye to make sure Buster was tracking him and not running.

Buster had his headphones on, and Sam could hear the atonal whine of spilled music from twenty feet away. As he came within five feet, Sam took note of the gold hoops running from the top of each of Buster's ears down to the lobes, only slightly hidden by his orange and blue locks. Sam counted eight hoops on each side and wondered if all the piercings had been done in one sitting.

When he was standing directly in front of Buster, Sam slid his left hand into his jacket pocket and palmed something. Buster only caught a glimpse, but it looked like a strip of paper.

Buster nodded to the beat of his music and gave Sam a smile with all the warmth of Everest. It reminded Sam of how he'd been feeling all day. Since leaving Jill, he could swear the blood in his veins had been replaced by liquid nitrogen, and it brought a crystalline clarity to his perspective. With his right hand, Sam fished his sunglasses from an inside pocket and slipped them on, then returned Buster's smile and held out his left hand, palm facing upwards.

"Here, Buster," he said. "I thought you might need this."

Buster tilted his head forward and frowned, at first not registering what it was, then not understanding why Sam was showing it to him.

It was a Band-Aid.

As Buster raised his head to ask the question, Sam extended his right hand and tore four gold hoops from Buster's left ear.

Buster screamed and staggered backwards. Sam let the Band-Aid fall to the ground and reached out again, this time with his left hand, and tore away four more hoops. Buster's agony was now symmetrical.

Buster's eyes bugged out in disbelief. When he raised both hands to his ears, Sam punched him in the nose. Blood spattered Sam's glasses as Buster fell backwards onto the sidewalk.

Buster was trying to dig his heels into the concrete and push himself as far way from Sam as possible, but Sam stepped almost casually around Buster until he was standing behind him. Buster froze as soon as Sam's shadow fell across his face. Sam bent at the waist and spoke quietly. "You don't look too good, Buster. Guess I should have brought two Band-Aids."

Buster spat blood. "You can't do this—my rights—it's fucking illegal. I could—" He stopped and spit again. "I could sue your ass."

"Illegal." Sam almost laughed. "That's funny, Buster. You mean like breaking and entering into someone's apartment?"

Buster tried to look defiant, but being upside and covered in blood, he was at a slight disadvantage. "*Loco.*"

"Maybe you should have thought of that before you tried to set me up."

Buster coughed and tried to sit up, but Sam moved a foot onto his chest, saying, "You were too easy to find, Buster."

Buster's eyes went wide, but he managed a half-hearted snarl before Sam put enough weight on his leg to push the air out of him.

"*Chingate,*" said Sam. "Fuck you, Buster."

Like most San Franciscans, Sam spoke enough Spanish to get around. And like most cops, the bulk of his vocabulary was profanity. Buster didn't seem offended, though. He had other things on his mind.

Buster saw spots and thought he was going to black out, which is when he realized their terrible mistake. The very thing that had emboldened Zorro to act had changed the playing field against them. Sam was no longer a cop. But they had assumed, unconsciously, that he would still act like one—tough but measured, careful to remain on his side of the law. But they had made this personal, and when Buster really thought about it, they didn't know a damn thing about Officer Sam as a person or as a man.

They didn't know that Sam hadn't felt like a cop in years, which is why he quit the force. He may not know what he was anymore, but *measured* probably wasn't one of the adjectives he'd choose. *Careful* wasn't on the list, either. On one hand, Sam was waking up, rediscovering that he was part of the human race, connected to the people around him. On the other hand, he wasn't all that sure he wanted to be, because some people were just assholes. Marie had always believed people were fundamentally good. As a cop, Sam had always believed the opposite.

Now he found himself standing somewhere between the two realities, and he felt with disturbing clarity his own ability to move from one to the other without missing a beat.

"Hey, Buster," he said gently, still looming over him. "Where's Zorro?"

Buster's fingers were criss-crossed with blood from his ravaged ears and nose, but his eyes had a calculated cruelty that even his pain couldn't hide. "OK, I tell you. Zorro is—"

Sam raised his foot directly over Buster's head and clucked his tongue.

"*No mames*, Buster," he chided. "Don't bullshit me."

Buster sneered and started to say something, then stopped himself and muttered, "I don't know."

Sam waited, his foot only inches from Buster's ruined nose.

Buster looked past the foot at Sam and said, "*Chupar es mi pinga.*"

"Wrong answer." The foot came down hard next to Buster's head and he sighed involuntarily, then gasped as Sam grabbed two handfuls of dreadlocks and dragged him across the parking lot.

"I thought these were extensions," grunted Sam. "Must have taken you a long time to get your hair to grow out like this."

Buster was kicking and cursing in a torrent of Spanish, English, and what sounded vaguely like Swedish, but Sam had all the leverage. When they reached Sam's car, he twisted his wrists violently clockwise, causing Buster to flip over onto his belly.

"*Maricon.*" Buster's voice was muffled by the pavement mashed against his face.

"Don't get your hopes up just because you're on your stomach," said Sam, who released Buster long enough to pop the trunk. "You're not my type." When Buster got on his hands and knees, Sam kicked him in the belly, just hard enough to knock the wind out of him. While Buster wheezed, Sam rummaged through his pockets and snagged his wallet, cell phone, and a knife Buster had shoved deep in his right front pocket. It was a butterfly knife, a fixed blade covered by hinged handles that swung apart to reveal the business end of the weapon. Once you understood the mechanism, the knife could be opened one-handed almost as quickly as a switchblade. Sam transferred the items to his own pockets. Then he grabbed Buster by the hair and belt, threw him in the trunk, and slammed it shut.

Sam scanned the street and noticed quite a few people watching him but trying very hard to appear as if they weren't. He didn't hear a siren and didn't expect to. He'd never thought of it from the perpetrator's point of view before, but that was one of the nice things about assaulting someone in this part of town. He slid behind the wheel and adjusted the rearview mirror, catching a glimpse of himself in the process. He paused and took off his sunglasses, studying his expression as if looking at a stranger.

He didn't really like what he saw, but it didn't bother him all that much, either. Sam backed out of the gas station and drove away in no particular hurry, like a man who had yet to decide which way he was going to turn.

Chapter Fifty-three

"Turn here."

Jerome ignored his brother and kept driving straight ahead. He wasn't positive that driving down Mission toward the Ferry Building was really any better than turning onto Market Street, but like most San Francisco residents, Jerome hated driving on Market. You couldn't turn left off Market; you couldn't park; the goddamned buses and trolleys took up half the street, and if one of the electric buses jumped free of its overhead wires, you might be stuck for half an hour.

Market Street sucked.

And Jerome couldn't abide how the city arbitrarily chose which parts of the street were going to be tourist-friendly and which parts would be ignored, often within the same block. On one side there might be some swanky shopping center and theater complex, while directly across the street was an abandoned storefront flanked by a ten-dollar whore and a homeless guy sleeping with his malnourished dog. The city had decided which corners were worth defending and turned its back on the rest. Jerome considered Market Street the perfect metaphor for the hypocrisy of city government. On one side it reeked of money. On the other, it stank of piss.

Lighten up, Jerome. All this responsibility was getting to him. He glanced over at his brother staring out the window as if pondering the secret of the universe. Larry's hiccups had subsided and he seemed neither stoned nor panicked, just pensive and strangely at peace. Jerome felt a pang of envy. He took a deep breath. OK, so he hadn't exactly quit the day job, but he had scored some points on Zorro—that had to count for something. Maybe it gave them leverage, but he couldn't figure out the angle that would get them out of this mess without pulling them even further into it.

"Hey Larry," he said. "We need a plan."

Larry nodded but didn't turn away from the window or say anything.

Jerome swiveled his head toward his brother and prodded. "Larry?"

Larry turned to face Jerome. "Yeah?"

"What do you think?"

"I think I'm gay."

A horn blared as Jerome swerved inadvertently into oncoming traffic. He leaned on his own as he passed a battered Honda and swung back into the right lane. When it was safe to steal a glance, Jerome saw that Larry had resumed his vigil at the window as if he'd just said something about the weather.

Jerome asked, "When did this happen?"

"It doesn't suddenly *happen*," said Larry. "I mean, it's not like I woke up with a cold."

"That's not what I meant," said Jerome, a little too quickly. "I mean, when did you…" He faltered and tried to regroup but was struggling to find the words. Before he could, Larry took over.

"Change teams?"

Jerome nodded.

"I don't think I changed teams," said Larry. "I think I always knew, in a way. Remember how when we were kids, I always liked to play with dolls?"

Jerome stole a glance at his brother. "Those were GI Joes."

"But they were still dolls, Jerome," said Larry. "Remember those little boxers they used to wear—"

Jerome cut him off with an abrupt, almost spasmodic gesture. "What about high school?" he asked. "You dated that girl, *wuzzername?*"

"Jenny," replied Larry, a wistful smile on his face. "We used to go to Star Trek conventions together. But it's not like we did it, or anything. We were…just friends. Now that I think about it, she may have been a lesbian. Or maybe just a fag hag."

"A fag hag?" Jerome grunted, secretly impressed his brother had the gay lingo down already. He wondered if Larry had been studying in his spare time, working up to this moment. "When were you gonna tell me?"

"I just realized it today," said Larry. "Like an epiphany."

"Epiphany," Jerome repeated slowly, thinking it was kind of a gay word choice.

"Yeah," said Larry. "I was thinking about you and Tamara, then Shayla, and I realized I wasn't interested in either of them. And the more I thought about it, I realized I'd never been interested. Go ahead and tell me I'm full of shit, but if you're not interested in those two girls, then you're probably gay."

"Or dead."

Larry laughed, a low, confident chuckle that made Jerome turn his way again. His brother was the picture of calm, a skinny white Buddha of serenity.

They drove in silence for a while, Jerome concluding after a few blocks that his brother's logic was flawless. Questions and rebuttals collided in his head like pinballs until only one remained. After a minute, he asked the only question that seemed to matter.

"Are you happy?"

Larry seemed to consider it, but his face already held the answer. So he said, "Just don't tell Mom."

It was Jerome's turn to laugh. He blinked and realized he had tears in his eyes.

Larry pretended not to notice. "I think it's been a long time since I liked my own reflection—sorry I've been such an asshole."

Jerome stared straight ahead through the windshield. "I haven't exactly been easy to live with."

"No," said Larry, "you haven't."

Jerome was thinking it was the longest conversation they'd ever had about their relationship, then realized it was the only one they'd ever had. But it was enough. He was relieved that Larry's sudden surge of gayness hadn't made him too chatty. As they turned onto their street he said, "We need a plan, bro."

Larry smiled. "I've got one."

"You do?" Jerome coasted to a stop in front of their building. "Shoot."

Larry turned in his seat. "I don't care about the money anymore, do you?"

Jerome started to object before he realized the first image that popped into his head was Tamara—not a visual of himself wearing a two-thousand dollar suit and shades, driving a vintage Caddy, which until yesterday had been one of his favorite fantasies. But he wanted to make sure he understood the question. "Is this like a double-jeopardy thing?"

Larry shook his head and grinned with the confidence of someone who realized his entire day had been a carefully delivered message, a road map to the rest of his life. "All this time we've been playing ball with Zorro, there's been a cop living next door."

"So?" asked Jerome.

"So why don't we change teams?"

Chapter Fifty-four

Gus decided to change teams. Just like that, he waved across the net at Rod and told him to double up with Judy before the next set. Gus wanted to play alongside Kathy, see if they fared any better. Bottom line, he was tired of losing and had decided that Judy's shitball serve was dragging him down.

The other three had played tennis with Gus long enough to know when he was in a mood, so nobody objected as they took their places around the court. But once the game started, Rod couldn't help himself. He started talking trash.

Rod was pushing seventy and had a wicked serve. Tall and lanky with most of his hair still in place, in the original mousy color, he fancied himself a ladies man. Wore a fedora when he wasn't playing tennis and cocked it whenever he saw a pretty lady, like he just waltzed off the silver screen like John Barrymore. Gus had caught him more than once making eyes at Gail but let it slide, figured they'd settle it on the court.

But lately Rod had started trash talking Gus on the court. For his part, Gus let that slide, too, the first few times. Figured Rod was suddenly confused about the difference between a gentleman's game like tennis and a little league baseball game where you razzed the batter. Rod was one of those coasters who had never worked very hard and retired early, when he was sixty-five, so Gus figured Alzheimer's had set in. But after a week of taking shit from across the net, Gus had had enough.

He'd seen Rod at the coffee shop, in the clubhouse, and he was the same as always. No signs of dementia. Alert, friendly, perfectly pleasant. *Congenial*, that was the word. Rod was one congenial guy. So Gus waited until after their usual set one day to ask congenial Rod what was his problem, why the sudden obnoxious banter?

"Gives me an edge," said Rod, leaning in close enough for Gus to smell his aftershave. "You've been taking me for two games for every one I win, Gus."

"That's because I practice every day."

"Been too long since I've won a set, no matter who I partner with, so I decided to change the playing field. Throw off your concentration. Think of it as a test of wills."

"You're serious."

Rod smiled, his teeth looking at lot younger than he did. "Deadly."

Gus stared at him, speechless, until he asked the only question he could think of.

"So you're going to keep making an ass of yourself, shouting at me over the net?"

Rod nodded as if a brilliant stock tip had been shared between them. "Precisely, old friend. What do you have to say about that?"

"Blow me."

Things had been a little tense between Gus and Rod ever since.

Gus got into position to serve. He bounced the ball a couple of times, then threw it high in the air. A perfect toss, the sun behind him. He was about to make contact when Rod shouted across the net.

"You tossed that ball like a lame, Gus. Your gout acting up?"

Gus lowered his racket, let the ball bounce, bounce, bounce next to his foot. He gave Rod a look, then picked up the ball and bounced it a few times, trying to regain his focus.

"You gonna serve or dribble, old man? This is tennis, not basketball."

Gus glanced over the net at Judy, who looked appropriately embarrassed at Rod's outburst even though she would be justified in being sore at Gus for changing teams. Judy had an eternally sunny disposition, even though she'd gone through a tough time during menopause when she decided she wanted to be a lesbian. Turns out most of the older lesbians in San Francisco were pissed off at men for one thing or another, probably deserved, but it gave their sexuality a decidedly activist edge. Far too angry for Judy, who was definitely a *glass is half full* kind of person. By contrast, she found that the younger lesbians were happy as clams about their Sapphic lifestyle. So Judy started hanging out with them, but then she realized that she was at least twenty if not thirty years older than her new friends, which made her feel like a dirty old lady. After five lonely years, she decided maybe she was straight, after all, and last May got married to the water aerobics instructor, a thoroughly nice guy who Gus always thought was gay.

"Hey Gus, you need a Geritol to get you going?" Rod was on a roll, and Gus wondered briefly if he'd stayed up the night before, writing these zingers down.

He shifted his gaze to Kathy, his new doubles partner. She was looking over her shoulder at him, her eyebrows raised, her expression saying she'd apologize for Rod if she thought it would make any difference. Kathy was sweet as syrup, the youngest in the group at fifty-eight, cursed with a backside so enormous that Gus could only see half the court whenever she took the net. He smiled at her as if to say don't worry about it. Then he got an idea.

Actually, it was less of an idea than an impulse. He looked at Rod standing dead center at the foot of the box, right where Gus was meant to serve, and he visualized the bastard wearing his fedora on the court. Turning to an imaginary crowd and waving, flashing that Pepsodent smile. Gail sitting in the crowd, charmed despite herself. Waving back.

The mental image got his blood boiling. *Nobody messes with my girl.*

That made him think of the cop down the hall. Gus had nothing against him, really, except he'd seen him twice now leaving Gail's apartment. Guy wasn't bad looking, and he had a way about him. Gail was a sucker for real men, that's how Gus had caught her eye. And just when he thought they were settling down, along comes this young buck with notions of becoming her back door man. No matter which was he turned, Gus was under siege.

Gus was suddenly the bull staring down Bugs Bunny, steam shooting from his nostrils, his eyes blood red. But he was Bugs, too. Cool, calculating. Smart as a hare.

He called out to Rod, no sound of anger or irritation in his voice.

"Hey Rod, you actually think you're gonna return this serve?"

Rod looked up, nonplussed. Clearly he never expected a rebuttal to his taunts. Gus in his tennis whites was too proper to play the verbal hardball Rod had been pitching across the net. This must be a stalling tactic.

"Yeah…yeah, I do Gus." Keep it short and snappy, thought Rod. Keep the pressure on.

Gus wore an expression that said he was going to ace Rod on the first serve. Rod squared his stance, legs wide. Straddling the middle of the box, in position to cut left or right. Just what Gus expected.

Gus threw the ball high in the air but made no attempt to hit it. Instead he stepped over the line and bolted toward the net, yanking a second ball from his tennis shorts and tossing it into the air, tracking its curve and timing it just right, his racket arcing through the air to find the ball at its zenith. By the time his racket smacked against the ball, Gus had cut the distance between himself and Rod by half the court, which gave Rod almost no room to maneuver and little time to react. Before he could dodge right or left, the ball hit Rod square in the crotch.

Gus thought it sounded like a hundred of those plastic packing bubbles popping all at once. Rod wasn't the only one with a wicked serve.

Judy gasped and Kathy dropped her racket. Gus gave both ladies an apologetic grin, then turned and headed toward the showers. He'd played enough tennis for one day and felt great. It was amazing how even a little exercise got your endorphins going and calmed you down.

As he walked away he half expected to her Rod hurling some verbal abuse his way, but none came. Rod was still yelling in pain at the top of his lungs.

Chapter Fifty-five

When Buster started yelling, Sam found an abandoned parking lot and drove over the speed bumps at thirty miles an hour. It took him two full circuits before his passenger settled down, at which point Sam pulled into the far corner of the lot and parked.

"Just need to make a phone call," he said as he revved the engine in warning. "Try to keep it down, OK?" Grabbing Buster's cell phone from the seat, he toggled through the numbers until he came to the last letter of the alphabet. A capital letter Z sat lonely at the end of the address book, no other incriminating letters necessary. Sam called up the numbers and studied them. There was no way to be sure, but the last four digits had that redundant pizza-parlor signature of a cell phone, not a house phone. Besides, he didn't think Zorro would have a landline phone—or even a cell phone contract, for that matter. Dealers bought prepaid phones and trashed them every few days.

Sam set down Buster's phone and fished his own from his jacket. It took him a minute to find the number he wanted. Sam counted eight rings before a gruff voice said, "Who is this?"

Sam smiled to himself. "That's a bullshit, question, Maury, coming from you—my name came up on that fancy caller ID thingy of yours." He held the phone away from his ear, waited a minute, and then said, "Call it whatever you want. I'm gonna call it a thingy as long as you keep busting my balls." The berating resumed as Sam made faces at himself in the rearview mirror, mimicking the imagined expressions of his former colleague. When the rant subsided, Sam responded by saying, "Retired? No, it was a leave of absence. I'm back on the job." Sam studied his face while he talked, surprised at how easily he lied. "I need to find a cell phone, don't know if it's moving, but I'm pretty sure it's in the city."

Sam read off the number from Buster's phone and waited while Maury Korovich, evil genius of the SFPD technical support group, sat somewhere in a windowless office on Bryant Street. Sam tried to visualize the room but the effort brought forth a sense-memory of stale body odor and grilled cheese sandwiches.

When Maury came back on the line, Sam said, "I don't need to keep him on the phone for three minutes or any of that Hollywood crap, right?" Once again the phone had to be held at arm's length as an angry diatribe spilled into the car. "No, I don't watch *CSI* or *24*," said Sam, trying to sound apologetic but doubting his own sincerity. Before he hung up, he added, "Call me back on this number, the one I called you on."

Sam looked at Buster's phone, the letter Z glowing blue and cold in the dark interior of the car. Dusk had swept over the city and brought enough fog to drop the temperature ten or fifteen degrees. Sam told himself he was just feeling the chill. He clenched the muscles in his jaw a few times before he pressed the button marked *Send*.

Sam held the phone gingerly to his right ear but almost dropped it when a male voice answered by saying, "*Sí?*" It was only a word, a single syllable, but the almost forgotten voice was all too familiar. Sam bit his tongue as he jammed his thumb against the *End* button and banished the voice back to Hell.

Thirty seconds later his own phone began to ring.

Chapter Fifty-six

Twisted Oliver picked up the phone, stared at it, then put it back in its cradle without dialing. He sat quietly for several minutes, wondering if he was going crazy.

Scowling, he shuffled through the papers on his desk before returning his watery gaze to his computer screen. Maybe he submitted the request to the lab incorrectly. He scanned the top of the glowing spreadsheet for the codes that indicated which tests would be run, then flicked his gaze to a sheet of paper clipped to the front of a manila folder. He compared names, dates, numbers.

He'd done this four times already, but Oliver believed in being thorough. He'd run the whole gamut of tests for Sam, as requested, and even told the lab to put this blood work at the top of priority jobs. He punched the keyboard and squinted through his glasses at the scientific names that appeared on the screen in a new window.

Well, well.

If you knew where to look, there were many flags for cause of death, and almost all could be seen in the blood. Oliver liked to think of the bloodstream as a person's chemical record—not just their overall health but their stress level, diet, even state of mind. Every emotional state had corresponding blood chemistry, from the soothing endorphins of exercise to the pheromones of sex or the adrenaline of exertion and stress. Even the depression of a suicide or the blind rage of homicide left their mark, if you knew how to find them.

As he read down the list, Oliver focused on the inconsistencies, chemical compounds out of sync with the alleged cause of death. There were two or three, but his eyes kept tripping on one in particular.

Prunus Dulcis.

"What the hell are you doing there?" he asked aloud, tapping the nail of his right index finger against the screen. When the screen didn't answer, Oliver sighed and looked back at his notes.

Severe impact trauma. Adrenaline signature. Blood oxygen saturation.

Oliver turned his gaze once again toward the phone.

It's not your job to figure it out, he told himself. *Just report the facts and move on—there are plenty of corpses waiting for you.*

The thought of handling dead flesh roused Oliver from his torpor, and this time he dialed. After four rings he heard the click of an answering machine, followed by Sam's measured tone. When the beep came, Oliver spoke clearly and precisely.

"Hello, Sam? I ran those tests on your landlord, and I might have found something…"

Chapter Fifty-seven

Flan spotted the cop from across the street and knew something had gone terribly wrong.

Flan's real name was Humberto, but since no one had called him that since his mother died, he thought of himself by the name given to him by Zorro's crew. There was something about criminal life that made nicknames an automatic part of the shared language, a shorthand way of identifying someone without all the social niceties or bullshit of civilian life. Someone called it as they saw it, and if the name stuck, that label was good enough for everyone.

Flan was named for a crème caramel served in Mexico, a slightly yellowish custard with a thin crust and a sweet filling, which he ate in such enormous quantities that his skin had taken on both the texture and vaguely cloying scent of the popular dessert. Flan weighed in at a respectable three hundred and twenty pounds, most of it extraneous fat that began at his chin and rolled like the breaking tide when he walked, and every day he thanked The Good Lord Jesús that he wasn't born Italian. He couldn't stand going through life known as Humberto the Chin.

The cop parked his convertible in front of a hydrant and scanned the street before wrapping his knuckles on the trunk and jaywalking toward the restaurant. The cop's gaze swept smoothly across the front door and didn't linger, but Flan knew he'd been made. He was hard to miss and had no illusions about his appearance—too fat for the NFL and too ugly and mean-looking to be wasting his time sitting in some cubicle trying to get his sausage-fingers to type on a keyboard. Just as Flan knew the guy in the sportcoat and jeans with the broad shoulders was a cop—even though he'd never seen him before—the cop would know Flan was Zorro's muscle. The only question was how to play it.

Flan decided to be sneaky. He quickly reached into his jacket and pulled out a cigarette and lighter, cupping his hand around the flame and looking as nonchalant as a three-hundred pound man can manage on short notice. Though his blood sugar was low, his brain seemed to be working just fine as Flan reasoned that the cop wasn't going to do anything rash. After all, he was a cop, not a triggerman for some rival gang.

Flan decided to let the cop go inside the restaurant rather than brace him at the door, then follow him as he navigated his way to Zorro's table. When he least expected it, Flan would come up behind him. Flan was surprisingly light on his feet for a big man and felt he could easily manage this maneuver, the idea being to intimidate the cop with his sudden appearance, as if he'd just materialized out of not-so-thin air. The cop would lose his nerve, Zorro would gain the upper hand in their exchange, and Flan would be rewarded appropriately.

Flan feigned a coughing attack as the cop brushed past him and headed through the front door and down the short hallway toward the reservations desk. He was about to follow when the cop took a sudden left, opened the door to the men's room, and disappeared.

Caray! This was going to throw off his timing. Flan counted to sixty, thinking that was plenty of time to take a piss, but when the cop didn't emerge, Flan figured the prissy bastard was washing his hands, so he kept counting until he hit a hundred.

Nothing. Flan started counting again as he tried to remember the layout of the men's room. Three stalls, two urinals, two sinks but no window. So there was no way the cop was going to sneak out, even if he made had a change of heart and decided to run. In that case he'd just come back through the front door.

Two hundred. Great, the guy suddenly had to take a shit. But Flan could sympathize. Sometimes just the thought of facing Zorro put his own bowels in an uproar. He'd give it another minute.

A young man wearing an expensive suit and a haircut to match left the restaurant and entered the men's room. Flan had noticed the guy when he arrived half an hour ago with his date, who was a reasonably plump tomato with red hair and fishnets. After a count of thirty-three the guy pushed open the door and returned to his table. *Didn't wash his hands*, thought Flan.

Three hundred.

Murrda. Flan knew the difference between a gang-banger and a career criminal like himself was the ability to stay flexible, think on your feet. That was what separated Zorro's men from the other gangs whose members wound up dead or in jail. New plan—take the cop down in the bathroom. Lock the door and scare him a little, then drag the *maricon* to Zorro's table or throw him out on the street.

The bathroom was on the left, halfway down a long hallway leading to the reservations desk and the restaurant. The desk was almost twenty feet away, so Flan figured that even if he made a little noise in the bathroom bouncing the cop off the walls, no one would notice. Inside the restaurant, most of the tables were full and it was noisy, the sound spilling down the hallway and out into the street where Flan stood. As he pushed open the door to the men's room, he flexed his fingers in anticipation, his knuckles cracking like castanets.

The barrel of the gun was behind his right ear before the door had swung closed. Flan's eyes went wide, but he didn't move. He recognized the cool, liquid feeling of the metal and had no illusions that the round shape against his skin might be a finger or ballpoint pen. As Flan tried to estimate the size of the barrel, a voice directly behind him spoke just above a whisper, as if the man that held the gun wasn't really there.

"A lot of cops favor the Glock," said Sam, pressing even closer to Flan, who stood frozen, hands out from his sides. "But the

Glock has no external safety, so misfires are very common. When the department first started issuing them, you wouldn't believe the number of leg shootings we had, cops shooting themselves as they pulled their guns out of their holsters. In the heat of the moment, it's no wonder a man's finger could slip."

Flan heard the distinctive sound of a hammer being cocked into place and tried but failed to control an involuntary shiver. The voice continued.

"Me, I like the Beretta. It has a safety that's easy to flick off with your thumb, and it has a hammer, which you just heard, that makes the first pull on the trigger really, really *easy*."

Flan took a deep breath and nodded his understanding. He heard a sniffing sound behind him.

"You smell nice," said Sam. "Almost sweet. Not at all what I expected." Flan was about to explain his nickname when Sam prodded him with the gun. "Handicap stall, *now*."

Flan shuffled forward, catching a glimpse of himself in the mirror over the sinks. It was a fleeting and only partial view, because turning his head wasn't really an option, but the expression on the cop's face gave Flan the distinct impression he wasn't bluffing. He began to sweat under his jacket, wondering if maybe this guy wasn't a cop after all.

Within the stall, one loop of the handcuffs was already locked around the pipe at the back of the toilet, the other dangling freely. Flan felt a sharp push of the gun against his ear and a simultaneous shove at the small of his back, and he staggered forward. When he reached the toilet, he turned his bulk around slowly, as nonthreatening as a three-hundred pound wall of flesh can be, and sank slowly onto his double-wide backside. Sam gestured with the gun and Flan fitted the loose cuff around his wrist—barely—and clicked it into place. Sitting there, chained to a toilet, he looked enormous, amorphous and almost sad.

Sam managed not to shed a single tear as he holstered the gun and headed toward the door. When he passed the sinks, he didn't bother looking in the mirror.

Sam had hit the jackpot. From the layout of the block, Sam was pretty sure this place didn't have a rear entrance. No other visible muscle suggested Zorro might actually be on a date.

An attractive young woman manned the reservations desk, her perfect chin lit from beneath by the halogen glow of a sinuous desk lamp. The effect made her eyes seem dark and huge, shadows stretching across her forehead, giving Sam the impression she was a beautiful alien sent to Earth for the sole purpose of welcoming him to this restaurant.

Sam gave her his most reassuring smile as he flipped his wallet open and closed and said, "Police." Her mouth opened and closed but no sound came out because Sam had already moved past her.

The restaurant was split into two parts. On the right was a traditional room filled with tables seating two or four, a long room running to a bar in the back. But to the left was an open courtyard where tables were arranged in rows, all the seats facing the exterior wall of the adjacent building, a five-story slab of gray cement. Normally not much of a view, but the restaurant had put it to good use and projected movies onto the surface of the wall, turning the courtyard into a cross between an intimate restaurant and a drive-in movie.

Sam had read about this place. To enhance the atmosphere, justify the prices, and avoid the issue of ambient noise, the restaurant showed foreign art films without the sound. Tonight a Japanese film about food loomed over the dinner guests. Marie had been a sucker for art films, and Sam recognized it from her collection. As he watched, the image on the wall cut to a scene of Japanese women dressed as pearl divers standing in the surf, the waves moving in an almost sensuous rhythm. As Sam scanned the courtyard, reflected light from the film flickered across the faces of the patrons, the strobe effect keeping time with the rocking of the waves.

A woman twenty feet away laughing at something her date had said. A man staring into the hypnotic light of his cell phone as he sent a text message, as if the phone was a crystal ball. A young woman in a too-tight dress leaning toward a man who had his left arm draped heavily over her shoulder, the man turning into the light to reveal teeth jagged and bent, reptilian fangs darting outward in all directions.

Bingo.

Sam moved quickly between tables and came up behind Zorro on the side opposite his date. With his left hand, Sam clamped down on Zorro's neck while his right pulled Buster's butterfly knife and swung the blade open with a sound like change falling. Zorro's head swung reflexively to the right as Sam brought the blade up and held the point directly below Zorro's right eye.

Zorro's mouth popped open with a wet smacking sound as his teeth disengaged from his lips, but no sound came out. He sat frozen as his eyes darted right and left, either searching for Flan or wondering when the other diners were going to turn away from the movie.

"*Hola* Zorro," said Sam, his voice like gravel. "Remember me?" Sam leaned across Zorro's shoulder just long enough for him to catch a glimpse of his assailant. Zorro grunted in recognition as he regained enough composure to close his mouth.

Sam glanced at Zorro's date to confirm his sudden appearance had the desired effect. She looked petrified, her right hand over her mouth in an almost theatrical gesture. He figured it was only a matter of time before her state of shock evaporated and she remembered she wasn't mute.

Sam tilted the point of the blade backward into the soft flesh below Zorro's eye. Zorro flinched, but Sam held his neck in an iron grip and forced his head forward. "Is this how you do it, Zorro? Do you scoop them out after they're already dead, or do it while they're still alive?" Sam twisted his wrist counterclockwise and heard Zorro gasp as the knife pricked his cheek. A thin trickle of blood ran over the back of Sam's hand.

On the screen, a young Japanese woman held an oyster shell in her hand and brought it to her mouth, the camera hovering only inches from her perfect skin. As she wrapped her mouth around the shell, the ragged edge caught on her lip and the camera zoomed even closer as blood pooled into the oyster. The image was jarring, erotic, and disturbing.

Zorro's date found her voice buried just below the surface of her fear and started to scream. Chairs screeched across the stone floor as people turned toward the girl, whose scream ascended rapidly into a wail. Sam didn't bother looking up but held the knife fast as he leaned close enough to whisper into Zorro's ear.

"Tag," he said. "You're it."

Sam flipped the knife closed and stood, turning his back on the crowd and the movie. Behind him on the wall, the girl with the bloody lip had rejoined her friends in the surf, the sea rolling back and forth as if waving goodbye.

The lovely alien from the reservations desk ran into the restaurant as Sam pocketed the knife and walked toward her with no sign of stopping. She looked at him accusingly.

"I thought you were the police."

"I was," said Sam. "But not anymore."

Chapter Fifty-eight

"I'm still a cop, you know."

Danny Rodriguez stated the obvious but didn't sound convincing, even to himself.

Sam smiled gently. "I thought you were off duty an hour ago."

Danny sighed. He yanked his badge off his hip and placed it deliberately on the bar between them. "This is a badge, Sam."

"I know," said Sam. "I've got one at home."

Danny's eyebrows shot up. "You were supposed to turn it in when you retired."

"I wanted a souvenir."

Danny laughed despite himself. "You mean something other than the shrapnel in your leg and the heartache?"

Sam didn't respond.

Danny tapped the badge. "You used to wear one, *amigo*."

"You're saying you won't help." Sam narrowed his eyes. "Is that what this speech is about?"

Danny scowled and snatched the badge off the table. He hadn't convinced himself, so why should his ex-partner buy his bullshit. He drummed his fingers on the bar and looked over his shoulder. There were other people in the restaurant but no one close, and the lesbian bartender was at the far end, washing glasses.

"You and I didn't know each other—not really—until we were partners," said Danny. He spoke slowly, his gaze somewhere beyond the walls of the restaurant. "Different years at the academy, and I spent some years in Narcotics before moving over to homicide. And your old partner, before me—"

"—James," said Sam.

"Right," said Danny. "A black guy, which is hard enough in San Francisco."

Sam nodded but didn't say anything. Cops used to joke that San Francisco was like a bag of Wonder Bread, all the bright colors on the outside wrapping—inside nothing but white. Hispanics quarantined in the Mission, blacks pushed all the way across the water to Oakland. A few scattered here and there in city council positions like chocolate sprinkles on vanilla ice cream, just because the mayor loved the taste of the word *diversity* when making speeches.

Danny said, "So you don't know what it was like coming up as a Latino cop with guys like Zorro crawling all over the Mission District like cockroaches. Other cops asking where you grew up, were you in a gang, got any friends in prison––wanting to make sure you won't get confused when it comes time to take a homeboy down."

"Assholes," muttered Sam.

"Maybe." Danny shrugged. "Not a lot of color-blind cops out there. But they had a point."

"Which was?"

Danny leaned forward and looked like he was going to spit. "Whenever the chip on my shoulder got too heavy, I had to remind myself that more than half the fuckheads we arrested came from my neighborhood. Gangs or no gangs, assholes like Zorro and Buster are the reason that I work twice as hard to get half the respect as other cops. I hate those fucking guys."

Sam didn't say anything. Danny had said it all.

Both men sat silently hunched over the bar until Danny said, "Of course I'll help." Sam squeezed his shoulder but Danny held up a warning finger. "But I won't break the law."

"I don't want you to break it," said Sam. "Just bend it a little."

"You've already got it as bent as a pretzel." To emphasize his point, Danny reached into the bowl of snack mix on the bar.

"I like pretzels." Sam grabbed a handful.

"We're cops," said Danny. "We're supposed to like donuts."

"I like 'em both."

"How bent?" Danny chewed for a minute, short angry crunches that mellowed by the time he swallowed. "Not reporting a crime, like your little tango with Buster—that's not too bent, because your story is just hearsay, not a confession."

"See?" said Sam. "Just like a pretzel."

Danny ignored him. "Not reporting your assault on Zorro, that's questionable, but—"

"—again, just a story I told you in a drunken rant."

Danny looked across his shoulder at his former partner. "You haven't finished your beer."

"That's also hearsay." Sam took a drink, set the glass down slowly. "I'm a lightweight these days."

"What about Buster? Where is he now?"

Sam looked straight ahead and spoke to Danny's reflection in the mirror behind the bar. "You know that gas station on the corner where he hangs out?"

Danny's reflection nodded as the Danny next to Sam grunted in acknowledgment.

"There's a dumpster behind it."

Reflected Danny frowned as the real Danny groaned. "When you allegedly deposited him in this alleged dumpster, what state was he in?"

"Physically, just a few scratches," said Sam. "Mostly cosmetic, around the ears."

"*The ears?*" Danny glanced sideways at his friend.

"You don't want to hear about it."

"You're right," replied Danny. "I don't."

"But as for his mental condition, I'd say he was pissed. *Mad as a hornet* might be the best way to describe it." Sam thought for a minute, then added, "And scared shitless."

"Of who?"

"You mean *whom.*"

"Fuck you," said Danny. "Afraid of you—or Zorro?"

"Probably a little of both. Zorro had Buster set me up, so he must have figured that's where I got his cell number."

Danny waved a hand dismissively. "Buster won't do shit."

"So no crime committed there," said Sam. "At least none that'll get reported."

"Swell," said Danny. "But not reporting a dead body—that's pushing it."

"That one's on me," said Sam. "Dead Walter is my responsibility."

"Is your responsibility—*is*?" Danny was incredulous. "You still haven't made the call?"

Sam grabbed a handful of pretzels. "I've been busy."

"Jesus."

Sam held up a hand that was meant to look reassuring, but it ended up looking just like a hand, so he put it back on the bar. Danny put his hands over his ears and said, "We're not having this conversation."

Sam finished his beer while Danny sang to himself, hands cupped and locked in place. Sam thought the tune might be *It's A Small World*, but he couldn't be sure—Danny did have a daughter at home. Sam signaled to the bartender, who smiled and moved down to pour him another beer.

Danny lowered his hands but waited until the bartender moved away before speaking. "Zorro's gotta kill you now—you realize that, right?"

"*Machismo.*"

"No small thing, in his world," said Danny. "You embarrassed him in public, in front of a woman no less."

"Wish you'd been there."

The laugh Danny had been fighting burst forth. "Me, too partner. Me, too."

They sat for a minute, both smiling, like the two old friends they were. After a minute Danny turned on his stool and dropped his voice. "You must have a plan, *pareja*. You always do."

Sam nodded. "It's messy."

"You figure he'll come for you tomorrow night?"

"Yeah," said Sam. "Tonight he's licking his wounds, and he doesn't move around during the daytime."

"But you can't be sure."

"No," said Sam. "I don't know anything for sure."

"I could arrest him," said Danny.

"For what?"

"I'll think of something."

Sam looked skeptical. "And hold him for how long?"

"Not long enough," said Danny. "Not long enough to keep you safe."

"So you want to hear my plan?"

"Absolutely not," replied Danny. "The less I know, the better."

"Agreed."

Danny blew out his cheeks. "But how messy is this plan?"

Sam seemed to think about it before saying, "Very."

Danny studied his friend for a long minute. "You're making this up as you go along."

Sam drained the last of his beer and nodded. "More or less."

Danny watched his reflection work the muscles in his jaw.

"So what do you expect me to do," he asked. "When the time comes?"

"Just be yourself," said Sam. "A good cop."

Chapter Fifty-nine

A good cop.

Buster almost laughed at the thought but started coughing, an involuntary spasm that drove his bruised ribs into his lungs, which made him cough even harder. He bent over the sink and spat blood, watching as the crimson tide swirled down the drain, his future right behind it.

A good cop. That's how Zorro had described Officer Sam, saying it like an insult. Calling the guy a pussy, letting Buster know they had nothing to worry about. Zorro predicting the future like some old gypsy minus the head scarf, bad perfume, and crystal ball.

All Buster had to do was raise his eyes to the mirror to remind himself how completely wrong Zorro had been. Both his ears were ravaged where the hoops had torn through—he looked like he'd been chewed on by a wolverine. The antibiotic ointment he'd smeared on them glistened in the weak fluorescent light of his bathroom.

He'd scrubbed the blood from his cheeks and tried brushing his teeth, but it hurt too much. Every sideways motion of the brush sent a jarring pulse through his busted nose, Newtonian physics applied to cartilage and pain.

Buster shifted his eyes to meet his own gaze but quickly looked away. He was hoping to find rage but would have settled for grim determination. Instead all he saw was fear.

He used to think Zorro knew everything. Heard everything. Saw everything. Someone held up a grocery store under Zorro's protection, the crew went down the next day. A new player started moving product around the Mission, he disappeared before his next sale. The stories were legend.

Now, looking at his miserable expression in the mirror, Buster realized he'd only *heard* those stories—but out on the street, he rarely saw evidence of Zorro's hand. Maybe Zorro wasn't so omnipotent after all. Maybe Zorro was just a bully that no one had stood up to until now. Until he fucked with the wrong guy.

Who knew it would be a guy like Sam?

No doubt Zorro was dangerous. One glance at that jar of eyeballs and you knew better than to fuck with the guy. He would kill you as soon as look at you. But he wasn't all-knowing, and he wasn't always right.

He had been wrong about Sam. Dead wrong.

Zorro said that being a good cop meant playing by the rules, but now Buster thought maybe it meant doing the right thing. Standing up, not taking any shit. Buster looked in the mirror and met his gaze, managed to hold it this time. Realized for the first time that he wasn't looking at a player or a *gangsta*—a G. That cop had played him like a punk, because that's what he was. That's what Zorro had made him.

Zorro wasn't someone you wanted to cross, but as it turned out, neither was Sam. And Buster had managed to cross them both. No matter which way he turned, Buster was caught in the middle, and when those two tangled it was going to get messy. Deep in his gut, Buster knew this was going to end badly.

Buster brought the scissors up and cut away the hair extensions. Blue and green strands fell into the sink and onto the floor, cotton candy from some nightmare carnival. When he got to his own hair, he brought out the electric clippers, moving from front to back until he was down to a quarter-inch of stubble. He dumped his grill in the garbage can, a twisted sliver of metal covered in blood and saliva. Took the rings off his fingers and the chains from around his neck.

For an instant he felt naked, almost dizzy, and thought he was going to be sick. Then he realized his ribs hurt a little less, as if a great weight had been removed from his chest. He took a tentative, deep breath and looked in the mirror again. Almost recognized the guy looking back at him, someone from a long time ago. A forgotten friend. Not a bad guy at all.

Buster nodded at his reflection, then turned and walked down the short hallway to his bedroom.

The duffle bag was packed and over his shoulder in less than fifteen minutes. He didn't look back at his bed or mourn the loss of his stereo. He left his keys on the counter and the door unlocked.

It took him five minutes to reach the BART station at 24th and Mission, the underground train that would take him through San Francisco in a straight shot, under San Francisco Bay and into Oakland. In less than an hour, with any luck, he'd be at Oakland airport.

Buster had a sister in Denver. She was a self-righteous bitch, and he hadn't spoken to her in ten years, and Denver sucked. Full of whitebread people, shitty weather, thin air that made you stupid. Goats, cows and other animals roaming around that Buster was pretty sure the locals liked to fuck when their dough-faced wives were on the rag. His sister married a goat-fucker, you could just tell by looking at the guy.

But family was family, and Buster needed a new start. He'd rather talk to his sister and fuck a goat than sit around waiting for some sick *pendejo* to come and cut his eyes out.

Buster arrived at the platform where the ticket machines stood all in a row like robots, red lights blinking a warning about a fare increase. Nearby was an escalator leading to the tracks. He reached into his pocket for some cash and felt the edge of a card. Pulling it out, he saw Sam's name and flinched involuntarily. It was the business card Sam had shoved in Buster's jacket, what seemed a lifetime ago.

He ran his index finger across the raised digits of the phone number and stood rigid on the platform as people brushed past him on either side. He imagined calling Sam and wondered what he would say. *Would he threaten him?* Not a chance. *Thank him?* Not likely.

Tell him that he wasn't a punk anymore. He wasn't Zorro's bitch. Maybe ask Sam to call off the dogs. Let him slip through the net. Walk away if he fingered Zorro.

Buster looked over his shoulder, an involuntary move that he suddenly realized he might be doing for the rest of his life.

He started to chew his lower lip but it hurt. Blinked and looked up from the card, found himself facing away from the ticket machines. Ten feet away stood a pay telephone, its silver key pad a little face staring him down, daring him to make the call. From the next level down, Buster could hear a train approaching.

Fishing in his pocket, Buster came up with a quarter and held it gently in his open palm. As the roar of the train shook the station, he chose heads and flipped the coin into the air.

Chapter Sixty

The phone scared the *bejesus* out of Larry and Jerome.

They'd been home for hours, talking through their plan. No television, no radio, just the sound of their own voices until maybe an hour ago, when it seemed there was nothing left to talk about. Larry lay on the couch, sipping Tab and staring out the window. Jerome sat in the kitchen watching the clock. In the perfect stillness of their thoughts, the phone sounded like a fire alarm.

Jerome grabbed the handset and grunted hello. Larry watched as his brother's brow furrowed and his expression changed from curiosity to wide-eyed disbelief.

"No can do, Z," Jerome said mildly. "We only had the one toaster." The wrinkled brow again, followed by, "Never mind, it's not important. We'd love to help, but that's boxing outside our weight class, know what I'm saying?" A pause, then Jerome nodded, as if expecting what he'd just heard. "Sure, we can do that, but that's all we can do. Yeah—crystal. *Adios*."

After Jerome hung up, Larry asked, "Zorro?"

Jerome nodded. "He changed his plan. Either that or the cop changed it for him."

"The cop didn't show?"

Jerome shrugged. "Got me. The only thing I know for sure is Zorro is pissed."

"How pissed?"

"Pissed enough to call us himself."

Larry thought about it. Zorro always worked through inter-mediaries. "What happened to Buster?"

Jerome raised his hands. "What am I, Google?"

"Sorry, what did he want?"

"He wanted to know if we'd kill the cop."

Larry spit Tab across the living room. Pulling a handker-chief from his pocket, he dabbed his mouth and said, "You're serious."

"You heard what I said about the toaster."

Larry took a deep breath. "Probably not the answer he wanted to hear."

"I don't know," replied Jerome. "I think he had to ask, you know? I mean, if we were willing to cross that line, it solves a lot of problems. But he didn't *want* me to say yes—there was something in his voice…"

Larry picked up the thought. "He wants to do it himself."

"Yeah," said Jerome. "So Zorro's coming here."

Larry shook his head as if shaking off a nightmare. "What does he expect us to do? Just sit here and wait for him?"

"Nope," said Jerome. "He wants us to keep tabs on the cop—he said he wants us to be his eyes."

"His eyes." Larry put his chin in his hands. His head felt incredibly heavy.

"He's going to kill the cop, then pay us for our trouble."

"Pay us?" Larry was incredulous.

"We help him get the cop off his ass, he gives us a bonus, then we're back in business."

"I'm done with this…*business*."

"Me too, bro," said Jerome. "But one last paycheck would make it a lot easier to kiss it goodbye."

Larry looked like he was about to get sick. "We don't have any choice, do we?"

"You want to change the plan?" asked Jerome. "We could run, you know."

Larry kept his head in his hands but his voice was firm. "It's a good plan."

"OK, we stick with the plan."

Larry sighed. "*His eyes*—he actually said that?"

Jerome nodded. "Those were his exact words."

Chapter Sixty-one

"They will be my eyes, and then I will eat theirs."

Zorro plucked an eyeball from his little jar of horrors, but Julio was unimpressed. Zorro was a pig, and Julio was getting tired of his monologues. He remembered when they were just getting started, struggling in turf wars with rival gangs. Zorro was one of the men, a natural leader, not someone who believed his own bullshit. Julio would come home with blood on his shirt and cash in his pocket. The good old days.

"We will kill everybody," said Zorro.

Julio shifted his size-fifteen shoes and frowned. "Everybody?"

Zorro sucked on his teeth and nodded. "The cop."

Julio held up his right hand and extended his thumb. "That's one—"

"—the brothers."

Julio opened his index and middle finger and held them high. "Two and three—but I thought they were your eyes?"

"After they spot the cop, they are just loose ends," said Zorro. "And tomorrow I tie them all up."

"You're going to tie them up, and then kill them?"

"No, idiot." Zorro shook his head. "I am tying up loose ends. I meant it metaphorically."

Julio nodded. What a *pendejo*. "So how are you going to kill them?"

"*We*," said Zorro. "*We* are going to kill them."

Julio shrugged—just another day at work. "OK, how are *we* going to kill them?"

Zorro held up his hands. "You have no suggestions?"

"I say we shoot them."

"Not very dramatic."

Julio took a deep breath and spoke very deliberately. "He is—or was—a cop, Zorro. He will have a gun. The brothers—if they don't run away tonight—will be suspicious. That makes three possible threats, and we are only two."

"But you, my friend, are a giant."

Julio held his arms out from his sides. "With only two hands. They live in an apartment building in the heart of the city."

"The guns will be too noisy then, no?"

"No," said Julio. "The noise will scare people. If they are afraid, they are more likely to stay in their apartments until the police come. But if they hear a struggle, who knows? Maybe they rush into the hallway to help, become a witness. And then—"

Zorro frowned. "We have to kill them, too."

"Guns are fast, Zorro. We go in, shoot, and run away."

"I thought you were going to make the brothers commit suicide."

"That was before."

"Before what?"

"Before you decided to kill the cop in his home."

Zorro grunted. "You're saying you can't do it?"

I hate this job, thought Julio. "I suppose I could...maybe. After we shoot them, we could put the guns in their hands, make it look like they came after the cop, but he shoots them at the same time."

"A Mexican standoff," said Zorro, clapping.

"We set them up, and then we run away." Julio felt it important to repeat the *run away* part, in case Zorro wasn't paying attention the first time.

Zorro frowned. "What about the eyes?"

Julio clenched his jaw but forced a smile. "You want to go to jail?"

Zorro didn't answer.

Julio sighed. "We could always get them later."

"From the morgue?"

"Sure."

Zorro seemed content. After a minute he said, "Any word from Buster?"

Julio shook his head. "The men are still looking. I think he's hiding, or he ran."

"Maybe the cop killed him."

Julio thought about it. "Maybe."

"When we find him, add Buster to the list."

"The list of loose ends?"

"You have another list?"

So this is how you lead your men. "I'll see to it myself," said Julio.

Zorro licked his lips. "We will use guns," he said, as if it had just occurred to him. "But what kind?"

"Big guns," said Julio. "The louder, the better."

Chapter Sixty-two

Sam drew his gun before he opened the door to his apartment.

He knew someone was waiting inside. The deadbolt had been turned before he left, and now it was unlocked. With his right shoe he flipped the corner of the doormat and saw that his spare key was missing. Given the events of the past forty-eight hours, leaving his key might not have been the best idea.

He flicked the safety off with his thumb and kicked the door open, crouching as he crossed the threshold, gun raised and held steady with both hands. Movement in his peripheral vision as he pivoted toward the kitchen just as Jill started to scream.

Jill's coffee mug crashed to the floor as her hands jumped into the universal sign for *please don't shoot me!* When the ceramic mug exploded, her scream came to an abrupt end. Sam lowered the gun and holstered it with a mildly embarrassed look on his face.

"Hi," was all he could manage. Sam bent to pick up the shards of ceramic at the same time she did—their knees collided and both fell ass-first onto the floor. When they stopped laughing, Jill said, "Sorry I screamed. I never—"

"—had a gun pointed at you before?"

Jill's eyes answered for her.

"Let's hope it's the last time." Sam stood and brushed off his pants. He took her right hand in his and pulled her to her feet, then kissed her lightly on the lips before stepping back and saying, "Sorry. I'm a little jumpy."

Jill forced a smile. "Rough night on the town?"

"Eventful."

"Want to talk about it?"

Sam took her hand again and led her over to the couch, where they sat, knees again touching. "You want me to?"

Jill gave a tentative nod. "But maybe later, OK?"

"Sure." Sam leaned back on the couch and tried to decompress. Still holding Jill's hand, he took a deep breath and closed his eyes. When he opened them, his gaze reflexively moved to the mantel, and what he saw there made him sit bolt upright. He released Jill's hand as he stood and crossed to the fireplace with a sudden sense of vertigo.

All the frames were where he'd left them, but every picture had been replaced, some restored, others new. But in every frame the eyes looked back at him. His own face, smiling. Danny, trying to look serious. And Marie, her eyes as full of love as ever.

"I hope you don't mind," said Jill. "You had told me where you kept your key, and I was going to make you dinner, but the pictures..." She faltered, then said, "I couldn't stand looking at them. So I snooped around a little in your closet and found that box of photographs..."

She stood behind him a few feet, hesitant, wondering if she'd crossed a line. When he spoke, she couldn't see the tears in his eyes, but she could hear the emotion in his voice.

"Thanks," he said simply. "This is better than any dinner."

"I should've left a note on the door. Didn't mean to startle—"

Sam turned and took her in his arms. As they embraced she backed toward the couch, a slow and awkward waltz that ended with her pulling him onto her as she fell. Within minutes they were on the floor and their clothes were scattered across the couch that Sam realized wasn't nearly wide enough.

Afterward Sam padded down the hall and returned with a blanket. Pulling cushions from the back of the couch, he made a makeshift bed and lay down facing the sliding glass doors and the night sky, Jill lying in the crook of his arm.

"That was nice," she said.

"You really do have a talent for understatement."

"Want to tell me about your night?"

Sam shook his head. "I'd hate to ruin the mood."

Jill ran a hand across his chest. "Fair enough. You can tell me later."

"Deal." Sam pulled her close. "How was your night?"

"After you left I kept working on the computer."

"Singing?"

"Some, then I took a break and did some real work—the kind that pays the rent."

"Websites," he asked. "Or graphic design?"

Jill paused as she gave him a squeeze. "Shalya came over for a while. We worked on their site. They're making a lot of changes."

Sam chuckled. "Those girls will be co-presidents one day."

"Of their own company?"

"Of the country."

"You really should visit the site."

"You won't get jealous?"

"It's some of my best work."

Sam lifted the corner of the blanket and looked at her with open admiration. "Ever think about having your own site?"

Jill snatched the blanket away from him. "I'm too modest."

Sam laughed. "Could've fooled me." After a minute he said, "Thanks for coming over. Next time—"

Jill put a hand over his mouth. "Next time I'll leave a message on the door." Her eyes went wide and she sat up, adding, "I forgot to tell you—"

"What?"

"Earlier," she said, pointing toward the kitchen and the phone sitting on the counter. "You got a message. I heard your machine pick up while I was rummaging around in your closet, so I didn't hear the message—only the last part when I came into the living room—but it sounded important."

Sam glanced toward the kitchen but didn't move. He was way too comfortable, even though his arm was falling asleep from the weight of Jill's body. He didn't want to move ever again. "Did you hear a name?"

Jill nodded against his shoulder. "Oliver. He said you should call him back."

Sam continued to look toward the kitchen but didn't budge.

"Maybe you should call him back," said Jill. "It might be good news."

"Not likely." Sam was about to describe Twisted Oliver's penchant for doom when there came a knock on the door.

"Shit." Sam stood, naked, and grabbed his gun from the counter.

"Who do you think it is?"

"I don't know," said Sam. "But it might be bad news."

Chapter Sixty-three

Sam held a pillow in his left hand and a gun in his right. The gun covered the door while the pillow covered his crotch.

He checked the peephole and sighed, relieved it wasn't Zorro knocking. But he wasn't expecting any visitors tonight, especially the two in the hallway. At his signal, Jill unlatched the deadbolt and pulled open the door. Sam took a step forward, gun raised.

Larry and Jerome raised their hands in perfect synchronization, as if they'd practiced as understudies for the touring company of Bob Fosse's *Chicago*. Their eyes became perfect circles to match their open mouths. Larry was the closer of the two, so Sam dropped the pillow and dragged him into the apartment before his vocal chords caught up with the expression on his face. Jerome came trailing behind.

Jill shoved the door closed behind them.

"We come in peace." Jerome kept his hands up.

Sam studied the startled pair before lowering the gun and saying, "Live long and prosper." Then he turned and walked back to the living room, where he set the gun on the mantle before reclaiming his pants from the floor. By the time he pulled them on, Jill had come over to sit on the couch. She curled her legs beneath her and watched the two brothers with an amused expression on her face.

Jill had thrown Sam's dress shirt on for cover, but her legs were bare and her breasts swayed suggestively under the fabric. Sam noticed Jerome taking mental snapshots for retrieval later and was going to say something when he realized Larry was looking at him in the same way. Frowning, he cleared his throat, which had the desired effect. Both brothers immediately tried to make eye contact with him.

"What do you want?" Sam asked.

"A beer would be great," replied Jerome. Larry smacked him on the shoulder. Jerome flinched and added, "Or coffee would be cool. Whatever's easier."

"We need your help." Larry cut in.

"With?"

The two brothers looked at each other. As if some silent exchange had taken place, Jerome turned and said, "With Zorro."

Sam took an involuntary step forward. "What do you know about Zorro?"

Larry looked at his feet. "It's a long story—"

Jerome nodded. "—about two brothers and their toaster..." Larry smacked him again but Jerome was on a roll. "...a story of hope, betrayal, and the search for true love—"

Larry managed to get his hand over Jerome's mouth long enough to say, "We're in trouble—" Jerome shrugged him off and added, "And so are you."

Sam stared at them and tried to figure out what was part of their act and what was the result of years of unsuccessful therapy. Finally, he gestured at two chairs adjacent to the coffee table and said, "What'll be, then? Beer?"

Larry sighed with visible relief and said, "Got any Tab?" Jerome shook his head in embarrassment and took the nearest chair.

A minute later Larry sat sipping a Diet Coke. Jerome held a bottle of beer. Jill gathered up her clothes and said her goodbyes. Sam walked her to the door and said, "You're welcome to stay."

She leaned forward and kissed him lightly on the mouth. "Tell me about it later."

Sam smiled. "Thanks for coming."

Jill lowered her voice. "I should be thanking *you* for that…"

Sam blushed despite himself. "OK, then. We're even." He stepped into the hall and watched until she reached her door and opened it. She waved once and then was gone. Sam turned and crossed into the kitchen, where he grabbed a beer of his own.

"OK, let's hear it," said Sam.

"Well," said Larry, "we make sandwiches—"

"—but not *just* sandwiches—," said Jerome.

"—we also make a lot of money—"

"—a *lot* of money—"

"—because Zorro is our business partner—"

"—sort of a *silent* partner, only—"

"—lately…"

"…he hasn't been so silent—"

It went on like that for almost an hour, neither brother finishing a single sentence. Their story was one long, unbroken narrative that Sam couldn't have interrupted if he'd tried.

When they had finished, Larry looked at his can of soda and said, "I have to pee."

"Me, too." Jerome placed his empty beer on the coffee table.

Sam almost shook his head in wonder. Maybe they were born Siamese twins, joined at the hip from birth? He gestured down the hall. "There's two. First right, or keep going through the master bedroom for the second one."

Jerome stood. "I'll make the long walk."

Larry followed him down the hallway. While they were gone Sam tossed his beer bottle into the recycling bin and started a pot of coffee. He suspected this was going to be a long night.

Next to the coffee pot, the Ziploc bag of cookies Gail had forced upon him sat neglected. Sam tried to remember all the flavors but only came up with *macaroon*. That morning seemed a lifetime ago. One day you're chatting with the nice old lady down the hall, a few days later you're waiting for someone to cut your eyes out.

Just to the right of the untouched cookies, the answering machine lobbied for his attention, its red eye blinking mournfully. Sam glared at it but it kept blinking, even when he didn't. Sam sighed. Sparing a glance down the hall, he pushed *play*.

Twisted Oliver's unctuous voice filled the room.

Sam stared at the answering machine as the tape unspooled, his expression changing from anxious to confused as he tried to reconcile what he was hearing with the more pressing problem of Zorro. It was a litany of medical terminology, chemical names, facts and figures, Oliver getting excited about puzzle pieces that still needed to be fit together. Words that needed to be translated into plain English. When the message was over Sam took a deep breath and looked at the clock to see if it was too late to call. Oliver and his theories would have to wait. Unless Sam could figure out how to survive the next twenty-four hours, Danny was going to have to connect the dots, right after he attended Sam's funeral.

The brothers returned to their respective chairs. Sam took the loveseat across from them and started asking questions. Cop questions, one right after another, not giving them time to think or manufacture any bullshit. He kept on them for half an hour, at which point they looked more exhausted than defensive. Finally, Sam leaned back in his chair. "It took balls coming here."

Larry and Jerome looked at each other, their expressions clear that they'd considered it an act of desperation.

"You could run," said Sam.

Jerome shook his head. "That never works. Seen too many movies."

Sam didn't argue. "You could have done what Zorro asked and set me up."

Larry frowned as Jerome said, "You think Zorro's gonna leave us alive, after he kills you?"

"Not a chance," said Sam. "He's planning to kill you both."

Larry sucked air through his teeth, as if hearing the threat spoken aloud had knocked the wind out of him. Jerome put a hand on his brother's shoulder and ground his teeth together before saying, "Zorro thinks he's going to kill us, but he's wrong."

"Sounds like you have a plan."

The brothers nodded in unison.

"Good," said Sam. "So do I."

Chapter Sixty-four

"That will never work."

Gail pulled the cookie sheet from the oven and surveyed the damage. The sugar cookies should have been the easiest to bake, but the oven was almost as old as she was, and the temperature fluctuated wildly from one rack to the next. The perfectly round cookies had risen uniformly in the middle, but some had brown edges. That would never do, not for company.

Shaking her head in disgust, Gail strode purposefully over to the garbage can, stomped the foot pedal and used her spatula to scrape the cookies into the trash.

"Should have used the top rack."

Grabbing a fresh cookie sheet, she painstakingly doled out equivalent masses of dough, her wrist as supple as a velvet rope. When she had finished the tray was covered by a perfectly symmetrical six-by-five matrix of sugar and flour.

"Much better," she said to her dead cat Simone.

Simone didn't answer, since she'd been buried more than five years ago, but she was still very much alive whenever Gail was in her kitchen.

Simone had lived with Gail long enough—almost eight years—for them to strike up quite a relationship. Like most relationships with cats, it was almost entirely on the cat's terms. Simone would shower Gail with affection by rubbing against her legs and shedding on her slacks, her couch, her bed. Cajole her with insistent purrs, chastise her with disapproving glances, berate her when she came home late. Once she had even demonstrated her great loyalty by leaving a present for Gail at the doorstop, a gray dormouse with a broken neck.

But Simone was an excellent listener, so it seemed only fair Gail should give Simone something in return.

Gail would talk nonstop to Simone while she baked, and in exchange Simone was given small tastes of the cookie batter. Depending on how Simone reacted, Gail knew if she was onto something. Gail remembered once adding some extra vanilla into a tollhouse recipe, then turning her back just long enough to check the oven. By the time she came back to add the chocolate chips half the batter was gone, Simone's whiskers sticking together. Gail whipped up another batch immediately and never went back to the original recipe.

It broke her heart when that cat died. For the longest time, Gail blamed herself. Maybe she should have been more careful about what she fed her. Taken her for walks. Not had her neutered. Brushed her more regularly. But then Gail got tired of feeling guilty and blamed the vet.

She got old, the vet said by way of explanation, as if the cat's age had been some kind of curse, a death spell of numerology. Not something you say to an old lady.

Then he chided her for feeding the cat cookie dough, saying it was bad for the cat's metabolism. Clogged the arteries, weakened the heart. The whole time, Gail felt like the vet was talking about her and not her cat, describing a time bomb that was set to explode somewhere in her *old* body. What a smug little prick he was, probably never let his kids have dessert. Looked like a teetotaler, too.

But Gail thanked him for his trouble, left the cookies she had baked, and silently prayed that his liver would explode. She kept that thought between her and the Almighty, which was easy because she was an agnostic, but the moral victory was hers. *Always be gracious*, her mother had said, *even when they treat you like dirt*. Even in grief, Gail was a class act.

But she never got another cat, even when the ASPCA came calling. She gave them money and a small bag of cookies but asked them to leave her alone.

She still talked to Simone whenever she baked, and tonight she was baking up a storm. She was expecting company. Eight, maybe ten people at least. It would take at least eight hours of baking to finish all the cookies she had planned.

She flicked on the oven light, checked the color, then took a quick inventory of her supplies. Ingredients were laid out across the counter in near-military formation. The standard bag of flour, a box of brown sugar, baking soda. A colorful assortment of bottles—flavors like vanilla and nutmeg, food coloring, other extracts designed to linger on the palette and compel even the most disciplined dieter to reach back into the jar for *just one more*. Bags of chocolate chips—semisweet—enough to make cookies till the end of time.

Gail's number one rule, *don't be stingy with the chocolate*.

Her eyes wandered toward the end of the counter where the liqueurs, nuts, and spices were arranged in a rainbow of temptation. More adult fare, a little kick in your cookie, a sweet afterthought to the drink in your hand.

Gail grabbed one of the bottles and titled it toward her mixing bowl, thinking *why not?* She hadn't had guests in some time, unless you counted her visits from Gus or her chats with the girls down the hall. Or her recent conversations with that nice man Sam.

He was an interesting one. Smart, and handsome—looked his age, not like a man trying to recapture his lost youth. And the saddest eyes she'd ever seen on a man. It almost brought a tear to her eye, thinking about the way that man talked about his wife.

"He's a keeper," she said, knowing Simone would have agreed with her. "Maybe I shouldn't have stirred him up like that, getting him poking around, but I couldn't help myself. Besides, I think it'll be good for him."

Simone made no comment.

"Fella like that needs to be out in the world meeting people." She bent down and cracked the over open a fraction of an inch. *Perfect.* "Like that nice girl Jill; such a lovely voice. I think it's good they met—good for everyone."

Simone didn't disagree.

Gail slid the tray out and smiled. Thirty perfect circles stood in formation, awaiting their deployment on the cooling tray. Then came the icing. "Maybe red this time, just for fun."

While the last batch cooled, Gail returned to her mixing, felt the soothing motion of her arm churning the batter. The honest feel of the wooden spoon in her hand. She loved cookies. Who cared if they weren't good for your body—they were good for the soul. She dipped a finger into the batter and brought it to her lips, smiled at the decadence of it.

Some people took all the joy out of life just trying to survive. The way Gail saw it, people like that got old long before she ever did, in spirit if not in body. Why all the fuss? Everybody died.

She thought about Simone, a cat who helped fill the void left by her dearly beloved, dead these long years. Her sweet Gus, still a spring chicken in his own eyes but catching up to her in aches and pains. That wonderful woman Marie, taken so young from that nice policeman. And even that dead bastard Ed. Almost made her want to get religion, just so he could burn in whatever circle of Hell was reserved for landlords.

Everybody died, but how many lived without regret? That was Gail's idea of heaven.

She took another scoop of batter and licked it off her bony finger. Life could be sweet if you just made it that way. She turned to the spot on the counter where Simone used to sit, imagined the cat giving her a disapproving look, waiting impatiently for its turn.

"Give me a break, you old sourpuss," said Gail as she treated herself to another lick. "I just want to have some fun before I die."

Chapter Sixty-five

On the chance he was going to be dead tomorrow, Sam decided to spend at least some of the time he had left on Earth looking at naked women.

By all rights, he should have been asleep. He was exhausted. Listening to Larry and Jerome was almost as grueling in its own way as grappling with Zorro's band of thugs. The brothers had left an hour ago and it was late, too late to walk down the hall and wake Jill. Late enough that Sam should be getting some rest while he could—sleep deprivation wasn't going to help keep him on his game. But the coffee had kicked in and Sam was restless. Too much caffeine and adrenaline for one day.

The first thing he did was open a kitchen drawer and pull out a pad and pen, which he used to take notes while he listened to Oliver's message a second time. Then he played it again, scribbling questions to himself. He drank more coffee until the pot was empty, cursed himself, then switched to beer, hoping the two would cancel each other out.

Then he went into the spare bedroom where he kept his files and pulled open drawers until he found his old phone list. He found Oliver's home number, dialed, and let it ring until it woke Oliver up. For some reason Sam didn't think Oliver slept like normal people or, if he did, Sam assumed it would be during the day inside a coffin.

Sam grilled Oliver for twenty minutes before thanking him and hanging up. Instead of feeling smarter, Sam only felt like asking more questions, but even Oliver had his limits. Part of the problem was that Ed's accelerated descent from the roof had taken place a lifetime ago, as far as Sam was concerned. With his own life in jeopardy, Sam was having trouble focusing.

Sam fired up what he still thought of as Marie's computer. While he waited for the operating system to launch, he returned to the kitchen for another beer. He opened an overhead cabinet and was delighted to find the bag of pretzels he'd hoped was there. Tearing it open, he returned to the office and sat in front of the computer. He still felt wide awake.

Jill hadn't exaggerated. The girls' website was intoxicating, beginning with the homepage. Some models and actresses looked great on film but surprisingly average or even awkward in person—but the camera loved them and made them more beautiful on film than in life. Given how spectacular Shayla and Tamara were in person, Sam couldn't imagine them looking any better, but the camera loved them, too. Maybe more than anyone.

The fact that they were often topless or naked in most of the photos didn't hurt, either. Sam felt himself stir and experienced a pang of guilt over Jill, but he reminded himself she had insisted he visit the site. She had a reason to be proud.

The navigation from one section of the site to another was ingenious, involving a click of the mouse or a scrolling move across some erogenous zone of the girls' anatomy. And since the cursor appeared as a hand icon, it only heightened the interactivity of the site. But the site had a sense of humor. The copy was irreverent, and most of the images were more playful than pornographic, the girls looking at the camera with a wink and a nod, letting their guests enjoy the view but making it clear they were in on the joke.

Like a blog or visual diary, Shayla and Tamara had written short entries for each day or night, searchable by date, each accompanied by a series of digital photos and usually a short video. Yesterday's entry had a series with Tamara painting her nails, topless, her long black hair barely concealing her breasts.

The day before revealed Shalya doing yoga on the rug wearing something that could pass for a thong if it were just a little bigger.

Sam clicked through all the sections, then randomly jumped around the archives. He noticed the site was topical, playing off current events. A week ago the girls took advantage of the World Poker Tour to have their own game of cards. While the tournament played on the TV next to the big bed, both girls sat half-dressed, knees touching, cards in their hands. A big pile of clothes suggested they were playing a game of strip poker. The blue orbs of Shayla's hair made a stunning contrast to the pink bedspread. Sam wondered if Jill consulted them on their wardrobe in addition to the art direction of the site.

Every time Sam clicked to watch a video, he was sent to a screen that asked for a password and invited him to enter his credit card if he wanted to join the site. He found himself visualizing his wallet on the kitchen counter and decided it was time for one last beer. He imagined anyone who visited the site more than once would succumb to temptation. After seeing some of the free photos, thirty bucks a month for hi-resolution video didn't seem so steep. He shook his head as he ran the math behind the site one more time. Even with only a few thousand members, those girls would have no trouble making the rent.

Sam shut down the computer and returned to the kitchen, wondering how many times he was going to walk back and forth between the two rooms before he felt tired. His pulse had quickened, but he couldn't tell if it was from all the walking or the naked pictures. Either way, he was getting old.

He dropped the half-eaten bag of pretzels on the counter, where Gail's cookies sang a siren song from inside their Ziploc. Somehow cookies and beer didn't sound too appealing, so Sam grabbed another handful of pretzels. While he stood munching, he thought about Gail's colorful descriptions and took the cookies out of the bag, one by one, and arranged them carefully on the counter. He moved one forward and another to the side, changing the pattern the way a quarterback in a scratch football game might move sticks and rocks while explaining a play to his teammates.

Sam chose a blood-red cookie with a cherry center for Zorro. He set that alongside two smaller cookies sprinkled with rock salt meant to represent Larry and Jerome. Shayla and Tamara were matching vanilla cookies dipped in chocolate, which looked sweet and decadent at the same time. Gus was a rich brown cookie with nuts. Danny got pink frosting. Gail became one of her almond cookies, and Sam gave himself a role as a macaroon. Jill was a Madeleine, classic, delicious, with the perfect contours of an Art Deco sculpture. Walter, sadly, was the one cookie that had broken into pieces, pulverized so thoroughly that it was impossible to tell what kind of cookie Walter had been.

Sam drank another beer and moved the cookies across his counter in a hypoglycemic ballet set to a tune that he couldn't quite place. He stared at the cherry cookie and hummed, trying to find the melody, seemingly unperturbed, until he abruptly smashed his right hand onto the counter and crushed Zorro's cookie into so many pieces that not only the king's horses but even the king's men were shit out of luck.

Sam took a deep breath and brushed crumbs off his hands into the sink. He suddenly felt exhausted, but he knew sleep wouldn't come, not yet.

Time to get your affairs in order.

Sam took the pad and began writing, standing at the kitchen counter, pausing every now and then to collect his thoughts. He finished his beer before he finished writing. When he was done, he scrounged around for an envelope and found one in his junk drawer. He wrote a short note on the back and laid the letter in plain view next to the coffee pot.

Sam stepped around the counter and over to the living room, where he looked out the window for a long time. He looked for patterns in the stars but couldn't find any.

Finally, he moved in front of the mantle and talked to Marie for almost an hour, just to hear the sound of her voice inside his head. They talked about everything and nothing, and in the end it calmed Sam enough that he was able to sit down and relax in one of the big, comfortable chairs. He kept talking but after a few minutes started to mumble, and soon the echoes of Marie's voice had faded away.

Sam closed his eyes and slept like a dead man.

Chapter Sixty-six

Larry leapt away from the ringing phone as if it were a cattle prod and he a wayward Holstein. When it rang a second time, all he could think to say was, "Aaaaah!"

Jerome grabbed his brother by the shoulders and forcibly sat him down on one of the bar stools, then reached across the counter and grabbed the phone. As he pushed the button to answer the call, Jerome glanced at the kitchen clock, a worried expression on his face.

"Z, you're early—"

Larry watched his brother grow paler with every nod of his head.

"Yeah, he's still there. Down the hall."

A long pause, and then, "No, we're not going anywhere. We want our money."

Jerome dropped the phone back into its cradle, the call over. Larry couldn't tell if Jerome had hung up on Zorro or the other way around.

Jerome clenched his jaw. "Zorro came sooner than Sam said he would."

Larry's eyes flicked to the clock. "They're here—*now*?"

Jerome nodded but didn't say anything.

"Does he know we're home or did you let him think we were somewhere else?"

Jerome sighed. "He called us on our home phone, Larry. Not on my cell."

Larry looked at the phone with revulsion, as if it had turned into a snake. He hated phones. Over the past few days they'd brought nothing but despair into his life. If somehow they managed to get out of this, he had a new mantra that he swore to live by.

"Never answer the phone," he said.

"Too late," said Jerome.

"You could have used call forwarding."

"I could have saved a bunch on car insurance, Larry, but I didn't. So much for looking backwards."

"We're fucked."

"We stick with the plan."

"Sam's plan or our plan?"

"Why am I the only one worried about our asses?"

"But they came early."

"That's Sam's problem."

Larry breathed in and out as if he might hyperventilate. "I like Sam."

"*Godammit*, Larry. That's got nothing to do with...with anything. I like staying out of jail. I like not getting killed. I think I like those things *more* than I like Sam, but that doesn't mean they won't happen."

Larry didn't answer. He looked over his shoulder toward the living room, his gaze moving desperately to the picture window and whatever lay beyond the glass.

Jerome walked to the front door to make sure the chain was pulled into place. He kept his eyes on the door as he took a seat next to his brother, then reached out and took Larry's hand. Both their palms were sweating, and Jerome was sure he could feel Larry's heartbeat through the pulse in his thumb. It felt like they were the same person, separated at birth but now rejoined, able to read each other's minds because they shared the same thoughts.

Maybe this wasn't such a good plan, after all.

Larry squeezed his brother's hand. "We could still run."

Jerome watched the door and shook his head sadly.

"Not any more."

Chapter Sixty-seven

Zorro was impressed that Julio had thought to bring duct tape.

The Golden Towers apartments had three daytime doormen for each of the three towers, but at night there was a lone security guard sitting on the ground floor of the main tower, looking through a plate glass window that fronted the courtyard. His job was to open the doors for residents who lost their keys or locked themselves out—or take emergency calls if someone burned their toast and thought pulling the fire alarm was an appropriate response.

But most nights the job consisted of sitting around on your ass until dawn, which is why Harold Laraby had taken it. He was going to school to become an electrical engineer but his classes didn't start until noon, so he could sleep in after staying up all night. And this job gave him the perfect environment to study. He was alone, it was utterly silent, and there was no TV or computer to distract him.

Only it hadn't worked out the way he had planned, because Harold had developed an uncontrollable obsession with celebrity news. He had tried to resist, but the media machine kept hitting him when his guard was down—during the morning news, in the checkout aisle, on the radio. Even NPR and Bravo had succumbed. It was one thing to avoid *US* or *People*, but now Brad and Angelina were everywhere, even *Vanity Fair* and *Time*.

Not to mention Jessica, who was on both *Teen People* and *Good Housekeeping* in the same month. Fucking *Good Housekeeping* wasn't safe anymore, for crying out loud. Harold very much doubted Jessica had ever kept a house, let alone a good one, but there she was right on the cover. No matter where Harold looked for serious reading material, the crack pipe of celebrity culture was thrust into his hands.

Somehow the tawdry gossip soothed him. If these people who had everything could become such train wrecks, maybe his problems weren't so hard to understand. Maybe his life wasn't so bad, after all. Reading about celebrities made him feel smarter, more emotionally stable, and more fulfilled.

Harold was halfway through an article about Britney going completely insane when his trance-like state was interrupted by a knock on the glass door of the office. He blinked for a minute to reconcile the shape with the sound. The knock had been gentle, almost feminine, but the guy standing on the other side of the door was a giant. Harold stepped closer and recoiled involuntarily at the man's face, which looked like it had been beaten with the ugly stick until the stick had broken. When the giant smiled it only added another layer of gruesome to the visage.

But the guy seemed friendly enough, and it's not like anyone ever stopped by for anything except a missing key or help with a stuck door. This building needed security like a donut shop needed a salad bar.

Harold had pushed open the door and launched into his pat *good evening* when the giant's right hand shot through the opening like a cobra. Harold went suddenly blind—his entire face was engulfed by the giant's palm, the heel of the hand forcing his mouth shut, making it impossible to breathe.

Harold backpedaled across the office but the giant kept pace. When Harold felt a second enormous hand grab the back of his neck, he knew it would be over soon. He prayed that he wouldn't feel a thing.

He didn't.

When he regained consciousness, Harold was so shocked and relieved to find himself alive, he started crying. The tears ran across his cheeks and over the duct tape covering his mouth. Blinking, he realized that he'd been moved to the storage closet adjacent to the bathroom. Dim light passed through a grill at the base of the door.

Harold was sitting down. His shoulders hurt. He tried to move his hands but couldn't. They were held fast by duct tape, as were his feet. He shifted his weight to no avail, but the effort revealed why he had been attacked.

Harold didn't sound right. More accurately, he didn't make a sound at all, because the telltale jangling of keys was gone. That sound that reminded him of miniature wind chimes, the sound that followed his every move since he took this cushy job. Harold knew without looking that his set of master keys had been taken.

Back in the courtyard, Julio held the roll of duct tape in one hand as he handed the keys to Zorro with the other.

"It's important to come prepared."

"He is still alive?"

Julio nodded.

"But he can identify you."

"There will be no mystery about who killed the cop, Zorro. Let's face facts. Only you would have the *cajones* to come into this neighborhood for revenge. And if they find you, then they find me."

"I will disappear," said Zorro. "For a while."

"So will I."

"Of course," Zorro said, a little too quickly. As if he wasn't concerned about Julio, or anyone except himself. Julio could disappear or go to jail, and it was all the same to Zorro.

"I will visit my mother in Guadalajara," Julio said.

"A good idea."

Julio heard the feigned interest in Zorro's voice and recalled the conversation between Zorro and the two brothers, when Jerome said they needed a fall guy. He remembered the way

Zorro had looked at him then. Perhaps after they killed the cop, Julio was just another loose end.

Julio turned to face his boss. "I might not come back."

Zorro met his gaze. The trees in the nearby park sighed in protest as the wind pushed them around. *The wind is a bully*, thought Julio. For a man who had spent his entire life leveraging his own freakish size to intimidate others, it was a strange thought. He absently picked at the roll of duct tape with his thumb as he waited for Zorro to make a move.

Finally Zorro broke eye contact and looked toward the top of the tower. "You are ready, then?"

Julio kept his eyes on Zorro. "Always."

"*Bueno.*" Zorro rattled the keys in his left hand. In his right was a shotgun, matte black with a pistol grip and short barrel. The grip and barrel length made it illegal in the state of California, but they also made it highly effective in close quarters. The five cartridges in the magazine were more than sufficient to clear a room.

Julio reached into his waistband and pulled out a handgun the size of a bazooka. It was a 50-caliber Desert Eagle, a semi-automatic pistol so large it could barely be held, let alone controlled, by anyone smaller than Arnold Schwarzenegger. The bullets were as big as twinkies and no less deadly. But in Julio's massive mitt the gun looked no larger than a nine millimeter, and the sharp angles made it appear even scarier than Julio himself.

Julio racked the slide to force a cartridge into the chamber, then jammed the gun back into his waistband.

"Let's get this over with."

Chapter Sixty-eight

One turn of the key and they were inside the cop's apartment.

Zorro wanted to kick down the door and barge in with guns blazing but agreed to try the key first. If they got lucky and could sneak inside, it would improve their chances of making it to the brothers' apartment before witnesses appeared in the hallway.

Zorro stood to one side of the door as Julio tried the key. It turned easily, and though Zorro was surprised to find the deadbolt open and the chain off, he wasn't going to look a gift horse in the mouth. That said, another thought occurred to Zorro that he didn't like one bit because it meant the brothers had betrayed him.

Maybe the cop isn't home.

Snoring put his fears to rest. The telltale sounds of slumber carpeted the room. Zorro took a tentative step into the apartment, Julio close behind. Once inside, they could tell the breathing was coming from the living room. Julio moved to the left, flanking Zorro as they crossed the foyer toward the open kitchen. To the left of the kitchen counter would be the living room.

Another step and the picture window was clearly visible. Zorro registered a few stars and the faint outline of trees backlit by a waxing moon. He followed the path of the moonlight into the room and froze.

The cop was sitting in a chair with his back to them, right arm dangling to the floor. From the sound of his breathing, he was dead to the world.

Soon you will be.

Zorro leveled the shotgun.

Julio carefully drew the hand cannon from his waistband and took aim.

Zorro fired first. The shotgun was deafening in the enclosed space of the apartment. Julio felt the concussion in his ears as flames leapt from the barrel. He watched as Zorro racked the shotgun and fired a second time, but it was like watching a silent movie. Julio's ears were ringing and he was deaf to the world. He still hadn't fired a single shot.

Zorro's face contorted with rage as spittle flew from his lips. He was shouting, veins bulging in his neck. Julio stood transfixed, as if Zorro's true animal nature had been revealed in the strobe from the gun barrel. Julio watched as Zorro fired a third time, then forced his gaze to shift to what was left of the cop.

The right hand was gone but the arm remained, a ragged tear at the end of the forearm where the hand should have been. The back of the chair had a gaping wound in it, a jagged hole through which Julio saw moonlight. He saw blood—wet and black in the shadows of the room—spattered across the window, the ceiling, and the mantle where the pictures were.

Where the pictures were.

The thought struck Julio like an ice pick. He scanned the ruined mantle as Zorro fired a fourth time, blue light blazing across the room for a split second.

The pictures weren't there.

The fourth blast caught the chair on the right, causing it to slowly, painfully spin in place. As it swiveled around in slow-motion Julio cringed, not at the sight of blood but in anticipation of their terrible mistake.

The ruined body of Walter—overweight blackmailer, B-movie mogul, and recently departed neighbor—slumped in the chair. Most of his chest was missing, his right hand was gone, and his empty eyes stared accusingly at Zorro. He looked less angry than hurt, as if he expected to be treated with just a little more dignity in the next life.

But Walter had the last laugh. In his lap was a tape recorder from which the sound of snoring still emanated, courtesy of Jerome. The nasal symphony of his nighttime allergies had been captured on tape after his evening of ecstasy with Tamara. The recording was Jerome's contribution to the plan.

The air was thick with the smell of death. Noxious fluids surrounded the chair and cordite filled the room, the aftermath of Zorro's carnage.

But Zorro wasn't finished.

Julio turned to see if Zorro had realized their predicament, but Zorro only had blood lust in his eyes. His nostrils flared like a bull as he racked the shotgun. He had one shot left and clearly he intended to use it.

Julio was about to say something, try to shout above the ringing in his ears, when he registered a subtle movement of Zorro's feet. He was pivoting on his left foot, shifting his weight around to the right. He was bringing the shotgun around in a tight arc, moving the barrel away from the body in the chair toward the only other person in the room.

Julio.

Zorro's crooked teeth curved into a cruel smile as he prepared to take his last shot. From less than five feet away, the shotgun would punch a hole in Julio the size of a basketball. Game over.

Julio took one giant step across the room and swung his pistol like a club, catching the barrel of the shotgun and knocking it to the left. Zorro held fast to the grip and started another arc toward Julio's face, but the 50-caliber pistol returned on the backswing and caught Zorro on the temple. He went down like a bag of corn meal.

Julio kicked Zorro savagely in the ribs, then grabbed the shotgun with his left hand and threw it across the room. He paused for an instant and contemplated the pistol in his right hand, then jammed it back under his belt—he wanted both hands free.

This is personal.

Julio's hand was wide enough to palm a basketball, so grabbing Zorro around the ankles and neck posed no serious challenge. His arms were long enough to hold Zorro at either end like an unwilling barbell, then hoist him over his head in a clean-and-jerk motion worthy of the Olympics. Zorro's arms were technically free but Julio had cut off his oxygen, so they flailed listlessly around the giant's head. With one hand squeezing Zorro around the neck and the other holding the legs tight, Julio turned and stepped into the hallway.

The twin urges of vengeance and escape battled for control of his next move.

He turned left and saw the end of the hallway where the wide glass door opened onto the fire escape. The door was reinforced with cross-hatched wires embedded in the glass, but Julio was confident he could kick it open. Besides, the door didn't seem to have a lock. It was probably against the fire code to lock an exit leading to a fire escape.

That gave Julio one escape route. A little climbing and then home free. The other would be the way they came in, down the hall to the elevators.

Julio turned in that direction and stopped dead in his tracks.

The cop who was supposed to be dead stood in the hallway. He had a thin smile on his face and a gun in his hand.

"Your move."

Sam shifted his thumb across the back of his pistol.

The ringing in Julio's ears had subsided enough that he could hear the familiar sound of a hammer being cocked. Having his hands up already was certainly convenient, but it presented another problem altogether.

Zorro was getting really heavy.

Chapter Sixty-nine

Larry spasmed with every blast of the shotgun, almost knocking himself and Jerome off their bar stools.

"Did you hear that?"

Jerome was sweating but managed to raise one eyebrow in what he hoped was a wry expression. *If you act cool, you just might be cool.*

"Bro, the whole fucking neighborhood heard *that*."

It sounded good when he said it, but Jerome didn't feel cool at all.

Jill's hands shook as she latched the door. Sam had just stepped into the hallway and told her to stay inside no matter what happened. She moved to the kitchen and rummaged through drawers until she found an ice pick. She tested the point and decided it would do the trick. Now she had to figure out where to hide.

Shalya and Tamara jumped when they heard the gunshots but stayed on the big bed. They tried to concentrate on painting each other's nails but took turns nervously glancing toward the cameras in their room. If they were going to be murdered, at least there would be witnesses. Thousands of them, from all over the world.

◇◇◇

Gail sat on her couch and held Gus' hands in hers, their knees touching.

"We should call the cops," said Gus.

Gail shook her head. "How long do you think it would take the police to arrive?"

Gus shrugged. "Five, ten minutes, tops."

"Too late."

"Too late?"

Gail nodded. "We'll all be dead by then."

Chapter Seventy

"He must be getting heavy," said Sam. "Even for a big guy like you."

Julio shrugged to show it was no big deal, but the motion made his shoulders ache. Fucking Zorro needed to lose some weight. Maybe there was saturated fat in sheep eyeballs.

Sam held the gun steady, his expression bland. Julio's eyes flicked past Sam toward the elevator, but the hallway remained empty. Then his gaze darted toward his belt, where the mammoth 50-caliber handgun had slipped across his belt to rub against his crotch. It was an itch he couldn't scratch without getting his head blown off.

Zorro grunted and tried to twist free. Julio held him fast but the struggle made Julio sway back and forth as if he were doing the hula in a private luau for Sam.

The cop was right, Julio had to make a move. This was humiliating.

The thought occurred to Julio just as Zorro managed to open his mouth and spit. A thin line of drool escaped the sieve of his ruined teeth, oozing onto Julio's forehead and into his eyes.

Chingalo! Julio clenched his mouth shut and blinked. He wanted to be able to look the cop in the eyes. He took a deep breath and tightened his grip. Above, he heard Zorro squeak like a dog's toy.

The cop held Julio's gaze, the gun steady.

Julio stood motionless for a long moment, then nodded at the cop.

Sam watched as Julio pivoted slowly on one foot, Zorro held high, the big finale of the hula. When Julio's weight had settled on the other foot his back was turned to Sam. Without looking over his shoulder, Julio took a tentative step toward the fire escape.

Sam kept the gun raised, waiting.

Two steps, three. Julio reached the glass door set high on the wall, then quickly released Zorro's legs, which dangled and bounced in mid-air like the limbs of a marionette. Julio pulled the door open and caught Zorro's legs before he could find the strength to start kicking.

Julio spared a glance over his shoulder and saw that Sam hadn't moved. Their eyes met and this time Sam nodded, slowly.

Julio turned and stepped onto the fire escape. He lowered Zorro until he was at shoulder level, then Julio took a second step to the railing and thrust his arms up and away from his body in one fluid motion, launching Zorro into space.

Zorro plummeted a hundred feet before he made any noise. Then his scream tore through the building like an altar boy's parents in search of a lawyer.

Chapter Seventy-one

The scream bounced off the walls, rattled the windows, and woke up everyone in the neighborhood. For Sam and his neighbors, it was a sound that was all too familiar.

Julio leaned over the railing of the fire escape. The courtyard was illuminated by streetlights, and he could just make out the scene two hundred feet below. He grunted in satisfaction, then turned to face Sam.

"I hit the penguins," Julio said with obvious pride.

Sam kept his gun raised. "Congratulations."

"You're welcome."

"I think you did us both a favor."

Julio shrugged. He was careful to keep his hands away from his belt.

Sam asked, "You want to come inside?"

Julio studied Sam for a moment, then shook his head. "I'm not going back to jail."

"Not my problem."

Julio nodded, then took a tentative step off the uppermost landing of the fire escape, lowering his weight onto the first rung of the ladder. It creaked in protest but held. Sam remained in the hallway but tracked Julio as he took another step down. Both of the giant's hands were on the railing now, his gun out of reach, but Sam stayed where he was. When Julio's head was the only thing visible through the window, he paused. The two men looked at each other, frozen in time. Sam spoke first.

"*Adios,*" he said. "And, well, *gracias.*"

"*De nada.*"

Sam lowered his gun when the top of Julio's head slipped out of sight. He counted to ten, then pulled a cell phone out of his pocket and pressed the call button.

It took Julio only three minutes to follow the zig-zag of the fire escape down to the ladder that lowered automatically when it took his weight. The ladder was positioned to blend with a sign that featured the name of the apartment complex, the vertical lines of the ladder forming the letter "L" in Golden Towers. Below the sign, an open archway on the ground floor led to the main entrance.

A jolting ride on the ladder, a short drop and Julio was standing in the courtyard looking up. He had kept his eyes on the top floor, just in case the cop changed his mind about following. But Julio didn't think he would.

The dead cop who wasn't dead. The cop who wasn't a cop anymore. Julio didn't know what to call him, so he decided to think of him as *the smart guy who outfoxed Zorro and could have shot me but didn't.* It had a nice ring to it.

Julio lowered his gaze and turned, facing the courtyard. The main entrance to the building was behind him. The night air was cool but clear, the light at street level more than sufficient to reveal his surroundings.

Unlike the dead landlord, Zorro did not explode on impact. Somehow his sinews, bones, and muscle held his torso together despite the crushing impact of the fall. Maybe there was high fiber in eyeballs. Or calcium.

Zorro was looking up at the stars, arms outstretched in supplication, head thrown back in rapture. Through his chest the beak of the mother penguin protruded majestically, reaching upwards to heaven in thanks for this unexpected bounty. Zorro was the catch of the day.

Julio took a deep breath and turned away. It was time to get the hell out of there.

That's when he realized he hadn't heard any sirens. After deafening gunfire and a scream that could wake the dead, no one had called *911*? Alarms went off somewhere inside his head, and instinctively Julio reached for the gun in his belt, but he froze before his hand made it halfway to his waist.

A large-caliber handgun was pressing against his temple directly behind his right eye socket. Julio could feel the blade of the forward sight digging into his flesh.

Danny Rodriguez slowly withdrew the gun as he stepped from the shadows of the archway into the courtyard. He wore his badge on the outside of his jacket, its metal surface glinting in the diffuse light from the streetlamps. From a distance of four feet, he kept the forty-five pointed at Julio's broad face. Just out of reach but too close to miss.

Julio shook his head, disgusted. He tried to think of something to say—something smart or tough—but the only thing that came to mind was the mantra that had been running through his head all week.

"I hate this fucking job."

"Don't worry, *ese*." Danny used his free hand to gesture toward the penguins. "I think you just resigned."

Chapter Seventy-two

"Maybe I should resign."

Sam looked at his ex-partner and shook his head. "C'mon, Danny."

"You did."

"I didn't resign," said Sam. "I retired. There's a difference."

"This is a mess."

"I said it would be."

"Easy for you to say—you're not the one who has to do all the paperwork."

Sam drank some tequila but didn't respond. The Globe restaurant stayed open until two A.M., which made it unique in a neighborhood where most kitchens closed by ten. At this hour there was always room at the bar, and tonight Sam and Danny had it all to themselves.

Julio had been taken into custody. His desire to stay out of prison was trumped by his more fervent desire to avoid getting shot in the face.

The coroner's wagon had left an hour ago, along with the uniformed cops and the lone crime scene technician. A meager crew by CSI standards, but this wasn't television. Danny and Sam had moved to the restaurant down the street so they could talk in private.

"They came early," Danny said. "Good thing you were ready."

"Yeah." Sam blew out his cheeks. "I knew it wouldn't be last night, but tonight—I thought they'd come later."

"Like one A.M."

"Exactly. In the middle of the night for sure, not at ten. Almost caught me with my pants down."

"I don't think patience is—*was*—one of Zorro's talents."

"Neither was flying," said Sam.

Both men took a sip of their tequila and stared at nothing for a minute, anticipating the conversation that neither one wanted to have but knew they couldn't avoid. The bartender had told them it was sipping tequila. The price of each shot convinced both men that sipping was probably a good idea.

"I'm going to start with the painfully obvious," said Danny. "Then you fill in the blanks."

"If I can."

Danny gave him a look. "Use your imagination—you're good at that."

Sam kept his mouth shut.

"Zorro is dead. Killed by Julio, who should have considered trying out for the Olympic shotput team."

"Or horseshoes."

"That's not an Olympic sport."

"It should be." Sam took a drink.

"And then we have Walter, who was—"

Sam cut in. "—*shot* by Zorro."

The two friends sat there, shoulder to shoulder, contemplating the importance of semantics when writing police reports.

"There's a difference between *shot* and *killed*," mused Danny.

"There is a difference, but does it *make* a difference?" Sam turned on his bar stool to face his old partner.

Danny met his gaze. "*Should* it make a difference?"

Sam shook his head. "Not in this case."

"You saying Zorro killed Walter?"

"I'm saying you stopped the bad guys," said Sam. "At the end of the day, isn't that the job?"

Danny studied his glass of tequila as if it were a crystal ball. Not finding any answers from looking at it, he tried drinking it in one gulp. Six dollars down the hatch. He hissed as the liquid burned his throat, then set the glass back on the bar.

"These days I'm not sure what the job is."

Sam threw his own drink back, then gestured for two more. "You stopped the bad guys." He felt pedantic for saying it again but needed to convince himself. "They're all dead or in jail."

"Walter was into *something*," said Danny, but it sounded half-hearted.

"And he's dead."

"Zorro must have had some connection to that apartment building—*inside* that building."

"You working Narcotics now, Danny?"

"Fuck you."

Sam laughed. "Fair enough. But if you were Zorro's connection and if—*if*—you were still alive, what would you do, now that Zorro's dead?"

"Find another line of work and keep my head down."

"Exactly."

"What about Ed?" asked Danny. "Your lovable landlord?"

"He's dead."

"You saying he got sideways with Zorro, too?"

"Julio's got quite an arm," said Sam.

"You saying Julio threw him off the building?"

"You could ask him."

"Throwing Zorro off the roof might get him a plea bargain," said Danny. "Or a fucking medal from the Mayor. But throwing a civilian off the roof, well…the judge might frown upon such behavior."

"You're saying he'll deny it."

"Wouldn't you?"

Sam took a deep breath, then exhaled loudly. "Know what I think?"

Danny said nothing.

"I think Ed was a bad guy." Sam tried to keep the edge from his voice. "You talk to anyone who lives on that floor, and they'll tell you the same thing."

"Guess you got to know your neighbors."

Sam nodded.

"Do you trust them?" asked Danny.

Sam seemed to consider the question before saying, "About as much as I trust myself."

Danny studied his friend and former partner for a long time. Finally, he said, "That's good enough for me."

Neither spoke for a minute. Sam finished his drink and turned toward Danny.

"When I was on the job," he said, "I used to say that I worked for the dead."

"I remember."

"I had it all wrong," said Sam. "I think we're supposed to work for the living."

"Is that what you're doing?"

"Yeah," said Sam. "That's my new job."

Chapter Seventy-three

When Sam got home, Jill was already there, standing in front of the mantle. She adjusted a picture frame on the far right, then took a step back.

"What do you think?"

Sam looked around the room. Blood stained the hardwood floor around the ruined chair. Gore splattered the curtains. The nearest sliding glass door was shattered. But the pictures were back on the mantle in precisely the same arrangement as before. It felt like home.

Sam sighed. "I think you're amazing."

Jill smiled, but her eyes darted left toward the kitchen.

"Anything else?"

Sam gestured toward the broken window. "I was going to ask if I could sleep at your place tonight." Then he studied her expression and added, "But you seem to have something on your mind."

Jill glanced to her left. "I read your letter."

"I figured you would."

Jill took a tentative step forward. "What are you going to do?"

"Let me ask you a question."

"OK."

"You think all our neighbors are still awake?"

Jill nodded. "Gail invited everyone over, after we'd all stuck our heads out. After the shooting was over.

"Imagine that." Sam held out his hand. "Come with me."

Sam led her out of the apartment and across the hall. He knocked lightly and tried the doorknob at the same time. It was unlocked.

Everyone was there.

Larry stood by the sliding glass doors talking to Gus, who was spreading his arms as if telling a story about the one that got away. Jerome sat on the loveseat next to Tamara, hanging on her every word. Shayla stood behind them rolling her eyes, then waved when she saw Jill.

Gail sat by herself in a big chair across from a matching chair that was empty. In between was her coffee table and an array of cookies that would make Martha Stewart envious. Sam whispered to Jill and she crossed the room toward Shayla.

Sam took the chair opposite Gail.

"Hello, young man." Gail gestured toward the table. "Want a cookie?"

Sam eyed the spread. "Any recommendations?"

Gail leaned forward and plucked a single cookie from a tray. It was a soft yellow and had wavy lines along the top.

"Can't go wrong with a Madeleine."

Sam took the cookie with his right thumb and index finger, held it at arms length for a minute, then popped it in his mouth. As he chewed he said, "I'd hate to get it wrong, Gail."

Gail lifted a cup and saucer off the table and took a sip of coffee, eying Sam over the rim.

"So you figured it out."

"I had a little help."

"Your wife always said you were a smart cookie."

"I'm still fuzzy about a few parts…" Sam let his voice trail off.

"Such as?" Gail set the cup down carefully.

"Ed didn't jump."

"No?"

Sam shook his head. "He was poisoned. Seems he ingested cyanide."

Gail reclaimed her coffee and held the cup high, her eyes steady on Sam as she drank.

Sam continued. "Apparently wild almonds contain—" He paused to take a sheet of paper from his inside jacket pocket. "*Glycoside amygdalin.* Did I say that right?"

Gail nodded. "It turns into hydrogen cyanide, also known as—"

Sam cut her off as he glanced at his cheat sheet. "Prussic acid."

"I used to be a botanist," Gail said. "Did you know that?"

"Learn something new every day." Sam pointed to a row of round cookies with tiny almond flakes on them. "*Prunus dulcis.*"

"Yes," said Gail. "Almonds.

"You did say those cookies were *to die for.*"

Gail smiled but said nothing.

"That's a helluva way to confess," said Sam.

"You can regulate the quantity," said Gail. "Depending on the result you want."

"You saying you weren't trying to kill me?"

Gail's nostrils flared. "What an insolent thing to say. Of course not. I was testing you."

"Testing."

"Seeing how smart you were—I take it you didn't try one?"

Sam shook his head.

"It would have only given you a stomach ache, I assure you." Gail pursed her lips. "Something to think about."

Sam gestured at the square cookies with the bright red centers. "Cherry."

Gail nodded.

"I read something about cherry laurel?"

"The Internet is certainly amazing," said Gail. "*Prunus caroliniana.* Another excellent source of, well…"

"Poison," said Sam.

"Indeed."

Sam leaned forward and poured himself a cup of coffee. Around the room his neighbors were talking, laughing. Everyone out of hearing range.

"So I have a few theories," said Sam.

"A few?"

Sam pointed at the cookies. "One involves progressive poisoning. Slow increases in the amount Ed ingested, say over a period of weeks, until it reached a saturation point, and when the cyanide really kicks in—"

Gail spread her fingers as if counting off the days of the week. "It can trigger asphyxiation, seizures, cardiac arrest..."

"But that's too risky," Sam said. "You might get a dose wrong, or symptoms might come on too fast, then he ends up in the hospital and not dead."

Gail set her cup down. "You have quite an imagination."

"The other option is to try for the maximum dosage all at once."

"Less risk."

"Perhaps," said Sam. "But it poses a problem—several, actually."

Gail said nothing.

"You couldn't pull it off by yourself," said Sam. He paused to look around the room, then settled his eyes back on Gail.

"You could call everyone together right now," said Gail. "Like Hercule Poirot in one of those Agatha Christie stories."

"I prefer Miss Marple," replied Sam. "And I'd rather keep this between us for now."

"As you wish. You were saying something about an accomplice."

"Well, for starters, Ed needed a boost over the fire escape. Unless he started seizing from the poison, couldn't take the pain and hurled himself twenty stories to put an end to his agony."

"Is that one or two theories?"

"It's an observation," said Sam. "And if I had to cast for the part, I think your boyfriend Gus is just the man for the job."

"He's very protective."

"I noticed."

"Go on."

"You mentioned the Internet," said Sam. "Have you visited Shayla and Tamara's site lately?"

Gail blushed slightly. "Scandalous."

"It's impressive, and not only because of their natural... um...abilities. The daily updates, the archives. There's a lot to explore."

"And what did you find?"

"There's a video in the archives," said Sam. "From a week ago, before Ed died. Nothing out of the ordinary. Two beautiful girls half-naked, painting their nails."

"So?"

"So Shalya's hair was blue."

Gail looked over her shoulder. Shalya's twin orbs of hair bobbed to and for as she talked to Jill. "But her hair is blue."

"*Is*," said Sam. "But it wasn't when I met her. And she told me she'd never been blue before. That means they swapped that day's video with one they made later. Now why would they do that?"

"I'm sure you have an answer."

"I think your relationship with Ed wasn't even cordial anymore," said Sam. "After all the shit he pulled to evict you, I doubt you could lure him upstairs, even for all the cookies in the world. But Shayla and Tamara, they're sirens—even Ulysses couldn't have resisted those two."

"They had their own run-ins with Ed," said Gail.

"Yeah, you made it a point to tell me about that. Guess that was part of the confession."

Gail didn't respond.

"I've spent some time with those two." said Sam. "They could talk a snake out of its skin, then sell it back to him at twice the price. Getting a dumb bastard like Ed upstairs wouldn't even be a challenge. So they coaxed Ed upstairs and fed him the cookies you baked, then Gus gave him a helping hand into space."

Gail raised her eyebrows. "There's only one problem with your theory."

"I know." Sam leaned back in his chair and ran his hands through his hair. "*I know.*"

Gail let her eyes drift around the room. "She's such a nice woman."

Sam followed her gaze until it landed on Jill. She was laughing at something Shayla had said, her head back, worry lines radiating out from her eyes making her look even more beautiful.

"Shayla and Tamara don't build their own website," Sam said. "They need Jill to make any changes."

"She's very talented," said Gail. "It is an impressive site."

Sam took a deep breath.

"Does she know that you know?" asked Gail.

"I wrote a letter. In case anything…"

"Got messy?"

Sam frowned. "Messy."

He scanned the room again, pausing on every face, each person he had met less than a week before.

"You know what's funny?" he asked.

Gail shook her head.

Sam gestured across the room with his chin. "Larry and Jerome."

"What about them?"

"They're the only innocent ones in the bunch."

"It's dangerous to jump to conclusions. As a policeman, you must know that."

"Let's get one thing straight, Gail."

"What?"

"I'm not a policeman," said Sam. "Not anymore."

"Glad to hear it."

"Or a judge," he added. "Or a jury."

"So who are you, young man?"

"Just a neighbor. A guy who lives down the hall."

Gail looked at him, her pale blue eyes so clear you could see right through them.

Sam held her gaze. Neither spoke for a long time. Around them, neighbors were talking and laughing, enjoying the little community created by the random chance of where they had found an apartment.

Gail spoke first.

"Ed was a bad man," she said simply. There was anger and something else in her eyes, something that made them shimmer with barely suppressed pain.

Sam didn't blink. "I know."

A litany of Ed's crimes ran through his mind. *Blackmail. Assault. Attempted rape. Harassment. Extortion. Conspiracy.* Then Sam thought of Marie and those horrible weeks at the end, the stupid fight over the doors. He decided to add *being an unrepentant asshole* to the list of transgressions.

Sam stood and stepped around the table to put a hand on Gail's shoulder.

"Thanks for the cookies, Gail."

Sam turned toward Jill. Gus noticed that Sam had vacated the chair and headed toward Gail. Everyone else kept talking. By the time Sam had made it halfway across the room, Jill spotted him and smiled. When he reached her, he pulled her aside and moved to the sliding glass doors. Pulling one open, he led her onto the balcony, then closed the door behind them.

Jill looked up at him, her eyes filled with anticipation and maybe a little apprehension.

"Do you want to have that talk?"

Sam pulled her close. "No."

"Later?"

Sam shook his head. "Never."

Jill pulled back, still in his embrace but at arm's length. She looked him up and down.

"Are you OK?"

"Don't I look OK?"

"I mean, are you going to be OK with this?" Jill swept her arm toward the people inside.

"This isn't about them."

Jill's eyes flooded, but her lashes stopped the tears from escaping.

"But can you live with this—with me?"

"That's not really the question, either," said Sam. "Is it?"

"Can you live with yourself?"

Sam pulled her close and kissed her.

"We'll see."

Acknowledgments

The story of Jump that was in my head became the book that is in your hands thanks to the passion of Barbara Peters and Rob Rosenwald combined with the hard work of everyone at Poisoned Pen Press.

Gracias to my agent, early readers and fellow authors for keeping the faith and embracing the madness.

Big thanks to my family and unending gratitude to my remarkable wife, Kathryn, and our daughters Clare and Helen for constant support and ongoing inspiration.

To receive a free catalog of Poisoned Pen Press titles, please contact us in one of the following ways:

Phone: 1-800-421-3976
Facsimile: 1-480-949-1707
Email: info@poisonedpenpress.com
Website: www.poisonedpenpress.com

Poisoned Pen Press
6962 E. First Ave. Ste. 103
Scottsdale, AZ 85251